MELODY OF MANA

✦ BOOK 6 ✦

MELODY OF MANA

◆ BOOK 6 ◆

WANDERING AGENT

Podium

Published in 2025 by Podium Publishing
www.podiumentertainment.com

Podium

MELODY
OF
MANA

✦ BOOK 6 ✦

CHAPTER 1

✦

QUIET EVENING

An alarm sounded. It was nothing more than a simple timer, not one made with gears and cogs, but rather, magic. It wasn't much, but it was something that most people of this world would never own, or ever even see with their own eyes. Well, at least, probably not in my lifetime, but there may be more mages someday. I could only hope.

I looked up from my work with a frown. Another day gone by, and I was still running into the same problem. The portals we'd been using were a mess. I had been in this world for years now and had come to love it, which is why I needed to address this clear threat before it backfired, explosively. I'd already seen what that looks like. Something nearly ripped its way into this reality, something that sent a shiver down my spine. I wasn't going to let that happen again. It needed to be stopped.

Unfortunately, that was far easier said than done. My research of late had been focused on attempts to stop the portals—or at the very least to alleviate the mess they could create if things went wrong. The emperor wasn't going to stop using them, not with how dependent he had become on their usefulness. He was at least looking into spreading them out, so that was . . . something.

Sadly, magical items had limits to their abilities. The creator of the magic system hadn't included everything I might want for the portals, particularly some way to smooth space back to where it should be. I didn't know if he'd left that out purposely, or if he hadn't realized it would be important, but here we were. Though I knew where he was, I also knew I couldn't get there. That fact was quite frustrating. It was impossible—or nearly impossible. Otherwise, I would have gone and dragged the old man out of his cave to make him find a way to fix this.

Theoretically, I could fix the portal issues with my own spells, but there was no insert function in the cores that would allow me to automate the task. At least there were a few tricks I was working on that could address some of my problems.

The little box I'd been tinkering with glowed faintly, and a compass-like arrow pointed off to the north. After trying and failing to find a way to smooth out space, I was opting for a different approach. If I couldn't fix things, I could at least automate the process to find the problems. This box was my solution.

Inside were a number of small pseudo-gates. They looked and, in some ways, acted like their larger cousins, except they never actually opened passages to each other. Instead, each one would attempt to form connections with the others, going through a sequence of lessening the allowable disturbance in the local space until they started failing. Once they did, all it took was a simple comparison to see which ones failed first and then triangulate a direction to the nearest spatial anomaly.

I'd gotten the idea from our own travel system. Our gates would fail to activate properly if there was too much turbulence, and having been stuck in a small town for so long, that fact had stuck with me. It wasn't how that feature was supposed to be used, but it worked.

There were failings, of course. The box only found the nearest disturbance, and because it couldn't tell me how big it was, it gave no indication as to how far it was either. This was still a massive step forward, and one I was keeping to myself for now. It wasn't fully completed, and there were still lots of kinks to work out within the system. Currently, it just pointed toward the nearest gate in our own network, a recent addition just near the city's southern gate.

I locked the box down with the built-in password—I didn't want anyone else using it—and headed out into my "official" lab. There purposely wasn't anything too important in there—just a few tools and some minor items I made for myself or my family—before heading up into the house proper.

I nearly face-planted into the maid, whose hand was reaching for the door as I walked into the main house.

"Oh, Miss Alana, I was just coming to tell you that dinner will be ready at your leisure," she said, slightly nervous. She was new; they all were.

I had a staff of five, but with how low labor costs were in this world, and how much a magic user like myself could earn, it hardly affected me to pay them all well. If anything, I'd need to add more staff soon, just for the household upkeep alone.

"Wonderful, what are we having tonight?" Technically, I approved all the menus, but honestly, I never paid much attention to them.

"I've been told that the cook has made a vegetable soup to start. The main course is roasted beef fillet with herbs, asparagus with a cream sauce, and a medley of root vegetables. For dessert, there are assorted fruits, lightly treated with sugar." Her words nearly stopped me.

"That's . . . lovely actually, thank you." I'd really come a long way from the little hut I'd been born in. "Is there anything else?"

"A bit of mail, miss. Several invitations and letters from Mister Ulanion and your mother, the latter of which was marked as important," she said as she followed me up to my bedroom.

"Invitations? Oh, goodness, it's nearing winter isn't it?" I said as I realized that people were wanting me to attend parties and the like.

"It is indeed, miss. Though I'm told they're nowhere near as formal as they used to be. I know how you hate those things."

I laughed as we entered my room. "I went to a few before the nobility ceased to be. Did you know that? Nothing could have been more formal."

The maid helped me change into something lighter than my working clothes for dinner. I didn't need the help, but it did make things easier. If I didn't let my staff do little things like this for me, they would worry I'd fire them. It was strange but also just how things were. Honestly, it was all too much sometimes.

"I didn't, miss. Were they nice?" she asked, making small talk.

"Very stuffy, and not my crowd. I performed illusions for them; I'm glad the tradition was dropped."

Dinner was a bit much, but overall the food was excellent. I'd found a cook who was on the older side, and he seemed to think that I needed to eat far fancier things than I was used to. After some prodding he'd stopped making multiple courses for all meals except dinner.

Afterward, I laid into the letters, starting with the one I had been anticipating the most. Ulanion sent me one daily if he couldn't come see me and filled them with sketches, descriptions of his thoughts, and poetry, either in my language or his native tongue. It was old-school romantic, and I loved it.

Frowning, I popped the seal on my mother's missive next. She went through her standard list of greetings, before directing me to the included instructions about which social events I should attend, and which to ignore. I'd had to remind her multiple times that I no longer lived under her rule, but she still wanted me to go to certain events. She did make it clear that there was one event I couldn't avoid, though, if only because the monarch was hosting.

That invitation had been put on the top of the pile, ostensibly by one of my staff. Emperor Durin and his wife were having a gathering this year at the former royal palace. It was mostly used for state functions now, but the night in question was the winter solstice, mercifully a few months from now. There would be an eclipse that very night, and they were getting people together to enjoy the spectacle.

With a sigh, I moved to the desk in my room. Even if there was a formula to it, writing out tons of responses was still a chore. The only one that took me any significant time to write was my response to my suitor, but that didn't bother me in the least.

CHAPTER 2

TAKING UP TEACHING

I sat opposite Mystien, both of us flipping through papers. While Dras had gone into production of gates, I'd managed to push myself into research and development, particularly, looking into how to defend them and what messes might be made by doing so. Progress was slow, particularly in convincing everyone that they needed to be more careful. Sadly, the new toy was bright and shiny, and everyone wanted a piece.

"Moving them like that isn't possible, Alana, as you already know. Emperor Durin wants the big public hub in the capitol and there's not a lot we can do to change that at this point," he said to one of my constant objections.

"It's too many in one place, Mystien. We've seen what can go wrong if things go completely sideways. There's a crater to prove it. You have visited the crater, haven't you?"

"If only to stop your pestering, yes, I have; though, it's becoming a mine now. It's an impressive mess, but there's more involved now, other powers are making demands to have it. I know how that irks you, but compromise must be made here."

I sighed. "Couldn't the Emperor just make them stop? I know his advisors are being annoyingly dense on this, but unless we can get these things safe, which I'm not convinced we can, we need to take more care."

"No man is a power unto himself. He could order it, but the pushback would be too strong; they're just too powerful. Heck, even getting those annoying alarms of yours installed was a pain. You wouldn't believe how many complaints I'm getting about mana usage alone on those."

The devices in question were a simple tool that kept an eye out for any growing spatial disturbances, and even I had to admit they sucked. They were mana hungry and had the annoying habit of going off when there was no need—getting any kind of a reading on the size of an issue was difficult if you didn't know how far away it was. The best they could really do was tell you if something was getting bigger or a new something was appearing nearby.

"Boo, what's the point in being a ruler if you can't fix issues like that?" I said.

"Careful now, you're beginning to sound like some of the rabble-rousers," he chided.

"I can't believe anyone would actually be that stupid. Do they not remember the old kingdom? Honestly, the emperor is downright generous compared to those bastards."

"Some do and think they can still get better yet. Some were part of the power of the old kingdom, and they've seen their own statuses decline. They are now all but saying they want that princeling to come back and 'reestablish order,' or some such nonsense. Some are still very young, Alana, and were children when the old order was in place, so they don't know what it was like."

"Yeah, I suppose I already knew that, but still . . . Anyway, I did have an idea the other day, but there are issues, and I'd like a second opinion," I said, changing the subject. That conversation wasn't going anywhere productive.

"I'm listening," he said.

"I'd like to check that old gate to Atal, the one they locked up. If it's working . . ."

"I'm afraid not even I have access to that, Alana. It's not being researched, just held because there appears to be an archmage on the other end who might not take kindly to us using it." That was fair, and while not quite true, since he seemed to tolerate me, Justin might not tolerate others. "At any rate, don't you have work to do?"

"Suppose I do have a class . . ."

I marched off to get started on one of my other duties, teaching. I was the first in what was now our little hall in the research facility, a room so kindly assigned to myself and the three I'd taken on. I watched as they joined me about twenty minutes later.

Two were men, one a woman. I'd taught the man the portal trick back at the fortress. The twins had been brought back, not because they cared in the very least about portals themselves, but because they had experience with the gate network, and were known to be trustworthy.

To their immense joy, all three had finally managed the spell. They were also eager to transport themselves to the bucket we'd set up on the other side for vomiting. Everyone was still struggling to perform the spell without using all of their mana, a challenge that had taken me some time to overcome.

This was the perfect opportunity for me to teach them something new.

"All right everyone, we're still going to be working on cleanup," I announced. "We'll take turns making gates, and those who aren't doing so will be on cleaning duty."

"We drawing straws to see who pukes first? Or maybe dice?" suggested the only of us who hadn't been on the trip to Atal. His name was Ian.

"Oh, I don't know. Leah went last time, so I guess it's just down to the two of you, isn't it?" I asked.

Robert and Ian played a version of rock, paper, scissors, with the latter winning.

A few moments later Robert was leaning over the bucket. "Why . . . why did I ever let you talk me into this?" he asked between heaves. "I hate this, and myself."

"I believe, brother dearest, that your literal comment when you convinced me was, 'Wouldn't being able to teleport be amazing?'" Leah answered without stopping the dance she was using to clean the smear in the local reality. I was happy she'd seen my ability to cast silently as a boon, and had learned to do it herself.

I cleaned the bucket with a quick casting and looked at them. "All right, Ian's next, and remember everyone . . ."

"Don't try to do too big a distortion at once, and don't let them get near each other," they all chanted in unison. I was so proud. Even Robert managed it while lying down.

The messes they made in space right now were small, barely bigger than what an average portal did when it was active. That was good because I needed them to stay that way while I grew my new order. It wouldn't be a priest order, no, for we weren't them, but a new group I was interested in making, one dedicated to keeping the local reality clear of any . . . messes that might attract attention. Bards that would work to protect the world, a good endeavor, I thought.

My students didn't know my plans for them, and they needn't. What I needed right now was to get my teaching methods down and start spreading the idea on how to fix things. I wasn't immortal, and I knew it. I didn't want those who came after me to die horribly, or let some chthonic monsters out onto the land. This world had quite enough problems as it was.

By the end of the day they were all quite exhausted, which was normal. I spent another few minutes after they'd left checking and rechecking to make sure that we weren't doing anything to the local space.

There was no way to be sure, but I'd already seen where I'd messed up before. While the clear signs of space being tied in knots slowly faded on their own, there was residue. These small, nearly invisible issues were likely what had caused the explosion before, but now I knew of them. Once my students were ready, I would assign them to clean up the gate areas, while completing their other tasks, of course. They weren't quite there yet though. My students were still leaving small fractures here and there, but we'd get there eventually.

CHAPTER 3

✦

TWILIGHT FALLING

Days off were a resource that I seldom had anymore. Not because of my actual job—my employers allowed plenty of time for me to go and do as I please—but I still had my own projects. Many of these weren't all that vital to me, just things that needed doing.

My house, even with its many amenities, was still lacking a lot of basics. Most of these old manors were just that, old. Beyond their warding they had decades' or centuries' worth of magical items inside them. Well at least they had had them. Fleeing nobility, soldiers taking over, and all the staff losing their jobs all of a sudden had stripped my home down to what couldn't be hauled off.

So there was only one thing for me to do to get those amenities back— make them. Sure, I could have bought them, but then I'd be inheriting someone else's work. Oftentimes, my work was universally better than commercially available stuff, and my inventions worked exactly the way I wanted them to.

I'd also taken up trying to push my core to its final level. It was an on-again, off-again project for years. This wasn't at all odd, as few people managed it, and the ones who did were considered superior. Many, though not all, teachers at my former academy had managed to reach the final level, along with people like Mystien. Others, though, had jobs that took so much of their time that they rarely managed to push their cores as far as they would go.

Using functions like "if," "and," and the like really sped things up for me, as did the fact that I spent quite a lot of time working on it. If I had to guess, I was less than a year from finally completing the damn thing. I didn't know if I should be happy or sad about it.

Today, however, I had other personal matters to attend to.

"What do you think of this cloth?" Mother asked as we looked around a rather familiar tailor's shop.

"That we really should let the professionals handle it. I do rather like the idea of a darker shade, though; maybe with pale yellow or white highlights?" I looked over at the proprietor, a bard named Marcus.

"I believe I have something like that. Oh wait, is this for viewing the eclipse?" he asked.

"Yes . . ."

"If you don't mind waiting an extra day or two, my newest apprentice is doing some magic with embroidery, really lovely work," he offered.

"Can I see some?" I asked.

"Test pieces are over here."

The pieces we were shown were small, and worked into a high-quality black velvet. The patterns were complex but fairly normal—skillfully done, yes, but not anything too unusual. What was special about them was the thread. Each one was done in a slightly different color, and they shone with waves of gentle light, before fading back into the dark cloth underneath.

"Magical materials?" I asked, looking over the work.

"Indeed, a species of goat that only lives in the very far north. Quite expensive to import, normally impossible, but with the empire being so much larger and more stable, I can now get small amounts. I'm told that the animals use it to blend into their surroundings, but when charged with just a little mana they will glow faintly like this. Though, in the interest of honesty I must inform you ladies that the effect only lasts for a year or less. Not something I'd suggest for many, but if you want something truly special . . ."

There were a number of materials like this. They found most of their use in enchantment, and the making of special garments. For whatever reason a number of magical beasts ended up with special properties in their bodies. Glowing was by far the most common, but magical swords were often put in sheaths and had handles made of bone or leather from a magical beast. Supposedly, there was even a species of mollusk at the coast whose shells made concrete much tougher.

Regardless of where they came from, though, all eventually failed, severely limiting their uses. Replacing handles on swords was fairly common. Enchanting the material would make it last longer, but not for-ever. I suspected that there was also some type of enchantment like this in the swords and other weapons the elves made, but that was considered a trade secret. The juicier rumor was about the Lovers' Marks, but that was top secret.

"I like it, can you make it into something appropriate for a ball with Emperor Durin?" I asked.

"Naturally," the bard replied. "Any other requests?"

"I'd like to be able to move freely in it. I know that's not really the style right now, but can you avoid anything too restrictive or heavy?" I asked.

"I have just the thing, but please understand that it might be a little chilly." He gave me a look.

"Not a problem. I solved being cold with a spell when I was a small child." That got me a laugh.

"What about shoes?" Mother asked. She'd gotten far too deep into fashion in the last few years for my liking; perhaps it was due to her lack of options when we'd been poorer.

"Mother, I have plenty of shoes. Including both black and deep blue formal boots from my personal cobbler," I answered.

"There are better shoemakers . . ." she began before my look silenced her. She knew I liked my personal contacts.

The rest of the day was spent at my house. After acquiring a small patch for color matching, I was nearly ready for the big night.

"So, when are you and Ulanion marrying?" Mother asked while we were looking through jewelry I hardly ever wore.

"I don't know," I responded.

"Hopefully soon. You know I've gotten both offers and rumors about you." I gave her a scathing look. "Oh, don't worry dear. I told all the offers that if they couldn't approach you themselves they could take a walk. The rumors on the other hand . . . Both of my children going after elves . . . it's considered very forward thinking. Most love the idea; though, one or two people did need to be removed from my list of acquaintances."

"Well, if they want an Elven spouse, all they have to do is be magically powerful and show up on their continent," I responded. "We'll get to it when we do, if we do."

"Well, I surely hope you do. Your brother has yet to promote me to grandmother, you know. Though, I doubt that's for lack of trying, if the way he and Etia look at each other is any indication."

"I'd rather not speculate on my brother's sex life, thank you."

* * *

It wasn't too long until the day of the party was upon me. For once nobody cared what I did that morning, since the event itself was set to run all night and into the morning. I enjoyed myself for that reason, taking a very long nap mid-afternoon before piddling around in my workshop for a while. A couple of hours before sunset I had to head upstairs and begin getting ready.

I took my time to prepare, making sure I was as clean and presentable as I'd ever been, even breaking out cosmetics. I hated them, but sometimes it paid to look your absolute best. As I looked at myself in the mirror, I had to admit, I did look my best, perhaps the best I ever had. My hair was up in braids and clothes perfect. Maybe I could do this slightly more often.

Ulanion came to pick me up, and it was clear someone had gotten to him. He matched me perfectly—long, militaristic clothes in the same fabric and embroidery as my own, a small sword in its sheath at his side. He looked like he'd been plucked from a painting, or maybe a play—the impeccably chiseled hero. He gave me a bright smile as I entered the entry, eyes wandering to drink me in, and I did the same.

"It seems a star has come down from the heavens to join me tonight," he said. Normally, he left the poetry to letters. I blushed.

"Just tonight?" I replied. "I had hoped to join you for longer than that."

"Well then, we'll have to make it happen, won't we?" He offered me his arm, and we walked to the carriage.

"Though I'd like to survive this one first," I whispered. He knew I hated formal events.

"Ah, indeed. On that note, would you care to join me for breakfast tomorrow morning?"

"Of course," I said. "Where are we going?"

"I got us a place at a restaurant in advance; hope you don't mind. I'd like to spend my morning talking to you about some things."

"I don't mind in the slightest; which one?" I asked.

He laughed and put a finger over his lips.

Down in a basement, behind a false wall in a workshop known only to one person, a box whirred. It had been left on in haste, its owner readying for the evening's events. Now the parts inside the box, which hadn't done much changing in months, sprang to life.

A needle, which had until now pointed to the same gate, spun wildly for a few moments before pointing in a new direction. Every few moments it shook like a fearful animal, twisting this way and that before returning to its new heading.

Lights all along the box began to glow, and a loud, keening alarm went off in an attempt to warn someone who was no longer nearby. It sang the fearful cry that something had happened.

Overhead, a maid heard the alarm and looked around. There were a few timed alarms in the house, installed by her mistress, but she couldn't find the source immediately. When she realized it was coming from the basement—a place she knew she was forbidden to go—she shrugged and made a note for her employer.

CHAPTER 4

ROYAL BALL

Never before had I been to the old royal palace in an official capacity. Sure, I'd been in the back rooms when I'd helped save Lief, but we were going through the proper entrance now, and I felt special. The small porte cochere shone with hanging lights as we passed into the large garden-like space beyond.

Even if we were on the list to get in, we were nowhere near the top of it. We were also marginally later than some people, and thus, had a sizable line in front of us. Someone like my father or Mystien might have been bumped to the front, but me? I still wasn't that high in the current government. Not to say that I wasn't welcome; I just wasn't one of the movers and shakers that made people seem important to others.

Not being known to many was an advantage, though, and one I wasn't eager to give up. I knew the emperor valued me and my experience, and to an extent even heeded my advice, and that was enough. To be valued by those who mattered while not painting an even bigger target on my back was a winning move in my book.

Still, the wait was long. Each of us had been checked at the entrance to verify who we were, and now there were even more carriages behind us. Once we were out of our carriage, we had to wait again until we were announced. It all seemed a tad overdone, but it was still a big party full of politicians.

What struck me most was the weapons. Every man was armed, some of the women too. Even some who were clearly wizards or bards, or even non-magic users, had some form of blade. For those not trained to fight, it was a dagger, but swords were equally popular. This never would have been allowed back on Earth, but it seemed that since most of us were walking weapons anyway, it didn't matter too much to the people here. I also suspected that there'd been some kind of cultural shift after that one disastrous ball I'd attended as a child, where tons of people had been caught off guard and murdered.

As we passed through, our names being taken and our entrance announced, we finally entered the main set of rooms for this party. There was a ballroom, several sitting rooms off to the side for people to freshen up, and some parlors. Most of the parlors were for taking short breaks or just cleaning up after waiting for so long. One of the servants turned to us as we came in, offering drinks.

"Drinks sir, miss?" he asked, holding out a small plate of some alcohol.

"No thank you," I responded. "I do have a question, though."

"Of course miss, how may I be of aid?"

"How are we to see the eclipse from inside? I thought we were going to be watching it tonight," I said.

"Ah, later in the evening the event is scheduled to move into the gardens. I'm assured it will be quite visible from there."

"Thank you."

"May I be of any further service?" he replied with a kind smile.

"No, thank you," I said, and Ulanion nodded along with me.

Soon enough, we met up with people we knew. There were plenty in attendance, either from work, or from my younger partying days. Of course I met with my parents too, chatting with some of Mother's friends between short rounds of dancing.

"Are you going to dance with anyone else?" she finally asked me when Ulanion and Father went to go get us drinks.

"I hadn't planned to, no."

She surprised me with a giggle. "Well, he is a nice one isn't he? I'm glad he seems as taken with you as you are with him."

"And here I thought you didn't like him," I quipped quietly.

"Oh, I like him just fine. Wish he'd hurry up, but he's not too bad." She gave me a kind smile. "I've tried to help you, Alana dear, but things are changing, aren't they? Personally, I still think your homemaking skills are atrocious, but . . . I'll try to be easier on you after you're married."

"But not before, huh?" I asked.

"No, before you're his wife, you're my daughter, and I'll see to it you'll be getting all the skills you need. If only because I love you." She nudged me gently as she spoke.

"Love you too, Mom."

The boys rejoined us, and Mother asked, "Have you gone to greet Queen Sophia yet?" She was the host after all.

"I haven't seen her at all, have you?"

"Someone should have told you," Father said. "She's in one of the parlors with the young prince."

That was odd, very much so. Young people might, and only might, come to a ball like this, though normally they did not. With less formal events there were younger crowds, but something like a royal gathering was generally adults only, and while I'd never met him, I knew the prince was very young.

Something about my face must have given away my thoughts because Mother spoke again. "The prince has been ill of late . . . so he stays near his mother. I hear that the priests are in negotiations to try and help him. Poor dear came down with one of the noble sicknesses, though I hear he's been rather more robust than most through it."

"I haven't met him," I said.

"He's a well-behaved young lad, and very polite," Father added with a kind grin. He and the emperor were old friends.

Ulanion and I quickly made our way to the royal couple. It was quite the faux pas to not greet the lady of the house, and if we went on like this too much longer, we'd be in clear violation. Now that we'd been told where she was and that she wasn't waiting for a grand entrance, it was prudent to greet her.

The line to see her was small, and reciting the standard greetings to the lady and man of the house was only a moment's work, and then she bid us rise.

"Ah, young miss Alana. My husband speaks well of you, about all the work you do for our empire," she said. "Though I don't believe I've heard of your companion?"

"I met with the team sent to Atal, your Majesty, and was convinced by her to come and see your beautiful lands," Ulanion said with a slight bow.

"Wonderful, wonderful. I have heard much of your own homeland, though never managed to see them."

It seemed like she was preparing to dismiss us when a small voice interjected. "Sir, are you an elf?"

Ulanion looked down at the little boy who'd been up until now hiding at his mother's side. His age was hard to guess, since he was pale and clearly not feeling his best. It was something I should have remembered from the announcement of his birth, but honestly I'd paid little attention.

"Why yes, I am, your Highness," Ulanion answered.

A servant whispered something into Emperor Durin's ear. Other than a few words of greeting, he'd been fairly quiet tonight, seeming contemplative. Now he was beginning to frown.

"I heard about elves, and how you do a lot of magic, and make a lot of items and . . ." the prince began to chatter excitedly.

"Osvald, manners," the queen gently chided.

"Oh . . . yes mother. It was nice to meet you, sir," he finally said, clearly a well-rehearsed line.

"I hope you two enjoy yourselves; the eclipse is sure to be magnificent." With the queen's dismissal, we bade her well and turned.

We hadn't made it far when I heard Durin lean over to speak to his wife. "Something's come up, dear, that I need to take care of; it shouldn't take long."

We returned to dancing, interspersed with light conversation among friends and acquaintances.

As the night wore on and everyone prepared to go outside for the big event, much of the merriment grew. It was into this slightly buzzing atmosphere that the initial far-off shouts penetrated.

CHAPTER 5

✦

ECLIPSE

It took only a few seconds for the first of the staff to charge into the ballroom declaring the castle was under attack. She was followed by guards from several directions, both to check on us and to inform others of the danger.

Soon enough, the attackers were upon us. Unlike the memory from my youth, these fools weren't attacking spoiled nobles, most of which were not trained. No, they were attacking the leaders of a battle-hardened army, and they hadn't brought anything comparable to a mana-eater to lead their assault. The first unit that stormed the room was obliterated by an onslaught of spells that shook the walls; the second entered more carefully, with half annihilated by potent physical magic users.

"Back, fools!" a loud voice called. "You've lost the chance at surprise." It was old, and quite familiar.

I watched as, through the smoke and debris of the now destroyed entry, a single man appeared. The cloud of dust and magical particulate flowed away from him in a light wave as he sauntered forward. The former dean, Lorrae walked before us as if he hadn't a care in the world, looking over the assembled fighters like he was examining students.

"A magnificent formation, truly well done. Now, where is . . ." his eyes scanned over us, finally settling on Mystien. "There you are. Knew I'd find you somewhere around here. Do tell me, are you the one who killed my grandson Rooke? Not many could have managed that feat."

"That was me," I responded before my mentor could, drawing Lorrae's eyes in my direction.

"Is that so? He cared for you, you know? Wanted you to join us, even if it seemed unlikely, and you killed him?" The old man seemed mostly saddened by my admission, not that I could blame him.

"I didn't have much choice, and after seeing how Selene was treated, I stand by my decision," I replied.

"I can respect that my dear, but sadly I must say goodbye now."

My former dean raised his hand lazily toward me, and a wave of force bore down on me like a mountain. Mystien was suddenly beside me, a shield pulsing forward to break the attack meant to smear me into the floor for killing Lorrae's grandchild.

"I'm afraid you'll need to deal with me first," said Mystien, the most powerful wizard under the imperial rule, his eyes hardening like the very depths of the abyss.

"Very well," Lorrae answered.

Powerful hands grabbed me, pulling me back as the two archmages launched at each other. I'd never seen a fight like this before. While I was no slouch, I certainly wasn't at their level yet. Lorrae charged forward on a pillar of light and force, only to be met by my mentor, who was sheathed in a meteor of blue water, the two crashing against each other and toward one of the walls.

As the two titans of magic tore from the room and into the nearby sky, they left a wake of destruction. As they made their exit, another party of warriors entered our room. It was a shame, as several of the wizards here were students of Mystien, and now had to meet the enemy war mages on their terms rather than help our mentor.

The fighting couldn't stay here, not with the war spells that were now being spun into existence. Huge balls of fire, and water clashed into one another, exploding in massive clouds of steam. Bolts and lines slammed into shields and counters as one by one the wizards joined the fray. I could even hear singing as attacking bards tried to bolster their defenses.

I barely had a chance to get my own shields up before a bolt of lightning crackled across the room. It slammed into the shields, discharging harmlessly around me as my father and brother blurred forward at the caster. Beside me, Ulanion caught a charging physical magic user, a quick silver flick from his sword separating head from body.

Quickly the fight devolved into a melee. Soldiers wearing shining armor entered in droves. These had to be the former nobles, as they seemed to fight in groups of three or four who moved as one. Our own people had been caught with their pants down, so to speak, and while we had the numbers, we lacked the gear that they were all well equipped with.

After a few more seconds, the ceiling above us finally began to crack and break, sending boulders tumbling into the melee. Somehow my father and John made it back to my side as Ulanion scooped me up and ran to one of the many side entrances.

"Mom!?" I asked frantically as our little team rushed down a hallway, only passing one or two quickly dispatched soldiers.

"Your mother was near the exit with the other non-combatants. They'll have fled, and our enemies will want to capture them anyway," Father said, leading us forward. "Focus now. We need to find the emperor—he wasn't in the ballroom and I fear he'll need backup."

"He said he had to go deal with something and left," I informed him.

"His office then; this way." Father led us onward, my own singing quickly building the magic around me.

We arrived in a hallway to see several guards in imperial armor being dispatched by a group of attackers, the last receiving a death blow just as we approached. The boys seemed to slow in their charge for a second before I loosed my own power. It had been some time since I'd really let go with lightning on someone. The bolt that arced through the men in our way left charred corpses in its wake.

"Damn, Alana, remind me not to pester you so much in the future, yeah?" John said, looking at the dead men as we passed.

As we were led into a small courtyard, another group intercepted us. They easily had numbers, but again, we were more of a powerhouse. A pair of knights stepped forward. Dad and John moved to take position. Before the fighting could start, there was an explosion from the tower—where our emperor's office was located.

"You two move on," Dad told us. "Sounds like Durin does indeed need backup."

"Right, we'll meet up when we've dealt with this lot," John agreed.

As we moved into the portcullis opposite us, I let loose a wave of light at the approaching men. It wasn't much, but the brief flash gave Dad and John a moment to move.

Ulanion kept carrying me as we flew through a hallway up a square stairwell. More dead and dying lined the floor. I could see attackers, as well as some I recognized as bodyguards only by their armor. Sadly, as we neared the top I heard the doors below being bashed in.

"You lot, to the courtyard to reinforce there," someone yelled. "The rest of you, with me to help His Majesty, go!"

Ulanion finally put me down. We were only two or three flights from the top. "Go invisible and see if you can help him," he said before leaning in to kiss me.

"You're not leaving me!" I nearly screamed, the sound of boots on the stairs below growing louder by the second.

"Can you hide both of us well enough?" he asked, knowing the answer.

I could, but it would be awkward, and moving at speed like that, or if he moved too far away, it would make him visible again. It would also be weaker against others who might see us.

I leaned in, meeting his lips with mine for a few precious seconds.

"I love you," he said.

"Don't die," I replied, then turned to keep going.

The invisibility spell wreathed me as I kept up the ascent, noticing the open sky above the stairs. More bodies and blood pooling into the carpet or splashed across the walls showed the way, up, up, up to the final meeting place.

When I made it to the top floor, it was missing. Debris of what was once an office were strewn about—splintered bits of wood and crushed stone, metal pieces bent and broken like modern art. I could see in all directions around me, the wind whipping my hair and pressing the ballgown against me. I was glad the dress allowed me to move freely.

The palace was in flames, and there was fighting everywhere. One section of the sky had the two archmages still duking it out, potent magics clashing as they struggled to see who between them was the mightiest or most skilled. The sky in every direction had flying wizards of lesser strength hurling projectiles down onto enemies, while bowmen below tried to swat them from the air from beneath what looked like bardic shields.

The city wasn't even spared. I could hear the alarm bells ringing. The old academy had shields up and appeared to be under assault from another force, impacts resonating against the wards. Above part of the lower city, a swirling cloud of stars flowed, the burning houses beneath them speaking to the nearby combat. Near one of the far walls green flames licked upward from some unknown battle.

I looked up above it all and saw the moon, a pale shadow slowly beginning to creep across it.

The eclipse had begun.

CHAPTER 6

✦

BATTLES

Lorrae

Once again I pulled back my mana, readying a new spell. Years I'd trained, using ancient documents, and now this upstart was matching me blow for blow. Honestly, I didn't know if I should be proud of him for growing so strong or immensely frustrated that he had.

I, of course, remembered Mystien from his youth. Back when I'd been but a teacher, not the man I was now. He'd come through the academy, surprising us all with his strength and potent understanding of the element of water. He was no match for me at that time of course, but certainly an up-and-comer.

With a flash, one of my many shields died. Now was not the time to reminisce.

A comet of water appeared from the air, streaking at me and promising death. With a wave I met it with a blazing burst of light, obliterating the projectile into a bursting cloud of steam. I responded with a lance of force, only for my own attack to be absorbed by a wall of liquid.

We flew in circles like sharks looking for the kill, both testing, prying, looking for any opening in the other's defenses. Neither could find one, and so for now it was a battle of attrition, launching spell after spell in hopes of wearing down the enemy's reserve of mana, until the time came for a finishing blow. This was, sadly, how most battles between potent wizards ended.

Another joined us for only a moment; one of his apprentices launched himself into the air at me, spewing magic. I swatted him from the air with little more than a blink. This was not a place for the young to involve themselves, and they should all know better.

I could read the expression on my opponent's face, the rage at seeing one of his men killed. He charged forward, blasting a line of his favored element in a pillar that could turn stone to nothing but dust. Water was powerful, but it could only do so much. My elements of choice met his with a blazing light. The point flash evaporated the center of his pillar, pushing outward on the rest and opening up an easy route for the rest of the construct to pierce it.

Moments passed, and the sky around us filled with billowing clouds. Second by second his pillar was pushed back. The man was nearly smart enough to beat me, altering the flow of the water inside, and even adding a few extra bolts, but it wasn't enough. He couldn't drop his attack, or I would kill him with mine, and in a straight battle of wills, I would win.

I had to squint as my drill approached him, the energies between us too bright for me to look upon without some tool. It didn't take long before the water broke, the construct failing. My spell shot across the night like a blaze, and through my enemy.

It was a sad conclusion, but inevitable. Slowly I began to descend to secure my enemy's body and take care of that damnable girl. I'd have to find her. Such a shame, since she, too, had seemed rather promising.

Suddenly the clouds formed by our battle closed in like a whirlpool, pouring in at me. I threw out a shield in every direction, trying to push back against the incoming spell. It shouldn't be . . . No, he must have figured it out, managed to understand the teleportation that the girl had used. It had been a trap.

I pulsed a circular shield outward, trying to evaporate the condensing water again. It worked, for a second, and then the boiling water fell back in. He'd managed to get me to fly headfirst into his spell's radius, like descending into a lake. The protective spells around me began to waver under the onslaught of compressed steam, so I switched my trajectory.

Upward, like an air-filled bucket at the bottom of the sea, I ascended. I needed to get out of this spell, out of the surrounding fluids.

Above me was the briefest flash of magic, and the other magus popped into existence, aiming another pillar. I sighed as it fell into me, unable to see him, but imagining that he was smiling as he cast the spell that would end this.

Emil

I was too old for this, far too old; we all were. Not that there was much choice. Durin had to die. There was no other way, and everyone agreed. If we could kill him, just him, maybe we could do something about all of his followers. We could call the nobles who'd survived his purge, and they'd come. While I doubted we could retake everything we'd lost, some part of the kingdom could rise again.

Men swarmed forward. Over half were lost already, and the remaining were mostly men like me who'd been trained and bought with promises of wealth, but I'd brought one or two of the weaker knights with me as well. Many of them disdained me, thinking me dishonorable or above my station, but honestly, after how far we'd all fallen, I couldn't care less. I took the men I could into a group of my own, and we'd deal with the rebels as we could.

Splitting up, some moved out into the courtyards, while another charged up to the emperor's office. The bastard had taken the king's old meeting chamber, something it had taken me quite a bit of effort to learn. I passed a few bodies on the stairs, recognizing the unit—those who'd been tasked with taking Durin and protecting our king. It looked like they'd taken out the enemy bodyguards at least.

As I followed behind my men, one of our knights passed me in the other direction, through the central opening of the stairwell at speed. He struck the banister one floor down from us, his back bending unnaturally with a sickening crunch. That boded poorly. A second later, he was joined by several of his fellows. While I didn't get a good look, they'd clearly been wounded before falling. The blood spraying as they passed us was a clear indication.

Our opponent made himself known soon enough, walking down the stairs like he was taking an afternoon stroll. In one hand he carried a bow, clearly taken from one of my men, with a quiver over his shoulder. His dark coat and fancy tunic shining with some kind of enchantment. Arrows shot forth, each landing in an eye-socket or at just the right angle to pierce a heart.

I brought up my crossbow, loosing at him a full volley, only to see the man drop, pulling one of my own people into the line of fire. It was almost lazy looking. Of course, the men who were left now weren't knights or casters and would be little threat to him unless he was surrounded, or careless.

The cranks and latches of the multi-shot crossbow I preferred struggled against me as the magic user cut through my men. Some caught arrows, some were simply pushed out over the handrail to their deaths, and a few received kicks that broke bones and crushed heads.

As I brought the mechanized crossbow up, his eyes flashed in my direction. I sensed some form of recognition, and then abysmal hate that set all my hairs on end. He turned and loosed an arrow at me which, by some miracle, thunked my weapon in line with my chest. Luckily, his was a bow meant for normal men, else the arrow would have penetrated the crossbow, me, and possibly part of the wall behind.

"He's out of arrows! CHARGE!" one of my few remaining men yelled.

"Idiot!" I managed to say before he moved.

The soldier was right, our enemy was out of ammo at least. As my man thrust at the descending warrior, our foe ducked. Through some twist I didn't catch, he flipped my soldier over the railing. The bow had been placed neatly on a corner post, the string under the soldier's chin. The poor lad was left to strangle, since somehow the wooden spar held.

The descending enemy was nearly upon me, making it to my flight after drawing a glowing sword and continuing his rampage. His sword was either traditionally enchanted or subjected to whatever the elves did that made theirs capable of slicing through pretty much anything non-magical; hard to tell which would be worse.

"Do tell," he said with a slight accent, nearly unnoticeable. Elven? "I heard of a man who looked like a viper, the torturer for the *king*. Might that be you?"

"I prefer the term 'head of intelligence,' if you don't mind," I responded, trying to get a clean shot on him.

"I'm sure you would," he said, cutting down the last of my men. I could see sweat on his brow and the rise and fall of his chest increasing, his efforts finally taking their toll.

Finally, I had an opening. Poisoned bolts had aided me in killing more than one monster over the years, and this would be no different. I pulled the trigger with practiced restraint, even though I wanted to yank the thing hard. I only had one chance.

The mechanism clicked but didn't move. My heart dropped as I saw the arrow in the gears, keeping them still.

He was before me, slapping away the crossbow before his hand wrapped around my neck like a vice. "But it was highly *unintelligent* to torture my friend Selene, or threaten the woman I love."

Durin

Our blades clashed, sparks lighting the night as the enchanted swords slammed against each other. The young man before me narrowed his brows as he met me blow for blow.

He was barely an adult, fiery and strong, clad in golden armor with a white cape and pauldrons, which had to be mostly for show. I, on the other hand, was getting on in years, in suave black with a light cloak for contrast. His crown of gold was pretty, but mine was made of sky-metal and had allowed me to contact my men in the castle and academy of the attack.

Our battle had started in my office, but after several explosions and falls we'd ended up here, on the roof of one of the buildings, the palace complex engulfed in battle and flames below us.

"There's no future in this, boy," I said, admonishing him as I charged, our blades meeting again. "You know this to be true. Surrender to me, and I show you mercy."

"Mercy? MERCY!? How many have you slaughtered in your conquest? You're a monster and nothing more, here to consume, and take, and destroy! Your very men shout their darkness to the heavens themselves!" I'd heard a number of objections like this over the years, and frankly, I found them amusing.

"My men have brought peace. I ended the wars by having the will to do what needed to be done," I responded while parrying one of his strikes. It landed on the tiles, shattering them.

Another clanging of steel as we exchanged a flurry of blows at speed, and he growled, self-righteousness flaring. "You slaughtered my father! You murdered my mother! You stole my birthright and this kingdom, you bastard!"

He screamed like the pained child he was, it was a shame that I couldn't have brought him under my banner before.

"Enough," I said, finally seeing a weakness in his form. "It is time to end this."

I thrust my sword into the well-hidden gap in his defenses, focusing as much of my strength into my blade as I could.

CHAPTER 7

✦

SOVEREIGNS' DEATH

It took me some time to find them in the chaos, but find them I did. I'd teleported myself to the roof and was weaving spell after spell into place. Hopefully they wouldn't be needed, but if for some reason the emperor was pushed back, or ended it and needed aid, I'd be here for him.

For the moment, however, there was little I could do. Emperor Durin and his enemy were too fast. I was slowly approaching, but getting too close would be like stepping into a human-sized blender. Their blades bounced and thrust at speeds I couldn't quite follow, driven by both physical speed and skill that I lacked, so I looked on in awe.

Durin saw an opening, and with both hands thrust forward. It was a trap, though, an intentional opening. I watched as, in the span of a mere second, the prince turned, his own sword sparking brightly as it skidded against the emperor's. Lief did a full rotation, spinning as his own two-handed blade turned, rose, and fell.

As the blade finished its arc, I watched Emperor Durin's head fall away from his body. The blow had been unexpected, and perfectly executed. My heart sank, knowing there was absolutely nothing I could do to save him now. The headless corpse fell, and blood sprayed all over the golden-dressed Lief, all over the rooftop, all over everything. I watched as the emperor's remains slid slowly down the roof before falling into the flames that were consuming the courtyard below.

Lief just stood there in golden armor, standing over the burning cityscape, stance proud, sword bloody under a full eclipse. As the moon was covered completely, it seemed to almost glow red, a fitting shade for what had happened, and what was still to come.

I never stopped casting. I wanted to scream, to cry out. The man whom I'd respected, and who'd led to so much good lay dead. There was no time for grief though. Spells were needed if I were to survive, if our country, in some form, were to survive, if my family were to survive. Later I would mourn, but right now, I needed to act.

The man who would be a king turned me, and slowly began walking my way.

"Alana?" he asked.

"Yeah."

"If you surrender now, I will grant you mercy. There is no need for any more blood to be spilled this day. The false ruler has fallen; let it end with him." I could see the cast of his gaze soften, but it was still uncompromising in what he would demand.

"Do you even understand what you've done?"

"I have ended the monster that killed my parents and stole my home. Now I will need to fix things, set them right," he declared.

"Durin was already fixing them. Perhaps you don't remember, perhaps you never understood, but under your father's rule the common folk suffered and died. The same under yours. Do you even care? Did the young man who seemed enamored with justice die when we came up from beneath the city streets?"

"You've no idea what you are speaking of, and I have little patience for it," he said, gaze getting harder again.

"I've no idea? I've no idea!? I lived through your father's rule, through the uncaring and malevolent dictations that starved and tortured without need. I saw Ice's End, I saw the way those in lands you took over were treated—starved, frozen to death, beaten. Only one of the commoners sent after me survived, and he turned in an instant, singing the praises of the man you just killed."

"That's how it is then," Lief said, eyes dark. "So be it."

He lunged before I could respond, blade whistling in the air. Physical magic users were fast, sometimes so fast it was near-impossible to see their movements, and Lief was on the upper end of power. I didn't need to respond, though, because he and I had different levels of knowledge.

His blade sliced through the air without resistance, my illusion barely wavering where it stood. Normally at this point I'd dispel it, but we weren't done yet.

"Did you think killing him would put things back the way they were, really?" My illusory form asked this question while I remained unseen and unheard by my opponent. "All you did was destroy the proper method of succession and cause more pain. Have no fear though. You won't have to see it."

He was still looking around when the bolt fell from above. The lightning was to test his defenses, and if possible stun him. I had worries, though, so I wasn't putting my all into it. That was fortunate because the roof's tiles cracked and shattered under the blast of electrical might.

The prince shrugged it off, but he was winded, worse than I was, if I were to guess, but there were problems for both of us. I could attack at range, and while most of what I could do probably wouldn't harm him, I had one or two options. I could chip away at him by hiding until a finishing blow, if I could land one. If he caught me, though, I was dead. The damage he could do would end me almost instantly. That was, if he could find me.

I danced away along the roof, weaving magic as I went. My steps made no sound, and my illusions reinforced my stealth. There was no need to be too close, just in case he started doing something insane.

Something insane like spinning like a top, which he quickly began doing. When he didn't catch me, he dashed forward and to the sides, blade slashing out randomly, trying to find my real body. I wove a few more illusory targets of myself, and small wavering bits of air, hoping he'd think they were where my invisibility wasn't perfect. I moved them out from him in a radius, even as I got further away.

He took the bait with perfection, aiming at them for precious seconds while I tried to come up with a better plan. This was working. They were cheap, and he was still burning through his stamina to kill them, but I doubted it would be enough.

I ran through some spells I knew, discarding some, setting others aside for now. Electricity was out; his ability to resist magic was too high, or his armor was too well warded for electric spells to do more than superficial damage, and it wasn't cheap. Illusions were good, but not long term.

One of my newer creations seemed best for this, so I brought it forth. It, too, was slow, but would serve far better to weaken him, perhaps even weaken him to the point of death if I could manage it. Sadly, it meant that I needed to let most of the illusions fade into nothingness while I directed my attention elsewhere.

"Come out and fight me like a man!" he yelled.

"Seriously? No," replied one of the images I'd conjured.

He stopped aiming for them, seeming to realize it was pointless, and started bolting at the larger empty spaces between them. That was going to be a problem soon, but first . . .

Lief slowed, looking around as one hand moved to the gorget covering his throat. His breathing was already becoming more labored, strained. For only a moment he hesitated, then his eyes widened as he realized what was going on.

"What's wrong?" my nearest illusion asked. "Choking on your own desires?"

"This is you," he said between shallow breaths.

It was working, but nowhere near as well as I'd hoped. He was just so resistant to magic that most spells flowed off him like water. When he realized what was happening, he strengthened his aura to fight against the foreign magic, which pushed back my spell, but not completely. He was still losing air, and soon he would fall.

There was something slick under my foot, and I nearly slipped while dancing around, but still a good distance away from the man who could very well kill me. My eyes looked down to see what I'd stepped in only to notice Durin's blood, a streak from where he'd fallen. There was quite a lot of it, and I'd missed it while concentrating on the battle.

As I tried to move away from it, I saw Lief's head snap in my direction, well the direction of the blood I was now tracking. Without hesitation, I leapt to the side, trying to get low. It was fortunate that I did because he became a blur in my direction, and a strange feeling blossomed along my arm.

It took me a moment to realize that his sword had cut me. It had been so fast, so quick that the pain didn't even register as such. I didn't have long though. He slowed his charge, pressing the sword into the tiles like some kind of makeshift brake, and turned. My spell was still working. He was still running out of time.

He pounced again, this time, stopping very close to me, his sword slamming into the roof and sending up debris. There was no time for deceit now. He'd gotten too close. So I screamed, letting all but the choking spell drop. With the blood trail he could find me anyway, so the illusions were pointless.

As I pushed my power into the sonic attack, he flinched in pain and jumped back. Perhaps he was intending to charge me again. Perhaps he just wanted to retreat from my scream radius. It didn't matter. He was in the air now and slow enough for me to see, something I'd been hoping for.

I snapped a portal open behind him, and another off to the side of the rooftop, somewhere I could see easily enough. It went against my desires to use these portal spells flippantly, but I had to end this. He was looking at me, so he couldn't see the mouth of the gateway until he'd passed it and began falling toward the ground.

I'd worn him down, so he didn't land cleanly, instead coming to a halt when he smashed into a bower in the flaming garden below. My aim was off. I'd been aiming for one of the more brightly burning areas, and he was still a good ten feet from it. That was less than optimal, but still something I could work with.

The prince struggled to catch his breath and disentangle himself from the wood and vine structure he now found himself atop, but I was having none of it. If he got up, he'd be back on this roof in moments, and I'd either have to run or die. No, this needed to end now. I needed to end it now.

I hastily opened another portal and pushed one of my spells through, one that I knew could withstand magical resistance. It had been a long time since I'd summoned ethanol, but I still remembered how; I'd practiced it until it came easily. It poured over the would-be king in a stream.

"What?" He blinked, confused, still struggling to draw breath.

Then I tossed a small flame through the portal to join it, and we were done.

Lief was covered in the flammable liquid, and in a second everything around him was blue and red flames. He gasped in pain and surprise, a mistake because it only made him inhale more smoke and fire, not air, which he desperately needed at this point. There was a brief scream. As strong as his body was, this wasn't magic, so his resistance to it was much less.

In a panic he threw himself at the sky, another portal pair brought him back down. More alcohol, more fire, more choking. Wash, rinse, repeat. I wasn't letting him out of the bed he'd made for himself. It wasn't long before I could see the last of his aura begin to fade, his superhuman body unable to keep up with the abuse it was being subjected to.

I didn't stop though. I kept the fire going until his body began to blacken and crack, until I was sure. There was no room for failure. With the damage he'd done tonight, I wasn't going to let him get one more chance.

The emperor was dead, his rival was dead, and all around me it looked like the battle was dying down. I wonder who won in the end? Did it really matter? Well, I supposed it would. Either I'd be killed by our enemies, or I would need to deal with the fallout with our allies. Neither sounded particularly good to me.

For now I contented myself with fixing up my sliced arm and collapsing. I still had mana—not a ton—so I wasn't going to pass out right now, but if things got any worse, I'd need to be rested. So for now, I lay down on the roof and watched as the eclipse ended. Someone somewhere would probably be suspicious about the timing, and maybe they were right. Perhaps the moon demanded blood for what occurred tonight. Then again, perhaps it was just a good time for an assault, and the movements of the moon and sun and world had nothing to do with it. I'd have thought the latter in my previous life, but magic was an undeniable fact in this one, and sometimes it surprised me.

"Alana, Alana!" came the cry that made me rise. Ulanion.

"I'm . . . well not fine, but not badly hurt," I said, sitting up.

"Thank goodness. I saw the blood and the damage, and . . ." I took a moment to look around and realized what he was talking about. The roof I was on was a disaster hovering above an even larger disaster.

"Yeah, sorry about that. I can see why you'd be worried." I looked him over as well, and he seemed mostly fine except for a small addition. "Ulanion, what's that?" I said, pointing.

"A gift for Selene. I think it will help her in the long run," he replied, the small bundle on his side shifting.

"It's bleeding . . ."

"So it is. I'll have to clean it up and give her a warning first, but there are things she should see with her own eyes, yes?"

I began to realize what I was looking at. "Is that . . . a human head?"

"The torturer," he replied.

"Oh, well I'm glad he's dead, but you'll traumatize the poor girl if you give her that," I said, hoping to dissuade him.

"Perhaps," he said, tapping his chin. "I think I'll tell her I have it and ask if she would like it. "That's unimportant though; what is important is that we find out what's going on."

"We won," came a voice from above, slowly landing near us. "At least in most places. Your father will be here momentarily. Where is the emperor?"

"Dead," I told Mystien. "Body fell off the roof over there where all the blood is."

He looked stunned. "How?"

"Lief, who is also dead. If you care to gather his body, too, it's the charred one over that way." I waved in the general direction of Lief's charred remains.

While Mystien was still processing what I'd said, my father and brother showed up. Everyone looked rough, but at least they were alive. Small victories. I had to give the full story to everyone. It wasn't pretty, but it was the truth. They wanted a breakdown of how it had happened.

"I don't know what to do," my father said.

"We'll have to support the empire of course, while it gets back on its feet," Mystien replied.

"That's unlikely to work," I said, tiredly, "but maybe if we act swiftly, power can be handed over to the queen quickly and without a fight."

"What do you mean?" Dad said sharply.

I thought back to all of the empires of my first world. Alexander the great, Julius Caesar. Most that rose with one ruler fell with that ruler, unless power could be handed over to the heir while the elder was still around, like the Japanese leader who had finally won their conflict. Without Durin around to put his son in power and make sure he stayed there, the chances that he made it to the throne were close to zero.

The queen was a better choice, a much better one. Women were far more respected as potential leaders in this world. Sadly, it meant that a lot of people would turn on her. As much as Queen Sophia was liked by many, she wasn't her husband. She had neither his charisma, nor his support from the institutions. Perhaps she could have if she'd wanted to before, but she'd taken a step back to let her husband bask in his royal seat, and now it would affect her negatively.

"Half of the generals will probably rebel in the next year. Some of the more powerful civil servants too. They'll fall upon each other for the throne of the empire like vultures on a carcass, and more than likely we'll split into several different states. Even the old empire to the east— a lot of their people like our rule more, but culturally they're still quite different."

"This is just the beginning," Mystien said, closing his eyes.

"Maybe, but if we act fast, we might be able to avoid all that," I said. "Someone needs to secure the fortress. The gates are too powerful, too dangerous. Someone needs to take the nexus we've been building in the capital and hold it, as well, bringing in whoever is in charge in that city if possible. With that, we might be able to hold out. If the gates are captured early enough, we'll still have the best logistics anywhere."

Everyone exchanged looks for a few moments. Most of them seemed surprised that I was suggesting this, but there really was no other way, not if they wanted the current family to keep ruling. I was kind of neutral on the queen, and the prince was a child, but I liked peace more than war.

"I can gather my apprentices, and we can put the fortress on lockdown—tell everyone there's been a disaster, but don't give too much information. Enough of my people are there," Mystien said.

"I know the hub overseer, Ron, and most of the soldiers. Good people . . . the general though . . ." Dad said, looking worried.

"Take enough of your people to kill him if need be, and don't tell him anything until your position there is secure, at least the gate hub. If I remember correctly, it's as fortified as it possibly can be."

"The queen?" Mystien asked.

"I'll tell her," I said. "Most of their guards are dead, and I can be gentle when I need to be."

"I'll go with you," Ulanion offered.

"Actually, if you don't mind," Mystien said, "since we're securing things, I've got a task for you. One of my former apprentices is currently the dean over at the academy. He'll need to be alerted that we need aid. A few of our people there are loyal and strong enough to be of great help."

"Dras, his apprentices, and my own students need to be gathered too. We need to know their disposition," I added.

Before we all broke off to take care of our individual assignments, Dad enlisted a few soldiers he knew he could trust and tasked them with guarding me. Triangulation would be my next job after informing the queen. If I knew the makeshift models they used, and I did, then it would have pointed straight at it. Getting the direction would be easy as pie, and if I was lucky, they'd lost so many they wouldn't realize they needed to shut it down.

The survivors of the party had gathered together in one of the side rooms. I was sure there'd been some effort to move the queen away from the chaos. Sure enough, she was there with her people, looking calm and composed. It was easy to tell that she'd stayed to alleviate fears, a good sign if she was to take over.

With soldiers in tow, I was brought to her quickly. I schooled my face, trying to look as calm and as supportive as I could.

"Your majesty, could we have a moment away from the crowd?" I asked after greeting her. It would be best if she heard this in private.

"Something important? A message from my husband?" She must have seen me wince at that question, because she continued. "He's not hurt, is he? Surely nothing the priests can't fix."

My face was the only answer she needed. I'd liked Durin. He'd done more than enough to earn my loyalty. I wasn't family, or some old friend, but when I had a moment, I would mourn his passing like everyone else.

"What happened to him?" she asked, calm facade breaking slightly.

"Please . . ." I really didn't want to do this in public.

"Tell me what happened to him, NOW." There was a flare of her aura with her voice.

"Lief . . ." I tried to form the words, but there was no easy way to say it, and she understood what I was trying to say.

"That is a lie! That is a lie!" She stood from her chair.

"Majesty, please," one of her guards said, moving forward to try and calm her down.

She slapped the man hard, and there was a brief flash of light. As he fell, I could see his veins darken and spread, causing the man to scream in agony. I knew bardic magic well. That spell though. That was no bardic spell; it was a priest spell.

"You, you! I'll kill you, you lying little bitch!" She drew back her hands, a glow spreading across them.

There was no time to sing, no time to dance, or cast any kind of spell. I fell back on my training, throwing out my aura with all I had to push against the incoming storm. I'd learned to resist spells. It was risky, hard, and generally not as good as a shield, but in this case I had no choice, so I pushed with all I had.

Her guards tried to move in to restrain her. Who knew if they'd known she was a priestess or not, but everyone knew that a priest who lost their mind was a danger to everyone. They failed to hold her back, of course. She threw bolts that could wither men into husks, only to be met by their formidable protections. Few were skilled at stopping that kind of magic, though, and while it looked like they'd survive, they went down quickly.

Their actions saved me though. I couldn't have survived very long under her full assault. They took the pressure off and bought me a second or two before she could turn back to me. The spell she used was pain, pain incarnate, and it was spreading. My body and magic fought it, but it still burned like fire. In the background, I could hear the panic as realization hit the crowd. Screams of "Death priest" and similar, as schooled mages grabbed whatever family they had and bolted.

I felt it as she turned back toward me, though, seemingly determined to end my life, if nothing else. Then it stopped, completely. I looked up in confusion, thinking I might see her winding up something truly nasty, but no. I was met with a very different image.

After she'd dropped her guards and sent everyone fleeing, it seemed our distressed ruler had forgotten to look around. My mother was there, the small dagger she carried for self-protection in hand, stabbing. As I tried to rise, I saw her rip it from the queen's neck, sending a spurt of blood into the air. It wasn't enough though. I could also see the wound being mended almost as fast as it had occurred. Mother didn't let up, though, stabbing once, twice more, from behind her. Then aiming up, just a few ribs down and thrusting as hard as she could, the knife turning in the wound again and again, straight in Sophia's heart.

The queen couldn't see her, but seemed to realize that she was done. In a last attempt at revenge, she flashed out once more. The wave of magic she released was weak in comparison to her previous spell, bouncing off my aura like a wave. There were only a few others in the room now, but those that weren't prepared dropped.

The queen gurgled something, her mouth moving one more time before she fell. I ignored her though, running for my mother. Behind her was the prince. He had also fallen from whatever spell the queen had let loose.

"Mother," I gasped as I fell down beside her, trying to get her attention.

"Mom," I said, shaking her gently, trying to wake her up, but she didn't move. She was pale and still.

"Mom, mom!" I tried to wake her, even singing a few notes to reach out with healing magic.

"Mommy?"

CHAPTER 9

✦

GRIEF

I was numb, cold. There was nothing. All around me there were screams and panic, but I felt like I'd been frozen in ice. Some people were still fleeing the room, or trying to fix the wave of mana that had been released when the queen had died. It was still hurting me, but it was nothing compared to the feeling of my mana refusing to go into my mother.

In my head, I knew what it meant, but my heart didn't want to accept it. She was dead, gone, and there was nothing I could do. But she was still here in my arms, still warm, still . . . so still, so very still. All the little movements were gone, and as I finally blinked, I felt like she was too. There was something about bodies. Once life was gone, it was just . . . gone. It was still her, but also not. Her soul, or whatever people called it, no longer dwelt there.

I felt it building—the pain, suffering, loss. Tears sprung as hope died, and I wanted to scream. I wanted to yell and weep and break things. I wanted to hurt those responsible, but they were all dead. The queen was dead, the stupid invaders were mostly dead, save a holdout here or there . . . There was nothing I could do. So I pushed it down, hid it. Tonight I had to feel nothing, not until it was over. It felt . . . wrong, but still, I grit my teeth, shaking for a few seconds until I could reach that freezing cold that had enveloped me only moments ago.

Some of the guardsmen were still trying to rise, trying to get up and do something. As I looked up, I saw a soldier running into the room. He had no aura, no power, but the look of fearful determination on his face was striking.

"What's happening?" he asked as he made his way over to where we were. "Someone yelled about a death priest!?"

"The queen . . . She . . . lost her mind when she learned Emperor Durin died, just started trying to kill people," one of the bodyguards said as he tried to rise. "That woman there stopped her, thank goodness. Where's the prince?" he asked, looking around.

"Over here, sir," the newcomer said, pointing to where the boy lay nearby.

"Bring him over," I said. "I'll try to heal him." The bodyguard looked at me with a mixture of emotions. "I was just the messenger of the emperor's death. Stop being stupid." I was low on patience or fucks to give at the moment, but I'd still try to save a child if I could.

The bodyguard looked hesitant, but there were no other likely candidates around. He placed a finger to the boy's neck, looking for a pulse, and closed his eyes, but brought him over.

"Sir, you can't . . ." another of the guards tried.

"No pulse. If she can save him, she must. If she can't, he's already gone."

I tried. I really did, but there was nothing I could do. The little boy who'd never get to grow up was just as gone as my mother was, as his mother was. By the end of it, the lingering effects of the attacks from the former queen were too painful, so I tended to myself after shaking my head at the surrounding guards and soldiers.

"What do we do?" one of the men asked, sounding lost.

"We need to contact . . . I'm not sure, actually. For now, just make sure the attackers are out of the castle, and we'll do what we can to restore order. We'll worry about everything else tomorrow. Save who and what we can tonight." It seemed the newcomer was taking control of this unit, a smaller scale action of what was likely to happen everywhere. Not that I particularly cared anymore.

"You," I said, looking at the man without magic. "What's your name?"

"Liam, miss . . ."

"Liam, go get me a tablecloth or something and help me wrap her up, and then I'm going home," I declared.

"Miss, the city is in chaos right now," he replied.

"Interesting, but that's not a tablecloth or something." I was done with these people tonight. I was taking my mother home, and I was going to figure out what I was doing after that, but for now, I just didn't care.

"It's not safe . . ." he continued, trying to dissuade me.

"I've killed men tonight, Liam, and if someone gets in my way, they will join the others. Tablecloth, now." He seemed to take that as the not-so-subtle threat that it was and moved at speed.

It took time, but soon enough young Liam was carrying my mother's body out to my carriage. Thankfully, it was somehow fine, parked right next to the others, with the horses all looking scared. The soldier laid Mother down gently in the back while I looked around for the driver, who appeared to have fled.

I didn't know how to drive a carriage like this properly, but I'd been around enough wagons over the years to have picked up the basics. I got in the seat, let loose the brake, and set off. I was lucky that during the fighting, something had destroyed the gate, or I would have had to deal with the people there. It looked like a massive beam of fire had melted it halfway into slag. They'd managed that before it had been shut, and it wasn't shutting again anytime soon. Most people were either trying to fortify the castle or panicking, so I drove right on through.

The city streets were empty. There weren't any sounds of fighting, and it looked like most people had decided to just hole up until morning and deal with what they found then. That made things easy for me, as other than a few odd looks from the one or two people running around, or the odd patrol, nobody got in my way. I probably did a poor job steering the carriage, but the horses were well trained, and they knew their business. All I had to do was point them in the right direction.

When I got to my house, I could see the wards in full action. There were one or two men, quite dead, on my lawn, but nothing else. As I approached, a hole opened near the entrance to let me in. I could do something like that, with a bit of effort, but someone must have seen me approaching. It wasn't the protocol I'd set up for emergencies, but at least they didn't get in my way.

"Ma'am, you're home. Are you . . . Ma'am?" The butler approached with a limp, a bloody rag tied around one leg. In his hands was a crossbow, his eyes wide as he looked at me.

"Something wrong?" I asked.

"I . . . Are you feeling well?" he asked.

"I will live. By the way, we have protocol for a reason. Next time follow them while the wards are up."

His eyes followed me with worry as I went to the back of the carriage and pulled out my mother, or what was left of her.

"Is that . . ."

"My mother. Get the door please." I could have asked him for help, but I wanted to do it myself; it seemed right.

I struggled to carry her inside the house proper, going off to one of the side rooms and gently laying her down on a couch there. Then I sat down, because I felt so very lost. I didn't know what to do, where to go, what to say. So I sat there, looking at her, thinking about her.

It happened slowly. The longer I sat there, going through my memories—all the times she'd been there for me, all the places we'd gone, all of it—the more I felt. My lips tingled strangely, and my eyes burned and watered no matter how many times I wiped them. I pushed it down again, tried to hide from my emotions once more. A shaking hand went for a cup of tea someone had brought me, and I looked down.

What I saw shocked me. It was me, but the eyes—my eyes—looked so wrong, so pained, so cold, and so angry. That was what the butler had seen that had shaken him so.

When I tried to raise them again, to look away, there was only one place for me to look. I closed my eyes, trying to block things out, and an image appeared there unbidden. I saw her, the way she looked at me when I was just a baby, and then I saw my own orbs in the tea. It was wrong, so, so wrong.

I felt the first tear streak down my cheek, and from there I couldn't stop. It was the crack that broke the dam I'd built to hold it all in. I took gasping breaths, trying to stop it, trying to hold it back, and failing. Tear after tear came as I took in shaking breaths. Finally, I opened my mouth, and I wailed in pain. It was a sound I hardly understood, yet was so, so familiar.

I didn't mean to put any magic into it, but the magic found its way anyway. As the low scream escaped me, the walls shook and cracked, paint peeling away. I let myself go for a while longer before finally crawling my way over to my mother's body. I buried my face in her shoulder one last time, and I wept until I could weep no more.

CHAPTER 10

✦

TURNABOUT IS FAIR PLAY

The thing about crying was, eventually you had to stop. It wasn't like you wanted to, or were really done, but at a certain point, you just ran out of tears. I wasn't sure when exactly this happened, or how long it took, but after a time I was fully spent. The day had been long, hard, and brutal, both physically and mentally, and the sleep that took me brought some peace.

A gentle voice and a hand upon my shoulder woke me from my place on the floor.

"Alana, Alana are you okay?" I opened my eyes to see Dras there, along with Charles, the young man Dras and I had saved from the underground all those years ago, and Lucien, one of my former teachers. Behind them were some of my staff, obviously somewhat roughed up, and a few others I didn't know.

"No, but I will be. What's happened, and why are you lot here?" I asked.

"Looking for you, young Dras here said that you never made it to your lab where you'd be safe," Lucien answered.

"I managed to drag the old man up after trying to get the lower city under control. Headed toward the fighting at the palace," Charles explained.

"And I met them there, where you were supposed to be. There's . . . a lot of reports, some very conflicting," Dras finished.

"Durin is dead, Lief cut his head off; I killed Lief; the queen tried to kill me for delivering the news; and Mom stabbed the bitch, any questions?" I explained groggily.

"The prince?" Charles asked.

"His mom went out with a big wave type spell, killed him and a lot of others, which is a shame. He might have been a good person to keep this from going completely sideways; both of them would have been if she'd not lost her mind. She was a priest, not a bard, by the way, which nobody seemed to know about." There were a lot of lowered eyes and worried looks. I understood that. This was a real mess we were in.

"So . . . who's the next in line?" one of their soldiers asked.

"No idea, but it doesn't matter. The most likely outcome will be civil war between all the major players. Factions will form in a matter of weeks. It's going to be bad," I told him. "But how did you get into my house anyway?"

"I've seen enough of your work to find holes and knew where to push. Nice setup. Took some time to break it," Dras answered.

I looked at my workers, who were not particularly impressing me tonight.

"We did try to get to you, miss, but whatever you did to the room seemed to have been registered as an attack; your designs isolated you from the rest of the complex." the same soldier said, indicating the wrecked walls and décor.

There were a lot of safety measures in place in the event of a registered problem, and isolation was one of them. Everything had been made fail-safe, of course. I could have gotten out with ease, but them getting in wasn't in the cards. It was there to stop fires, explosions, and similar things from spreading too quickly in the event one of those things happened.

"Anything else to report?" I asked. His explanation made sense, but I would be examining my emergency procedures and some people's continued employment after this fiasco.

"Um . . . there's an alarm going off in your workshop. I left a note for you, but I don't think you've gotten to it yet . . ." one of the maids answered.

That got me up instantly. There were few, precious few, things that set off alarms down there, and if one of them was going off, it needed to be addressed quickly. I didn't hesitate as I quickly left the room, several people following as I took down any remaining protections in my way. These were my wards. I'd made them, I knew them, and they knew me. Even if every alarm in the house had been set off, not much would stop me from walking where I pleased.

"Alana, what's going on?" Dras asked as he followed me out into the hall.

"I don't know yet, but I have suspicions," I replied. "Is the fighting still ongoing?"

"Most of the enemies have retreated for the moment, but some are still popping up here and there."

"Good." I didn't bother to control the anger in my voice. These people had invaded my home city, and if they were fool enough to leave a door open to their base, I would be destroying them.

I proceeded down all the stairs and into my workshop. Most of the people with us stayed behind, but I didn't object to Dras, Lucien, or Charles coming with me. After this fiasco I'd be moving my shop anyway. Dras whistled at the outer room; he understood my setup well. Lucien, too, looked impressed. I understood he knew the basics of making magical items, but it wasn't something I'd ever seen him actually do. Charles, on the other hand, followed something only he saw on the floor—footprints or a wear pattern or something else—and raised an eyebrow at a seemingly normal bookshelf. He never ceased to surprise me. I really needed to find a good countermeasure against him and those like him.

With a quick movement, I opened my inner shop. The source of the alarm had been muffled, but now it was clear why it was triggered.

Dras's eyes bulged, but the other two didn't know exactly what they were looking at. My equipment in here was the real deal, something akin to what we had in our lab, and some of it better, in my opinion. I'd designed a fair amount of the workshops for the government's facilities, making tools to their specifications. These, on the other hand, were mine, and mine were far more exacting. It wasn't even inaccurate to say that I'd had magical tools describe the dimensions of rare metals in math to make sure each was perfect.

"Fucking shit, woman," he whispered.

"Kindly put your eyes back in your head, and we'll get on with it," I said as I walked over to the screaming box.

My portal detector was going absolutely wild, which I should have expected. Those that the prince and his toadies had been using were messy on the best of days, and I was quite sure that he hadn't bothered to clean up after himself when he'd made it. That wasn't surprising. He didn't understand them, not really; he just used them. This thing was made to pick up messes, and it had found a new, and quite large one.

I pulled out a few maps and began looking where it was pointing, comparing angles for our enemy's direction in three dimensions.

"I can't be sure, but my guess is that they set up a portal in the city, somewhere in the underground probably." It made sense since there were a lot of hidey holes down there, which were painfully hard to get to if you didn't know where they were.

"Sorry, what now!?" Lucien said. He wasn't government, and we'd not gone fully public yet.

"Huh, guess you're in on that now, aren't you?" I said. "Want to come help us kill the bastards who caused all this?"

"One, yes, they attacked my home, and two, you seriously figured out how to teleport?"

I smiled for the first time in a while. "Charles, could you bring my mother's body down here? I'm locking her in my shop until we can get around to burial. Then, we're going to need as many soldiers as we can gather. I think Dad and Mystien took the best with them, but we need a few more yet, particularly someone with excavation experience. We're going to find what little pus-filled boil these men came from and lance it."

While the boys went and gathered up who they could, I set up a makeshift morgue. I couldn't freeze time, but I could make things cold with ease.

In only a couple of hours we'd managed to assemble a force. One of Dad's subordinates had chipped in, along with several of the teachers from the academy. They'd be doing the digging while I pointed. It had taken a few minutes to figure out where exactly the enemy was, but I'd guessed right—definitely the undercity, between the richer and poorer districts. There were almost certainly some tunnels they were using to go up and down, but those could be found later.

"That way, forty-five-degree angle, approximately three hundred yards," I stated to the wizards who were in charge of boring.

I was impressed at their speed. These guys certainly knew their business. The city street disappeared in an instant, and a tunnel quickly formed. Rock flowed and moved, and soon we made it into the lower layers, busting through someone's basement, more rock, and then some tunnels, which were more tightly packed than I'd expected.

Soon enough, we broke through to the cavern they were using for their base, and the first wave of knights burst through. The invaders clearly hadn't been expecting this, as they didn't even have enough time to panic. Our fastest knights led the way, cutting and slicing with swiftness until they reached the gate, and then they piled through before anyone could stop them. Their job, first and foremost, was to take both sides. It was not to be broken this time. This time we were taking the fight to their base. We might not be the ones who secured the assets that would be needed in the near future, but we were certainly going to be the ones to end this threat once and for all.

CHAPTER 11

✦

REBEL BASE

I wasn't as fast as the knights who led the way, and they certainly didn't want me to come with them, but I wasn't going to be denied. My tracker was strapped to my side and deactivated, and I strode forward. I had armor, even if I rarely used it, kept from my time at the academy and maintained over the years. It was in need of an update at some point, but it would do.

The current portal was smaller than the last, and our men had to duck while passing through. Luckily, I was shorter than most of them. Behind me blood was flowing, as the soldiers I'd brought with me slaughtered all resistance. I didn't get a good view of things up ahead until I had passed the gateway, and when I did, I was unimpressed.

The enemy had set up a small room for passage, but their defenses were pathetic. There were very few guards, few enough that they were now all downed by the knights. I saw no automatic shutoffs, no grilles to cover the gate in case of emergency, and even the doors were just that, doors. The other gate pair was nearby, and thankfully it was deactivated. That accounted for all three gates Selene had made for them, and it was excellent news they'd not deployed it yet.

"Knight," I said to one of the men who came through moments after me. "Take that back to the other side and get it up our tunnel, now." I pointed to one of the other gate pairs; it would make a good backup in case we lost the active one.

"Ma'am," he responded, grabbing the item and hefting it up. I liked it when people didn't question me.

No, bad Alana, no letting power go to your head. Remember last time. I mentally chastised myself. It was a good idea to remind myself that I shouldn't be a tyrant.

We appeared to be underground, and as I followed along in the trail of destruction I realized that our enemy had really gone all in. There were very few soldiers left behind, and those that were . . . well, they fell like sheep before those accompanying me, and I'd only brought second-rate soldiers myself. The enchantments were well done, but they were being broken one by one through sheer brute force. There was no need for subtlety here, not for us, and it wasn't like we actually planned to hold this place when it was all said and done.

However, what I found as I made my way into the deeper halls and rooms wasn't warriors, but primarily women and children, huddling, waiting. They were waiting until their loved ones returned from a battle few, if any, would survive—husbands and sons, and a few daughters to try and topple our empire. I supposed, in a sense, they'd succeeded. The emperor was dead, as was his family, but still their "victory" had cost them everything.

I wondered how things would have gone if I had surrendered to Lief. Most likely, Dad and Mystien would have just ripped him in half, but what if they, too, had lost their fights? What would he have done with his sister, Queen Sophia? What about his nephew, who now lay cold, without life? Would my mother have survived? Would I have also perished in the end? I supposed it didn't matter; the past was the past.

Those who didn't fight were being taken as prisoners, and there were a lot of them. Since most were civilians, we weren't just going on a rampage. There was no need to kill these people. Most of the empire's soldiers knew what it was like to be repressed from their former lives, and the idea of mercy where possible had been drilled into them. I passed quickly and unopposed through dining halls and offices, and ended up in a nursery.

That room more than others disturbed me. It seemed there were several children dead. They appeared uninjured, at least on the outside. Their caretaker was here as well, a beheaded woman, and near her lay a small bottle. The children in this room were not with parents, and were all dressed the same, and poorly.

"What happened here?" I asked one of our soldiers as he looked over the few crying babies.

"Not sure, nor about all these kids. That one," he said, spitting on the body of the woman, "was poisoning them; got most of them before we breached the room. I'll never understand these people. Why kill kids? Whose kids even are these?"

Another soldier, a bard and medic was going body to body, checking each for life. I didn't envy him, as I knew trying healing spells on the dead awarded awful feedback, but he seemed to be taking it in stride.

"Got a live one," he said, kneeling over a little girl, perhaps eight years old. "Someone sing for me." The soldier and I both joined him for a moment as he pulled the poison from her, the girl's eyes fluttering open at him.

"I don't feel good," the girl said. "I wanna go home." She had a faint accent, almost like the people from Ice's End.

"Can you get them all out? Quick as you can, in case we run into any other problems. Someone is going to answer for this," I said.

At his confirmation, I turned and left. It would be a task, but I hoped they managed it. It's not like there were any active battles between there and the portal.

Eventually, I heard some fighting at the far end of one of the halls and headed toward it. I found a small unit locked in battle with what looked to be the last of the resistance in the base. This hall was separated from the others by thicker walls, and they appeared to have found something important.

Five soldiers in the old kingdom's colors faced off against three of ours. I was still singing up some lightning as one of ours fell. These men were stronger than the others. Odd. They turned when they heard my voice, and one caught a sword in the gut for his troubles. The remaining two imperial warriors blocked the hall, keeping them from charging me for the precious seconds it took for me to bring the thunder.

The bolt arced across the hallway and through my opponents, shaking the walls and flashing brilliant white-blue. It didn't kill them, but it did throw them enough for the knights to finish the fight, blades falling on the men who'd been stunned by my spell. Fights were like that sometimes— settled in an instant when one side had some type of advantage.

The soldiers quickly made sure the path forward was clear before nodding back at me and rushing the door. That, it turned out, had been a mistake on their part, as a red cone of fury slammed into them the instant they kicked the door down. It wasn't long range, but even from this far back, I felt the heat as the men in front of me were blasted by some ferocious fire spell.

I saw her there, framed in the charred doorway. She looked sort of like me—pale, blonde, blue eyes—but she was paler, her hair platinum to my own darker blonde, and her eyes ice to my sapphire. She was also prettier than I was, a little taller, a little lither. She stood in a white and blue gown with a crown atop her head. Her hands were surrounded by dark red flames. She had been the source of the last spell.

I also knew her, or of her at least. There had been talk that Lief had taken a wife, the daughter of the former lord of Ice's End. There was some discussion about how that marriage had gone down. The people of that city didn't believe for a second that she'd gone to him willingly after he'd murdered her father and taken her city.

"Surrender, please, just surrender," I begged. If the rumors were true, this was just another victim. Even if they weren't, I didn't want to kill this woman. What was the point? I'd come here for vengeance, but after all I'd seen—the sad state of the place and the dead—I was just tired.

Her eyes were terrified, scared of who knew what. Maybe she'd been told we were brutes, maybe she feared what would become of her if she gave up. I didn't know. I couldn't know. What I did know was that she began forming another spell, the fires around her hands condensing into a sphere near her belly.

She was no battle-mage, and I wasn't going to give her a chance. I didn't want to kill her, but I valued my own life too. The power was already built up within me, and it was hardly an effort to let another bolt of pale blue death strike her down.

Unlike the guards, the soldiers, the knights, she had no defenses. She wasn't trained to resist magic, wasn't trained to throw off any of the effects. She had no enchanted armor to keep her safe, just a gown. My spell blasted into the poor woman's body, and as it did, so her own spell detonated in her hands, sending her sprawling back.

There were no other hallways breaching off of this one, no other directions to go. Behind me was already cleared, so I strode forward, past dead men and into her room.

"Why?" I asked, looking down at her. She was gone, quite dead from either my magic or her own, eyes cast to the side.

My answer came in the form of a small scream and the beginnings of wailing from nearby. I followed the dead woman's gaze to a cradle, tucked back into a corner away from any lines of sight.

"Oh," I sighed in recognition.

CHAPTER 12

✦

GOODBYE, PRINCESS

I looked down at the child in her crib. She was small, less than a year old, if I had to guess, with lovely blonde hair that fell over her eyes. She cried, cried for a mother who'd never return to her, because of me.

It made sense now why the would-be queen had fought so hard, as I stood over the babe. To her, losing meant her baby would likely see one of several horrid fates, so there was no option but to fight in her mind. I could respect that; it was the right thing to do, and if I'd known . . . could I have done much? Could I have convinced the powers that were in the process of reestablishing a new order to just let them live peacefully? Probably not, if I was being honest with myself.

If they'd been captured by our unit, one of only a few things could have happened. They could either be used as tools or, more likely, just killed. My dad was a good guy, as was Mystien, but they also knew there was no option. We couldn't leave our enemies someone to rally around, and this kid could be just that.

I reached down, brushing the hair from her face. I didn't even know her name. The right thing to do from a military standpoint would be to kill her here and now, make it quick and painless and burn the evidence. Smash her skull against the stones and be done with it; it would be so easy.

I sang briefly, reaching out and touching each of the fallen nearby with healing mana. They were all dead, all gone—that made things easier, no witnesses. It wouldn't take much for me to burn this room and blame it on the queen, a last desperate spell to keep us from capturing her, from taking her.

"I'm sorry, darling, that I killed your mommy and daddy. Don't worry though. Everything's going to be okay," I said, wiping away her tears, "Everything's going to be okay."

I began singing in earnest now, weaving spells quickly, as I had much to do, and who knew how much time to do it in. The room around me got a quick once-over, soaking everything in ethanol. I wove silence and invisibility to hide what I would do. While I worked, I pulled off the baby's clothes. They were far, far too extravagant, too easy to recognize who this little girl might be.

I'd dyed my hair before with actual dye, and while I didn't have any now, I was going to use magic to try and improvise. I managed to darken her hair by a few shades. Hopefully it would be enough to keep anyone from recognizing her, and then I scooped her up in a holding spell. I hastily added my old warming spell to it, remembering how fragile a baby at her age would be, and then we left the room, and I lit the fire.

The invisible, silent, nude infant hovered nearby as we made our way out. If I could pull this off, if I could just make this happen, it would be enough. Just this one decent thing on this night of horrors. I couldn't save the world, or the empire, or our emperor, but maybe, just maybe, I could save this child.

I made my way back to the nursery, that room of horrors. It was perhaps one of the few places here that could help me. The deaths of all those innocent children were horrible, but perhaps the chaos would allow me to slip this little one in. That could work, right?

People were still working, several retrieving the few surviving children, and moving them out. The bard I'd seen working earlier had managed to save only a couple of the older ones, but many of the youngest still lived.

"There's a fire down further in," I said to the soldiers trying to give aid. "Evacuate them all now—grab the worst and get them out. I'll stay with the rest until you return. Go."

The medic responded quickly, understanding the form of triage this world used. He didn't even stop singing, trying to pull the poison out of the child he was working on as he hauled the kid from the room, right for the exit. Some of them were already in the midst of being removed from the room, and the soldiers grabbed up as many as they safely could, promising to come back and send help.

"I've got it for the moment," I insisted. "Go, quickly."

As soon as the room cleared, I leapt into action. There were things I couldn't do in front of others right now, not if this was going to work.

Luckily, all the diapers, blankets, and extra clothes for the kids were stored nearby, so redressing the little princess as one of these abused infants was a simple prospect. A soldier walked in, and I nearly lost my composure. I tightened up for a second and then quickly remembered that I didn't even have to lie; redressing a baby was something people did all the time. Nervously, my hands finished up as he and several others returned to grab up more of the little ones and get them out. Then, I did something extremely difficult.

With a careful move, I passed off the crying little princess to one of the soldiers, pushing her gently into his arms. "Get her out," I said. "Poor thing has seen enough tonight." Then, I looked down at her and said, "Good luck, sweetheart."

He sped off, and while it was hard not to be nervous, there were others who needed help. Sure, I'd been the one to start the fire and really make things worse here, but there still was a fire, and while it wasn't an immediate danger, I still wanted all of these children out and safe.

As the last of the children were being evacuated, a group of mages came running down the hall toward us.

"We heard there's a fire; need to put it out," the leader explained when I stopped him.

"No," I said in a moment of inspiration. "It's already taken a lot of the last room, at least it had when I was there, and it'll drive anyone still hiding up. Don't stop it; just slow it down. Not like we're keeping this place anyway." He smiled in cruel understanding, and they continued on. I wasn't his direct commander, but I was one of the higher-ups on this particular mission, so he'd do as I said unless ordered otherwise by his commander.

Cleanup and evacuation went fairly smoothly after that. There were a few little hiccups here and there, but that happened with everything. All in all, we lost very few men, and the victory would shatter what was left of the supporters of Bergond. After tonight, if any of the old nobility had thought about joining them, I suspected they would abandon those thoughts. Lief was dead, his queen was dead, their child was officially dead. I might be able to hide the fact that I was at least partially responsible for the deaths of nearly all the royals tonight . . .

As I made it back to the surface, I thought about it more. There was close to no chance that I wouldn't be blamed for some, perhaps all, of the royal deaths tonight. It would depend on who knew what, but I might well be getting a moniker like "king-killer," or something similar, by the end of this, if I was unlucky. Even if I was lucky, people knew I was involved.

Perhaps going to the Elven lands for the next decade or two would be a good idea . . .

That would leave my family here unsupported though; not something I really wanted to do. Dad would want to stay, and while I might be able to convince John, he was pretty dug in too. I would also be abandoning Dras and Mystien when they needed me most, and I wasn't sure I had the heart for that. I wasn't sure what I'd end up doing, but I had a feeling retirement from the public eye would be best, or at least setting up somewhere very secure.

On the surface, a few buildings had been chosen for the most immediate processing of prisoners and the like. When I arrived, there were already problems brewing. Someone had brought in priests from the Shield, if not just to take the rescued kids to one of their orphanages, then to act as observers, watching how we processed the prisoners. Accusations could be worse than truth, of course. The priests did not look pleased as they stood around, one of them in an animated argument with one of our knights.

"You cannot just show up with several dozen children, many of which have been clearly *poisoned*, and not have an explanation for it!" the very displeased caster said, leaning toward the nervous looking soldier.

My father's subordinate, and the provider of most of the troops for this action, was called over, and I met him there. Another fight tonight, with people we had no problems with, was out of the question. I arrived just behind him, laying a hand on his shoulder.

"Can you handle the prisoners here?" I asked. "Not something I'm good with, but I can talk to the Shield."

The man looked relieved and nodded briskly, uttering a quick "thank you" before he left.

The priest, on the other hand, looked less pleased. "Well?" he asked.

"Well, I'm tired, and your bishop will want a report anyway. Why don't I go speak with him? Better than repeating myself several times. It's still Bishop Theodore right, or has he retired?" I wanted off the field for the night, and throwing him off seemed the best way to take the wind out of his sails.

"Er . . . it is. Do you know the bishop?" he asked.

"Indeed, and while he's an asshole, we've at least dealt with each other with . . . acceptable results in the past."

He snorted at my description of his nominal leader. Seems I wasn't the only one who thought he was a twat. "Very well, let's go see him then."

CHAPTER 13

◆

MORNING TALKS

As I finished my explanation of the night's events, I looked at the bishop. His hands were clenched until the knuckles shone white beneath the skin, teeth gritting almost audibly. I'd only been in his office once or twice before, and it didn't look like it had changed much.

There were some things, of course, that I left out of my story. The details of the portals, and the fact that the young princess had survived and was coming into his care shortly. He didn't need to know, nobody did; it would only cause problems. I also made up how Lief's wife—sex slave, mistress? Honestly, I wasn't totally clear—had gone fire heavy on her chamber. Telling him that I'd hoped for her surrender and would have accepted it was no lie.

"The prisoners. I want them," he said with a growl.

"Get in line. There are some we might hand over, but that's going to be up to either Father or Mystien. I can trust you to take care of the children at least, can't I?" I responded.

It was odd looking at him now. When I was a child, he was so intimidating. He was so much stronger than me, with connections, subordinates, and sheer magical might; not so anymore. I had plenty of friends in high places, several subordinates of my own, and based on the few times his aura had flared over the course of my explanation of the goings on, I was stronger too. It was odd sometimes, knowing how much I'd grown, but also refreshing because he couldn't bully me anymore, regardless of what he wanted.

"Of course, of course, poor innocent dears. We'll see that they're raised well, if we can't find their families. I think we've got a couple of priests in

Ice's End still, after the whole debacle there. Would you mind seeing to it that I can get messages to them?"

"Again, things are . . . complicated right now. I'll know more in the next day or two."

"Yes, a real shame. Durin was a great man. Ah, forgive me, my condolences for your mother as well." He really did sound sincere. The bishop reached into one of his cabinets and pulled out a small bottle and a pair of glasses.

After a confirming nod, he poured me a drink. I was trying to keep the small tears that were forming in my eyes from going anywhere, and he politely tried to ignore them. There were still . . . a lot of emotions about my mother, complicated ones that I'd not had enough time to process completely.

"Thank you," I said.

"To those who died well before their time," he uttered, raising his glass.

We clinked glasses, and I sipped my drink in silence, looking down at the liquid. "You need better wine," I said.

"Hah! Even this is something I only drink rarely. The temples don't pay for such frivolities. I received this as a gift a few years back, else I wouldn't have any at all." His laugh was only halfhearted. He was as tired as I was, it seemed.

"Being a priest sounds miserable. Maybe that's why Sophia hid her own clerical status?" I thought aloud.

"I suspect her family had something to do with that. Being royalty and all, they probably didn't want us to take her. I trust you can see why we would have, though. There is a precedent for priests who aren't completely bound to us, if circumstances are right." Even he didn't seem overly convinced.

"Pfft, the reputation of the orders says otherwise. I suspect she'd have had an 'accident' at some point had she tried to just remain a princess and not trained with you."

He gave me a sharp look. "I've tried to be polite, Alana, and while I know you and I don't like each other, I would ask that we remain civil. You're not completely wrong. In all likelihood, she would have been assassinated by someone had we known the true depths of what was going on. Surely you can see why though? Had she not been stopped when she was, the destruction that one woman could have loosed on this city would have made the attacks by her idiot brother and his cronies look like child's play."

We spent a few moments staring each other down. He was right; we really didn't like each other. Sure, we'd found something we could agree on, and perhaps I could even laugh at the wine thing, but we weren't friends. Sadly, he was also right about me being ruder than I was proper.

"My apologies. I could have worded that better; and yes, I do get it. She managed to cause panic and death in seconds; that's some scary stuff." I lowered my head. No need to make another enemy, particularly when I was in the wrong.

"We've both had a rather long and stressful night. Let us put this aside, shall we? There's still much to do, and it's better to focus on the future."

We finished our drinks in silence, the mood rather dead. I could have left, but it just didn't feel right to waste something he'd been keeping for years. I really didn't want any more, since I had no clue what would be coming in the next couple of hours.

"All right, while I would love to sit and drink, I do need to check on things, and perhaps get some sleep," I declared once my glass was empty.

"Not the worst idea I've heard."

As I finally left into the bright morning light, I stopped and sighed. I looked up and down the street. It was mostly peaceful in this section of town, but I still hadn't seen what was going on elsewhere. That could wait, since surely we'd be getting reports, and I really needed some proper sleep.

I briefly considered trying to go see Kala. I knew she'd probably be at the temple for the Lovers, doing . . . whatever they did all day. It would be nice to see her again—a friend and someone I'd really trusted—but it had been so long, and I was always so busy. I made the commitment to go and visit later, after sending a letter first.

Home called to me, and soon enough I found myself there. The parts of the city I passed were still in a form of lockdown. People were aware that something had happened, but no official announcement yet as to what. The high-ranking people of the city were all either putting out fires or holed up in warded estates, waiting for the storm to blow over. Somehow it seemed unlikely that the latter would happen any time soon.

My butler had at least learned from his mistake and ran me through the full entry procedure when I got home, before informing me that I had a guest.

"Who?" I asked. Not many were permitted when we were locked down.

"Mister Ulanion," he replied. "He arrived a bit ago and is currently in the sitting room."

I found him there, snoozing on one of my couches. He had propped his head up on one of his hands and was snoring ever so slightly, the cup of tea in front of him forgotten. I lightly placed a hand on his shoulder, and his eyes opened immediately.

"There are guest rooms with beds, you know," I chided.

"But then I'd be missing out on this wonderful sitting room," he said, smirking.

I sat down next to him, cuddling in briefly. I wanted someone to hold me, and he was not only pretty good for the job, but had the good sense to be present for it. "Looks like we missed our breakfast appointment," I said.

"Huh, seems like so long ago now," he replied, looking off into the distance. Some nights were indeed like that.

"Yeah, you said you wanted to talk?"

"Now's probably not the best time for that."

"If there's one thing I can say for sure based on last night, it's that there's no time like now."

"You're right, not really the way I wanted this to go, but . . ." He rose and turned to me, taking my hands in his, and I was instantly awake. This was something major. "Alana, I was hoping that you'd do me the great honor of marrying me."

CHAPTER 14

✦

ORDERS

So you said yes, obviously," Kala opined.

"Yeah, but we're not having the ceremony for a while. Things being what they are, I'm afraid to have any kind of reception afterward."

"That's simply not acceptable, Alana. You must have some type of reception, if not for yourself, then for others. It's also a way to let people know that you really did it." My eyebrow raised in a challenging manner, and she continued, "There are situations where people come out and say that a wedding wasn't done officially, or properly, or whatever."

"I'll consider it. Will you officiate for us?" I asked.

"I'd love to," she replied. "However, I am in an odd situation myself."

"Care to share?"

"Only if you keep it in confidence." At my vigorous nod she continued. "My own fiancé wants a far larger event than I do. He has a big family, and I don't really talk to mine much."

I blinked a few times. "Hold on, you're engaged? To a man no less? I thought you were more . . ."

"I want children, and I have a finite amount of time to make that happen. For both of us it's more like . . . a business arrangement. He wants at least one heir, and I want several, which he doesn't mind. His family is old, magical, but not old nobility, and they're well off. He also doesn't care if I have a . . . paramour, so long as it's not another man, so we came to terms." She stirred her tea as she talked.

"That's really weird to me, Kala," I said.

"Well, Alana, that would be because you've always hated social obligations. Though, I'll say you seem to have ended up with more than a few of them." Her tone told me I'd overstepped, so I quickly changed the subject.

"On another note, I won't be in town much for the foreseeable future. Things going like they are," I said.

"That bad?"

"Chances are in the next few months, we'll be in a civil war. It's already tense, according to Dad. He moved quick, so we have most of the infrastructure under our faction's control, but . . . with the emperor and queen gone, there's a lot of arguing about succession. I've also been told to keep my opinions to myself in no uncertain terms." Nobody had liked my idea of a constitutional republic.

"They're giving you orders?" She was shocked. I'd been a pain about sticking my nose in places in the past.

"I was there when Durin died, and when Sophia died, and when their son died, and in the middle of all of it. There are several generals putting forth the idea that I might have been responsible, under Father's orders."

She sucked in her breath, "Oh, that's why . . ."

"There are a couple of guards in the hallway, yeah. Not all bad though. I got some concessions, a pet project or two I've wanted to put forward for a while. You know, we could use a priest, or a priestess. If your fiancé passes inspection, maybe he can come too." We spent a moment smiling at each other.

"Depends on what it is, I suppose . . ."

My offer wasn't all sunshine and roses. I'd been reactive too many times. I'd gotten better over the years, but this was just one more step. I had my location now, and it was time to recruit, because I wanted people loyal to me staffing it. Not Father, not Mystien, not some ruler far off, or my family. *Me*. We needed a priest regardless, and Kala was on the short-list. It helped that she was a priestess of Lovers, so she could officiate weddings, and Lover's Marks, and all that good stuff. I suspected at some point someone would need those services.

My students were the first to agree to join me in my endeavor. After them, Dras was pulled along with his crew. Charles had agreed to join me, with little effort; though, I had to find a place for his wife. She refused to spend too much time away from her husband—a real lovebird, apparently. I'd even pulled my old uncle Barro out of retirement so we could have a blacksmith if we needed one.

Selene was already on site and dug in like a tick. Upon hearing my proposal, she'd agreed without hesitation—it helped that I did this after Ulanion gave her the sack that contained a certain head—and she cried into our collective arms for over an hour. The fact that I would be improving the warding significantly helped a lot too.

When I asked Lucien if he wanted to work for me, he and his son asked me to repeat my offer and then laughed themselves to tears. I took that as a no.

Some of my maids had managed to get in because they'd already been vetted; my former butler did not. They joined a number of staff that had been suggested by others in the faction, small in numbers and all limited in influence. I'd made it clear that I would be the one setting rules for my project, nobody else.

Etia was the most divisive person to join us, at least in my opinion. I had rather complex feelings about my former teacher, my brother's wife. She was likable but weird. I might have pushed back had my brother not informed me that she was with child. He wanted her in the safest place he could imagine—with me, warding with all my might. After the attack, someone had told him of my home's security features in the city. That someone was no longer in my employ.

I stood in one of the boxes overlooking the small arena, back in the shadows as the public display was underway. The prisoners, those I and others had captured, were all in one of the massive complexes, which had been built ages ago for sporting events and rare punishments, like these. Each was bound to a pole, their arms above their heads. There were less than three hundred prisoners by the looks of it.

The four highest priests for the region, along with my father, stood on a platform. The stands were packed to the brim. The wealthy, the poor, those in between. Tickets had been handed out in the streets; the people ate this stuff up.

"You have violated the laws of nature," the high priest of the Vine declared.

"You have wandered far and well outside of where you should with your actions," said a man in sandals and worn robes, who nobody here really knew well.

"You have violated the love a caretaker should have for children, and perverted it beyond reckoning," the high priestess of the Lovers announced. The members of her order and the others looked upon the captives with rage.

"You have broken every covenant of war through senseless slaughter, slavery, and murder," Bishop Theodore finally announced.

I'd been told that it was very rare for the various orders to hand down such a public judgment, but it showed the public that the ruling authority supported them without question. It also served as an example to others what could happen if they engaged in too many violations against their precepts.

"But you have surrendered, and for that, your lives will be spared," Father said.

I didn't know all of them. The first to declare that they'd not tell their captors anything had been handed over to the Shield in front of the other captives; the rest had sung like canaries afterward. I hadn't been told what their punishment would be, only that as a ranking member of society, I was to be here.

"You shall live, and those of your children we found shall as well; they are innocent. Your worst crime was the killing of innocent children, so you shall have no more to bear. Your names extinct, your lines ended. Afterward you shall be exiled to a far-off place to live out your remaining days, while your young are raised to aid others." There was a collective gasp as their punishment was handed down.

There had to be a silencing enchantment somewhere down there, because several of the prisoners were clearly screaming. It didn't matter, though, as before each woman a priestess came, pressing her hand to the lower part of her belly and letting forth a light, and before each man a priest did the same, only lower.

I had to hold onto Ulanion as I watched in horror—an act that was just inches short of genocide, and not because of race, religion, etc., but their actions that served as justification. I wasn't the only one shaken, judging by some of the faces in the crowd.

"That's . . . What the fuck?" I stammered out, reminding myself that for all the forward-thinking people that might be around, the justice of this world was still medieval, and angry priests were monstrously dangerous.

CHAPTER 15

◆

MOVING IN

I stepped through the portal, the last one I'd need to for a while, and looked upon my new facility. Durin's former fortress was already remote, and it was impenetrable—the perfect place for someone trying to avoid attention. Having the hub here was a big plus, since it allowed me to keep an eye on the gateways.

My first stop was my new suite. I hadn't taken the former owner's rooms, as that seemed . . . improper. Kala was getting those instead, after the wealth of overdone furniture was moved out and redistributed into more useful ventures. She still had plenty of nice pieces, but not the gold encrusted and silk covered items a monarch needed for impressions.

The suite wasn't empty of course, with my personal attendants buzzing about as Ulanion made the general rooms habitable. I'd probably spend a considerable amount of time getting it all perfectly to my liking, but the maids knew how I kept my previous home, so they were setting it up similarly.

"Fancy meeting you here," I said to my lover as I crept up behind him. "Though we are living under the same roof now. Scandalous."

"In a massive facility, in different rooms," he pointed out with a chuckle.

"Oh? And yet here you are, in my chambers," I teased. He knew he was more than welcome.

"Deliveries, love. How are things going?"

"Just got in, wanted to change out of my traveling clothes before going to check on everyone. Sadly, I have lots to do before dinner." It was the truth, and something I couldn't avoid.

I grabbed some more comfortable clothing and moved behind a screen one of my staff had quickly erected upon hearing me declare my intention. I teased Ulanion while they were around, but they knew the difference between that and more serious intent on my part.

"How are the soldiers settling in?" I asked, as I began undressing.

"Good, you brought along a lot of scouts, though, didn't you?"

"Yes, I want to know everything about the area, and we're already well defended. The more warning we have about anyone trying to approach, the better." I said. "If we're prepared, there's not much that can pry us out right now, and when I'm done, there will be even less. You and Charles both already know your business, so I'll leave you to it. If you need anything, let me know and I'll do what I can."

"Are we looking for something particular?"

"Go over the older scouting reports first, and then figure out if anything was missed. Like I said, I trust the two of you to know what to look for. I don't expect any for a while yet, but best to prepare." I turned to the maid, who was now helping me into my fresh outfit, "Little tighter . . . perfect."

I didn't need the staff. I could dress myself and set up my own dressing screen; or not. It wasn't like I cared much with Ulanion. Though, they were making things legitimately easier for me rather than harder. Sure, I'd be rearranging things before too long, but everything was in the correct general area, and I didn't have to worry about setting anything up. Help with clasps, getting a bath ready, and having things handy when I needed them was . . . convenient.

"How do I look?" I asked as I came out.

"Excellent, of course," he said without missing a beat.

"Good answer." I gave him a quick kiss and before pushing off and heading out with a smile and wave.

The wing we were dedicating to labs was my next stop. It was likely one of the biggest wings, and it was a flurry of activity already. Luckily, everyone was here, so calling them together only took a few minutes. Selene was with Dras's team for now; she'd been on the back-burner for a while.

"All right, everyone, points of business. Has everyone had a chance to meet yet? I know some of you haven't worked together much . . ." I began. We had brief introductions, and then we got into the meat and bones.

"I know it will be difficult, but we're changing our goals for now. With the empire in rough shape, we don't need many more gates. So instead, we'll be moving in the direction of research and development. Dras and his team will be doing most of the setup for design and testing, while mine works on developing spells and rechecking for spatial anomalies in the region. We are now able to check places we couldn't before. I don't want anything nasty in our backyard. Any questions?"

"Yes, what exactly are we developing? New gate models?" One of Dras's students inquired.

"Not presently, but rather detection systems for active gates and any spatial oddities. If we can manage some way to stop them, or redirect them with the current tools available, that too," I answered.

"That'll be a fun challenge. I'm not sure there are runes for that built into the system, or even for detection." I liked this guy's attitude and smiled.

"You'll be provided with a working detector. It's still a prototype, but I'm hoping you can refine and rework it into something much more useful. I'd like to do it myself, but there will be more draws on my time, and more eyes on the prototype may be the solution." Several people blinked. That I had such a thing wasn't yet known to many.

"Suppose we'll be working on perfecting portal spells?" Leah piped in.

"Quite so, and if you have any ideas for future trainees where vomiting is concerned, look into those. I'd also like you cleaning up around the portal room, making sure there's no massive warping that we haven't noticed yet, if you can."

After everyone was set to their new tasks, I retired to my private lab. Most of my belongings from my previous lab were transported to this new one, but security would be my number one priority. Perhaps I was paranoid, but I wanted to know if someone other than me came in here. I wanted to know, and I wanted to make sure that it was taken care of. To that end, I had a number of ideas.

As soon as I finished with the basics on my lab and personal quarters, I'd be upgrading the building in full. It was a daunting prospect, but I wasn't holding back. Internal communications, detection of any external ones from radios that were under the control of the now opposed factions. The portal room would be a huge point of concern as well. All of that was on my docket, as well as anything that popped up, and a few political concerns.

I groaned as I considered the latter. There were two people who needed talking to that I wouldn't trust anyone else with, and it was going to be a nightmare. They hated each other, and I needed to make sure that contact with them wouldn't be broken. I was also unsure if I could even contact one of them, but all that could wait until Father had finished delivering a certain package to one of our outlying locations.

CHAPTER 16

◆

A SMALL INTERVENTION

I was meditating, looking at my completed core. Three levels, one built upon another. It had taken a lot of hard work to get here, but now I needed to use my core to its full potential.

Most people never got to level three, and for those who did, it usually took decades. Between my trick for quick growth and my long time of hard work, I'd done it in a fraction of the time. That was good, because what I wanted next would never work with a lesser core.

The final level was almost never achieved because most considered it a waste of effort. You could do so much with only having reached the second level, so why bother? There was a reason though. As you built and built upon it, your ability to make progressively more complex items increased in leaps and bounds.

It wasn't the limit of the core that was the issue. It was the limit of what people thought to do with it. Once in a while someone would come along and think to use it to do massive spellworks. The core was needed for things like that, but it was needed for other things as well. The best use of a fully complete core was for the creation of highly complex items.

You could brute force most larger things, either using switches or manual controls, or just make them simple. Most wards, even very good ones, were simplistic, meaning there were few openings. But, if you wanted something to be able to respond in a myriad of ways, depending on what occurred—to adjust and be ready for a number of situations, to run huge calculations and spit out what it found—it required a finesse that lesser works couldn't match, and processing power these simple means lacked.

What I wanted to do was more complicated than normal. I wanted to create something that was capable of finding any dimensional issues on a grand scale and warning us about them. I had the sensor already, and that was a good start, but it was the difference between a compass and a GPS device. Or, I suppose in my case, something more like what they used for detecting earthquakes and atomic bombs, which was fitting because of how dangerous these things were.

The system itself consisted of a large number of sensors, spread out at known locations, which were looking for any dimensional issues nearby. They were then communicating with a central node at the fortress, where all the big work was taking place. There were a number of safeguards on the remote sensors, mostly to detect if they were being moved, but that was of little concern to me.

Once the data was collected, the central unit processed the most likely location through triangulation, and estimated the size of each disturbance as it was found. That would be nice, but I'd also added in a function to ignore the known locations of our gates, unless they showed an unusually high disturbance. Finally, it spat out where everything was; I didn't bother trying to put a map in it, as I knew those were only of middling accuracy at best.

For now, though, I was still looking for bugs. It wasn't possible to change this thing when it was complete, so I didn't want to waste time and resources if there was some small issue. I was going through everything with a fine-toothed comb, and while I had hopes that it would work as intended, I was also a realist. This first one would, if I could get it going, function. The next one or two, I might get it right.

As I stirred from my trance, a light hand landed on me. I knew its owner instantly and smiled.

"Good afternoon, what brings you here today?" I asked the elf.

"Etia asked me to get you. She was somewhat concerned since you missed both lunch and dinner."

"Crap, seriously? I must have gotten distracted."

"I figured as much," he answered sagely, "but talk to her first, then we'll see about food."

With a quick look to check that nothing had changed with the gate I'd had brought here, I sighed. I'd been trying to activate it now and then but only got flashes of a connection, which was far less than ideal. There was someone I really wanted to speak to. With nothing else to do for the moment, I left my room to find my sister-in-law. When I found her, I instinctively looked down at her belly; she was starting to show.

"Did you need something?" I asked politely.

"Yes, can we talk?" she asked. I led her to the gardens, one of the less used areas of the compound.

"Brother?" I asked, raising an eyebrow.

"Yes, he just sent me a letter. I'm rather concerned about your father," she said nervously. "He said he's . . ."

"Not the same, yes. I've been getting fewer letters from him recently, and they've been shorter. Mother's death hit him hard, but I think he's trying to hide it, trying to deal with the grief on his own. I'm not sure there's much we can do for him right now, unless he lets us." I frowned as I spoke; it wasn't good.

One of the most powerful men, not only magically but also politically, was having problems. Father had always been there, seemingly happy and ready to do what was right, but . . . he was different now. His letters were colder. The few times I'd spoken to him recently, he seemed more withdrawn. I didn't know what to do about it, or if I should do anything, as we all mourn in our own way.

I'd thrown myself into work to hide from the pain. My brother had become harder, less foolish and more serious over the last month or so. Perhaps this was how my father was dealing with it—becoming withdrawn, curt; I honestly didn't know.

"Perhaps you could ask your mentor to speak with him? I know they are close," Etia suggested.

"I have, and he has, I think, but the fact of the matter is that Dad is mourning. Just don't know if this is the healthiest way for him to do so," I explained. "At least he's not erratic or anything. How's Brother been the last few times you've seen him?" My family came by every now and then, if only because they needed to use the gates.

"Less joking, at least on the surface. Deep down he's still the same man, but between your mother's death and my current condition, I think he's stressed." We passed some lovely flowers, something made by Sophia through selective breeding and magic. I'd not known just how much of that she'd done until recently. "I'm more worried about you."

"Me?" I asked, a smidge incredulous.

"In the last month, how many times have you gone out to do something you enjoy?" she asked.

"I enjoy my work," I replied.

"That isn't what I mean. Have you gone out for a fun activity, or even danced? I do remember you doing quite well in my class, and you seemed to like it. When's the last time you danced just for the joy of doing it?"

"Mmm . . ." I hummed as I thought, a tad indecisive.

"Yes, that's what I thought. Did you know that some of the younger individuals here are still using that old hot spring you found? I've even gone myself a few times, though I'm picky about the pools I use. I think they're going to have a celebration soon for the spring, even if there's no spring here," she rattled off.

"You're going to push this, aren't you?" I asked, tiredly.

"Yes, yes I am. I don't want to see things fall apart even more than they already are. With the armies maneuvering the way they are, I think the only reason we've had peace is because people are trying to figure things out. Perhaps it lasts until the next harvest, or perhaps the fighting starts before then, but soon there will be battles."

I wanted to grumble about it, but she was probably right. She was also trying to help, and genuinely, if I were any judge; so, I couldn't really be that mad at her.

"Fine, I'll go. So, been thinking of names?" I asked, hoping to change the subject to something that wasn't about me.

"John and I discussed that. If it's a boy, I'm thinking Omos, after my father. He died to a beast many years ago. If it's a girl, John was thinking maybe Amara. I wanted to get your thoughts on that first though." She looked at me hesitantly, as if worried that I'd take offense to the suggestion.

"I think those are wonderful names." I had to look away as I considered it. Amara was a good name, my mother's name. "She'd be honored."

CHAPTER 17

✦

NIGHT OFF

I stood in the small central square where I'd once killed a former teacher. Looking around, it was odd to be back here again, back at this place that had once been so nice but was now filled with unpleasant memories. The square itself was bedecked in small paper lamps, and if I had to guess, they were being lit with magic.

There were as many traditions for spring as there were settlements in these lands. I'd never attended any traditional events in my home village, because I'd been too young. Normally, a village would slaughter several animals and have a small meal with games and food when times were good. Times had not been so good in my younger years.

All of this was done after the planting, of course, and to celebrate the new year. Winter was harsh, even in the milder places in our country, and spring initiated a flurry of work. That work was followed by much lighter labors until harvest, another time when large festivals were held.

"This is all quite strange to me," Ulanion said as we munched on some prepared snacks.

"Me too. I never really went to the spring festival in Lithere. I was working or in school, and it's more for adults," I agreed.

"More for adults?"

"When else might people get together to 'plant their seed' with one another. Good time for young couples." I raised my eyebrows at him, and he laughed.

"When you put it that way, I guess it does make sense," he said, returning the gesture.

"Harvest was bigger when I was little too. Spring is more of a city holiday, harvest more for the countryside. Mostly because it's when like all of the work is finally done for the year, and you basically go hide in your house for several months."

"The weather on this continent is weird. I hope you understand that."

"What's it like where you're from? Hot and steamy most of the time?" He didn't miss the smile, and I was glad.

"Yeah, or raining. You guys missed the rainy season during your visit, and we hadn't had a real winter for years. Those are a right mess, but at least we get a warning beforehand." He leaned back, stretching, and I leaned forward, waiting.

"Seriously though? It gets cold? Aren't you all in the hottest section of the world?"

"Only once every few decades. It's something magical, but you'd need to ask one of the people who studies it to get a real explanation on why it happens." He shrugged, clearly not having the answers, then flicked his eyes from me to the square, where dancing had begun. "Join me?"

"Thought you'd never ask."

I had to admit, this wasn't like other places I'd been. The elves had their style of dance, fast and with lots of hip movement. The rich had theirs, slow and fancy. This though, this was something else altogether. This dance style was similar to what the peasants had done, and what farming communities still did, to celebrate the turning of the year. There was no formality to it. The movements were generally proscribed. It was fun though, just fun; no worries and no stress about where or what you had to be. You could just be.

So I went with it. I laughed and twisted; I moved with just Ulanion, or with a group, to the wild, informal music. Many of our people were from villages like mine, or from cities like Lithere. They led us in dance after dance until late into the night, when I swayed, held close with my face buried in Ulanion's shirt, resting.

The night was nearly perfect, the air warm and rich from the billowing steam that never seemed to escape the little valley. Sometimes a cool breeze would blow through, and after bestowing a refreshing jolt, it would pass, replaced by the pleasant air once again.

Since I was in charge of our new headquarters, managing to reserve one of the little rooms that were being built up had been easy as pie. It had its own bath, which was wonderfully warm and served as an easy spot to have a cozy night without having to go home. It also meant we'd be undisturbed until morning.

I made it back to the fortress by early afternoon the next day and was extraordinarily refreshed. It was a perfect little mini-vacation, even if only one night. I would need to schedule something like that more often. Perhaps we could institute a proper vacation policy here. That would be a real change from how this world generally handled such things.

As soon as I stepped through the portal, though, my day began to go downhill. Several of the soldiers were up in arms, and before I had time to register what was going on, one of my students, Leah, approached me in a rush.

"Thank goodness, there you are! Unrecognized portal, miss, on the premises, activated five minutes ago."

"What!? Where?" I tried not to shout, but struggled.

"In your lab," Leah replied. "Just happened, and when you didn't respond when we called there . . . we'd feared something had gone wrong. There's a breaching team readying to go in."

I power walked to my lab, all the relief melting like snow in a volcano. The looseness in my muscles that my good night had helped me achieve was gone, replaced with tight tension as I walked up to the team of heavily armored knights, preparing to try and break down the door to my workshop.

"I've got the door, you guys lead," I commanded, and the leader of the team nodded as I got my personal shields up.

With a quick movement, the door popped open and they rushed, shields held out before them. It was almost like looking at video of a SWAT team entering a home, and in practice it was similar, but with less guns and more magic. I heard them sweep the room, looking for any threats as they shouted at one another.

Eventually, their commander came back out with an envelope in hand.

"Er, there's a gate in here, ma'am. Did you know that?" he asked.

My face fell, one hand massaging a temple. "Yes, my apologies," I said. "I moved that in there a while back. I've been trying to get my system to ignore the place, but I must have left one of the alarms on and tripped it. Is there anyone in there?" I knew there was only one person who'd activate it, and if he didn't want to be seen, he wouldn't be.

"No, ma'am, just a letter in front of it. Policy says we should check things like this for poison . . ." He seemed concerned about my reaction that he would need to take something obviously intended for me without my permission.

"Then do so," I said. "We have protocol for a reason. Mind if I speak with your men for a moment?" I was glad he was sticking to procedure here, so I gave him a kind smile.

"Of course," he answered briskly.

I gave a brief apology to the team for wasting their time, explaining that I'd made an error and thanking them for such a quick and well-executed response. I didn't like to admit my failings, but I'd learned a lot of things from Durin's rule, and one of those was that treating your people well tended to work well. Following someone who freely admitted to making mistakes and who praised actions in response to potential threats built trust in the system. It was also a safeguard so that when things really did go wrong, there wasn't a lack of response due to fear of reprisal.

It took hours for me to finally get the letter back. It came from a staff member who stated that they were unsure what in the world it said, but it didn't display any indication of poison or any odd residue of magic. There were a few magical substances out there that were pretty unpleasant, after all. I'd not wasted time waiting though. Instead, I tracked down the alarm that had alerted everyone and changed the parameters ever so slightly to prevent this from happening again.

The letter had a list of instructions from Justin, telling me to send a lamp through the portal if I needed a meeting with a color code to indicate the severity of the situation. He also told me how he would respond, which was by returning my lamp when things were ready on his end. I was warned against trying to venture through until he responded, as it might be dangerous to do so.

It took less than ten minutes to make a hand-sized light with a bright blue radiance and toss it through. The message was simple—"Large issue, not immediately dangerous, and I hoped to see him soon."

CHAPTER 18

✦

CONSULTATION

When the time came and the signal was given, I stepped through the portal. The world around me stretched, but I emerged out the other side perfectly fine, if a little disoriented. There was a definite lag between one side and the other, and it was super weird.

The room I was in was empty and blank, all white with light coming from seemingly everywhere. I couldn't even be perfectly sure where the walls were as I looked around, since it all just blended together as one. I started to move forward cautiously when a bubble popped into existence around me and I shifted again.

The second teleport was worse than the portals I used for personal transport. Though, I had to admit, those had improved markedly. At least there was no visible disturbance in the space around me as I reappeared. This time in a slightly more comfortable room, Justin's den.

"That is disorienting," I said as the ancient mage made his way into the room and sat down, motioning me to the couch opposite him.

"I assume this isn't just a social visit, given how many times you tried to activate the portal," he said calmly, leaning back.

"No, it isn't. I ran into something a while back that spooked me nastily. Hoping you might have a way to prevent it from happening again, or at least advise me on it."

He raised an eyebrow. "While I'm rather fond of our people in a general sense, I feel the need to express that I am not at your beck and call, young lady."

"I never meant to insinuate that you were. If this weren't serious and something that I thought you'd understand, I wouldn't be here. It involves the portals," I explained. Justin was nice enough, but I got the feeling that if I bugged him about trivial nonsense, that might end, at least if I didn't come prepared with something funny—he'd found one of my predecessors to be fun, or so Justin had told me.

"All right, let's hear it then," he declared.

I launched into the story of how one of our portal makers had been captured and subsequently tortured into making several for one of our enemies. How she'd done so, but left off even the most basic of safety measures, and my tests that followed.

As I explained to Justin the tests I'd attempted, I could see his eyebrows furrowing, and when I got to the rail-gun attempt, I thought his brows might well meet.

"The potential power of a weapon like that isn't to be underestimated. I do hope you didn't destroy anything important."

"No, though the explosion was pretty impressive. The weapon didn't function at all. As a point of fact, it did . . . something to the space around it that was quite energetic. I was then left with what I could only describe as a distortion on a massive scale," I answered.

"I'm aware that spatial magic, if improperly cast, can have effects on the area, but those tend to dissipate on their own, and they're not too bad. What were the measurements?"

I handed over a notebook. I had long since gathered up all the estimated sizes in preparation for this questioning, and organized them into something concise.

"There were more distortions in the area than I realized when it happened, from the other experiments. It cascaded through them, even though it looked like they'd all closed by the time I did it."

"Those residual effects seem to disappear, but they really just shrink. The rate is logarithmic," he said, flipping the pages as he spoke. "They do seem to eventually hit zero, or at least lower than any detector I've made can find. I like your notes, by the way, if not what they say."

"What do you mean about the rate?" I asked.

"The smaller they get, the longer it takes for them to shrink. Goodness! Is the size of this crater correct? It would take something the level of high explosives to do that."

"Of course, though that was the smallest of the issues. The gate disruption area was enormous, and then there was whatever was looking at us as I tried to fix it," I explained.

"The last page, what do you mean about something outside? Outside of what?" he asked.

"Reality, as far as I can tell. Justin, I felt something . . . something . . . I don't know, terrifying, absolutely terrifying, like it was trying to look at us, and . . . and . . ." I shivered and rubbed my arms at the memory.

"That isn't something I can really quantify. You're sure about it as well?" he said, rubbing his chin.

"I wasn't the only one who felt it, though I think I got the worst of it, being at the center of the spell and all. I'd rather you not try to repeat the experiment, because I got the feeling that if things had been just a little different, something horrible would have happened," I said as low as I could, knowing scientists always repeated experiments.

"I'll abstain if you say it was that bad. Also have to think about how to stop this from happening again. You have the stone still, right? The one I gave you?"

"Locked in a vault, and all of our current portal makers are accounted for under my supervision. I managed to get that right, at least," I answered.

I couldn't actually open the vault on my own. It had originally been keyed to Durin, but after his death, we'd managed to crack it. Mystien and I had successive layers to keep it, and a few more nasties, locked down tight.

"Glad to hear it. I'll need to run some numbers. It could take a few weeks, but no more than that." He handed me back my notes.

"Don't you want to keep them?" I asked. "I did make this copy for you."

"Elves have an eidetic memory. Well, pure-blooded ones do, at least. This ability diminishes as their bloodline becomes diluted with human blood."

"That is completely and utterly fucking unfair," I said.

That earned me a chuckle. "It is, isn't it?"

It did indeed take him a few weeks to get back to me, and after another series of teleports, I found myself in a different room. This one had a number of chalkboards, all covered with math that was so far beyond me, it hurt.

"This is one of the most interesting problems I've ever seen, young Alana, and I've seen a lot," the ancient magus said as he sipped some tea.

"Any idea what happened then?" I asked.

"Yes, you made ripples in the area outside of this universe. Not something I even expected to be possible," he answered calmly. "I'm impressed."

"So, what's out there?" I inquired.

"Nothing, or at least there should be nothing."

"Well, there's something," I said.

"Allow me to explain. There is nothing—no matter, no known energy. There isn't even time and space out there. All of those concepts fall apart when we talk about things outside of a universe. If there is something, it is so foreign to what we know as real that it would be like magic all over again, only worse, because it wouldn't be native to our world. I can't express well how much anything outside of a universe really does not relate to us in sensible ways, completely outside most of what we consider as conceptually possible." He shook his head as he looked at the equations.

"Our previous world didn't have magic," I said.

"Oh, I suspect it did, only limited or somehow repressed. Not sure why or how, though, and it doesn't matter. I'll figure it out when I get back. For now, though, it is clear that there are some large issues with the current portal structure. Can you guarantee that no more are being made?" He seemed concerned.

"I've shifted all of our research into tracking and cleaning up the residue, so yes. The gates are completely off production. Why?"

"Because clearly they shouldn't be made at all. I need to find a way to make sure this doesn't happen again, or permanently stop their production; perhaps both." That last bit sent my hair standing on end.

"It sounds like you're considering hurting my people," I said cautiously.

"I briefly considered it. Killing all of you would be expedient and solve the issue quite cleanly. It would cause all kinds of other problems, though, ones that I don't care to deal with."

That was only somewhat comforting.

CHAPTER 19

A VISIT

I was overseeing the reworking of our defenses around the portals when word came in that my brother had arrived. It was expected that he'd be arriving soon, but I hadn't been told exactly when that would be. There was so much to do to get this place up to my standards; it was taking all of my time. My lab had finally been set up to an acceptable level, but I had some ideas in mind for a few more additions.

"Hey there, little sister," he said as I hugged him. "Making some additions?"

"I'm separating the portals," I explained. "They're each getting their own area with separate defensive wardings."

"Okay, why?"

I wanted to roll my eyes, but he and his were among those supporting me, so I held back. "So that if someone attacks the portal room, we don't lose everything all at once. The defenses on the other ends are not in my control, and there is a distinctly non-zero chance of that happening. Point in fact, we still don't have access to the other ends of about ten of our portals."

"That number might increase soon too. I just got word that General Ozen just declared himself emperor and is demanding everyone now bow to his rule. Father wants me to go to some of our locations and double-check security."

"I'll note it, and add the portals in his locations to our 'outgoing only' list. The other generals respond yet?" I asked.

"No, but by my reckoning, we'll have at least two more declare the same. Tyron may or may not, but frankly it won't matter; he has few forces anyway. I'm also here to tell you that father is making an announcement of his own soon." John seemed tired, rubbing his eyes as we walked to one of the meeting rooms.

"Shouldn't we discuss that in private?" I asked.

"No, no point. Everyone who knows anything already knows. He's not going the full emperor route though. For now, he's just declaring that he and Mystien will be the administrators until a new ruler can be found. We think that'll go down better, and it doesn't force anything for the moment. He is fully rejecting all other claimants, though, so we expect trouble, quite literally, any day."

"You and me both. How is my old mentor, by the way?" I asked as I closed the doors and set the privacy wards in place.

"Old, and with the new baby—"

"The what now!?" I turned to him, hoping to see some humor in his eyes.

"Yeah, his . . . mistress or whatever gave birth a few days ago, healthy little girl." I stared at him in shock. "So, you didn't know he had one of those either?" As I continued to stare, he began laughing.

"Did dad know?" I asked.

"Sort of. Apparently, she lived in Hazelwood when we were kids and has been after the old codger for years. They kept the whole thing super quiet when she moved in with him. With his propensity for keeping his private life completely separate from work, it was more than any of us expected."

"What's with old wizards and their paranoid secrets?" I asked, tired by it all.

"Says the girl running the secret portal fortress hidden in the frozen wasteland, and adding literally every single magical protection she can," he said, chuckling at me.

"Yeah, but I'd at least tell you guys if I was like, pregnant!" It was exasperating. "Also, he's ancient now, what, he's like seventy or so."

He shrugged. "Kid looks healthy, and he's happy. Not sure what else to say about it."

"Wonderful. Did you just come to let me in on the news then? I'm happy and all, but rather busy, and I doubt he'd want me to come anyway," I huffed, sitting down on the couch.

"Maybe, but I thought you'd want to know. Now if you don't mind, I'd rather like to go see my wife."

My brother didn't stay long, busy as he was, but it was nice to see family every now and then. I needed to make time for that at some point, some imaginary time when we weren't all out of our minds busy with work or something. Then again they could always come see me too. I did have portals to nearly everywhere.

A few days later I was called out to check a ward issue. One of our expansions was running into a snag putting things in place. My afternoon was spent going over them with a fine-toothed comb, because even though they were copied from the same exact wards we were using in all of the other portal rooms, they were experiencing some kind of interference.

After several hours, I managed to localize the issue to a section of the room—previously, it had been a rather empty courtyard—that was sending out some odd responses to our spells. The strange part was that there wasn't anything there. Nothing, just a section of blank stone.

"Grab Dras and Ulanion," I said to an assistant. "We may have part of the old warding scheme buried here, and if so, we'll need to take it out. Shields up, everyone. There shouldn't be much mana left in it, but let's not risk it."

Removing an old warding was easy, if you knew where it was coming from, what it was connected to, and had the right equipment. Sadly, a lot of warding wasn't done centrally, as there were limits to the size of a core, but rather more locally. Even the dorms back at my old school had been on their own wards.

"More of them?" Dras asked incredulously as he joined me.

"Yeah, this is what, the third time this week?" I replied. We had found several such issues during renovations, though most were minor—things like temperature control wards that were ancient with just enough mana to keep messing with things around them.

"This procedure is a pain," he said, irritated that we always had to have extra staff on hand.

"Maybe, but I know you understand why. Do you remember the elevators in the Elven compound? Those things had fail-safes on their fail-safes."

He sighed, and then Ulanion added his two cents. "It's a good design policy, but we do need to get on with it." He was here just in case anything had been growing and feeding off the ambient magic.

Dras began his work, his hands moving as he pulled in magic and formed a small testing drill; the ward shouldn't be deep. I watched him, thinking how far he'd come since we'd first met, so far from the boy who could wield only fire. It was nice watching your friends grow, seeing them become more.

It took only moments for a section of the flagstones to collapse, falling in upon itself in a painfully loud clatter. We all looked at each other, and Dras began to make a small force bridge out to the hole. There was a ringing there, but one that sounded faltering, pained, and a slight flickering light emanated from the opening.

As we peeked over the edge, Ulanion asked, "What exactly happened to the man who built this place?"

"Ristolian," I answered. "We all assumed he died, but seeing as nobody else was here at the time, we couldn't confirm it."

"I assume we're going in?" Dras asked.

"You assume correctly," I said. "Do you mind?"

The three of us entered the hole, and as we did, lights flicked on all around us. Old magic sprang to life, as power—a lot of power—was redirected from somewhere, charging the various structures, one by one, in a way that shouldn't have been possible without some source.

"That's . . ." Dras whispered.

"Yeah, hate to say it, but let's not touch anything just yet," I said, looking out into the small room we now found ourselves in. The many tools were now whizzing to life in jolts, only to fail again moments later.

CHAPTER 20

✦

THE OFFICE

Everything in this room was dangerous. Well most of it, but we'd be treating it all as dangerous. Several items were trying to come on and failing, to multiple effects. A quick once-over confirmed my fears.

"It's the items themselves failing. Whoever built this place didn't bother seeing to it that the items inside would last long, and I'd wager no one has taken care of this place since Ristolian," I said as I backed off from the piece I'd been examining.

Rust and decay would damage and destroy even the safest of magical constructs eventually. Within stone they lasted longer, but if something wasn't done to turn them all off, they would degrade eventually. These items were not yet fully broken, but not working as they should.

"Agreed, and there's no way to tell what they were supposed to do. What I'm curious about is the power though," Dras added, rubbing his chin. "Where are they getting it, and how much is there?"

"Well, we're going to have to find the source so we can disconnect this mess and dispose of it all too." Any power source for this would be useful, and I'd love to study it, but the items needed to go. They were the rough equivalent of nuclear waste.

The room we found ourselves in was some form of workshop, not unlike my own. The tools were mostly variants of what the academy used. Though, they were degraded enough that it was hard to tell what the differences were. There was a stone door at the end of the hall with a reader beside it—just a box on the wall—but we'd get to that eventually.

For now, we needed to start removing equipment. One by one, we identified the power inputs and began to destroy them. It looked like the room had been set up to turn everything on when someone entered, and none of the items were hidden or anything.

When we were down to nothing but lights we turned to the door. I couldn't see anything to clearly indicate what we were supposed to do.

"Thoughts?" Dras asked after joining me in my examination.

"No idea, but it's old," I replied. "Just break it down?"

"Yeah, I've got nothing better."

Dras's spell shattered the door like it was made of glass, sending splinters everywhere. Whatever protections it had, or used to have, weren't enough to stop Dras's magic from breaking it to bits.

It also set off an alarm, a loud one. The lights flashed to red, and before I could even react, Ulanion had scooped me up. I felt him turning toward our exit, and then he stopped. The reason became clear as soon as my eyes caught it. There was a glowing red energy field crackling all along the walls and the floor of the room. It was opaque. If I couldn't see where I was teleporting, it was not safe to try it.

"That's not good; that's not good at all!" I shouted in panic.

"No, really?!" Dras said sarcastically as he began to move into the hall. "Quick, we need an exit."

Ulanion put me down, and we quickly made our way into the hall. There looked to be about five doors along it, none clearly marked. The one at the far end of the hallway was much larger and more heavily warded. The opposite end of the hallway had something far more ominous, a large golem that was slowly coming to life.

"Guys . . ." I pointed before I began putting up shields, singing them into place as fast as I could.

The golem laboriously disconnected itself from the wall and began to walk toward us. "Intruders in Headmaster's offices detected. You will come with me," it commanded with a mechanical voice.

Dras responded with an explosion of fire, while Ulanion drew his sword and I spun up lightning, not thinking I had much else. The golem let us, seemingly waiting for us to do something else. As the blasts hit it one after another, it didn't even flinch.

"It's tough," Dras said, looking for any damage on the construct's body, and finding no signs of any.

"Resistance detected. Deploying non-lethal countermeasures." It lifted its arm, and lights began to display all along the limb.

We felt nothing through the shields, but it was clear this was some form of wind spell, based on the amount of dust and debris being blown around.

"At least it's not trying to squish us," Ulanion said. "This wind won't do much."

"It was probably supposed to be something else in the past, or maybe pin students breaking in. Listen to it—it's still referring to a 'headmaster,' so it probably thinks we're . . . Woah . . ." As I was speaking, I began to feel sort of off, and then dizziness overtook me, and I almost fell.

"What?" Ulanion began, stumbling himself.

"How is it?" Dras asked, similarly confused.

"Gas! It's not wind—it's gas, prob . . . prob . . . oh." I managed to sit down on my own as the whole world started to make *woo woo woo* sounds. I briefly gave a halfhearted attempt at singing some air into my face but couldn't hold a tune or concentrate at all as everything spun around me.

Dras was down too, slumping against the other wall with his head lolling about. Ulanion made a run at the creature, only to fall and end up sprawled out foolishly. I couldn't help laughing at him; it was so funny.

"You're cute," I slurred, unable to stop myself from giggling. As I laid on the cool floor, I felt like I was floating, and my limbs were tingly.

"Saturation level reached. Relocating troublemakers." I felt myself being picked up and carried somewhere. I couldn't figure out where we were going, though, and didn't really care.

Soon enough, I found myself sitting in an uncomfortable chair, my companions on either side of me, and all of us slowly starting to come back to our senses. There was an empty chair as well, like the place had been set up to accommodate four people to sit on this side of a sizable desk. The desk was littered with a few discolored papers and covered in dust.

The most important thing about it, though, was the skeleton sitting at the head of it. It looked like we'd finally found Ristolian, sitting in his office in what must have, at some point, been a plush little throne.

"One day I'm going to learn," I finally said, leaning back in the wooden seat, "not to go underground, not ever."

"It's not that bad," Ulanion said groggily as he pinched himself. "That was the most pleasant take-down I think I've ever suffered, at least, and effective."

"Something I will be adding to my own spells soon," I said, trying to check my toes as I sucked in air.

"Ugh, she's not complaining about how bad it was, only that it's every freaking time we end up underground. It really is like this with you, isn't it Alana?" Dras said while trying to blink. "What was that anyway?"

"Laughing gas, if I had to judge, non-lethal, and a good move if it's trying to just stop disobedient students."

"Fun, but I'd rather be able to do it myself. Any side-effects?" he asked. Drugs were a known thing in this world.

"Not with this little exposure." I began to look around, hoping to find some way out of this.

I began to rise but heard a voice from behind me. "The headmaster has been alerted. You will remain where you are until the headmaster arrives." That got me to quickly sit back down.

"Any ideas on what to do about this thing?" Dras asked. "It looks like my spell didn't even touch it." I turned to look at the golem. These things were always a problem.

"A few, but none that we can do here and without any supplies. There should also be some way to turn it off, or some commands. Not sure what to do, really. Ask it questions, perhaps?" I looked at the golem again. "Um, it looks like the headmaster is here. May we leave?" I asked innocently, pointing toward the skeleton.

"The headmaster has been alerted. You will remain where you are until the headmaster arrives." It appeared to understand that I was addressing it, but it didn't have a response to that particular question.

"I think the headmaster is hurt. Could you call for help?" I requested hopefully.

"The headmaster has been alerted. You will remain where you are until the headmaster arrives," it repeated mechanically.

"Maybe we can take it down?" Ulanion suggested.

"If we damage it but don't break it, the thing might escalate to significantly more lethal measures, depending on how it was made," I answered thoughtfully, killing that idea.

We went back and forth, trying to come up with something for nearly half an hour. The emergency teams would already have been alerted, but they weren't here, meaning they couldn't yet break into the wards.

"Pfft, this sucks, and I need to pee," I finally declared in frustration. As I mulled it over, though, that pinged an idea. "Hey, golem, can I go to the bathroom?"

"I do not know, can you?" it asked, sounding awfully sarcastic for an automaton.

"If your creator wasn't dead, I would punch you in your smug face," I mumbled. "*May* I go to the bathroom?" I asked, louder.

"You may," it stated, pointing to a door near the side of the office.

"May I go as well?" Dras asked.

"Only one at a time," it said, turning toward him and looking rather menacing.

"Okay, I'll see what I can manage. See you soon." With that, I rose and headed to the room it indicated, hoping that it was at least clean and that the plumbing still worked.

CHAPTER 21

◆

BATHROOM PASS

The provided restroom wasn't at all clean, seeing as it hadn't been used in centuries, but it had plumbing. The mana started flowing around the section of this building again. So too did the water. I idly wondered where in the world the water was draining to, but I had other concerns.

That golem was potent, made by a very skilled mage to defend his personal quarters. It was clearly holding back now, but who knew if it would continue to do so when faced with a real threat. That real threat was my men, who were absolutely going to be breaking in here at some point to disable it. We would succeed, too, but I cringed at the idea of the potential losses.

So it needed to go, and there were only a few ways to make that happen. Ideally, there would be a way to make it shut down on its own, but I was dubious. Barring that, we at least needed to cut off the mana supply to the golem, we could just back off and let it drain itself. The golems beneath Lithere had managed to keep themselves going, but they were in a much denser region of mana, and this one had been on some kind of charging station before we came in. That would be my first target.

Before I could do any of that, though, I needed to get out of this bathroom. Would the golem know to check on me if I took too long? Hard to say. Constructs like that were often not very smart, but they were locked into what they could do. If its creator hadn't thought to put that in the programming, it wouldn't be checking on me, there was no way of knowing. Constructs like the golem were the work of years of trial and error, and trying to find a hole in its programming within mere minutes was unlikely to succeed easily.

I ran my fingers over the walls, looking for a weak spot in the wards. Care needed to be taken now because the defenses were already up, and I didn't want to attract attention. Minutes passed as I examined each wall, frowning.

"Damn, he was thorough," I said out loud. It was good work, after all.

As I washed the accumulated dust of my actions from my hands again, I looked at the faucet. I'd not thought of that one. There was a hole in the wall already, built and installed there. In theory, it might be possible to add a small water-making spell to the faucet itself and negate the weakness, but Ristolian seemed to have been locked into old ideas, so he'd used pipes instead.

A quick bit of work and I could see that the entry of this water line did clearly bypass the wards in the walls, sending a smile across my face. Disassembling the whole thing was somewhat of a pain, and I had to freeze and chip away the ice inside it before I made a hole in the warding, but it worked.

Normally, a small hole out into the hallway wouldn't have been particularly useful, but if I could see somewhere, I could make a portal there safely. So, that's what I did. I stepped through and waited, not knowing if or when our large metallic companion would come out into the hall. It would depend on what kind of senses it had.

A few moments and no sound of it headed my way, I began to slink away from the office. The halls were still and silent as I backtracked where we'd come from through the tracks of dust on the floor.

The place really was filthy, but not quite as bad as I might have feared. There wasn't much down here to rot or go bad, other than the building itself, so dust was limited, and there weren't any signs of insects or rodents getting in. It was more like a tomb to an ancient pharaoh, quiet and undisturbed.

The golem's creche was where we'd last seen it, stuck along the wall with a number of inputs for mana and signals from the building. I began to carefully examine it. On the side of the holder were two large red buttons, both covered by glass. The top one read, in English, "Attack" and ostensibly set the golem to a far more aggressive stance. The bottom button, separated by nearly a foot, read, similarly, "Emergency Stop," which one would hope would do just that.

My concern, and the only reason I'd not already begun pressing the latter button, was what I knew about the maker of this fortress. By all accounts, Ristolian had enjoyed jokes, and switching his buttons around to screw over an enemy would fit right in with the few stories I'd heard of him. There was also a slim chance that both buttons were traps.

After a sizable amount of observation of the display, I came to a conclusion. I didn't know what either would do. One or both could be traps, and there was simply no way for me to discern from this object alone which would do what.

"Okay, so he liked jokes and pranks, but would he do that here? The English makes it clear these were for him, or maybe Justin . . . Did Justin ever come here? Not important. It may also work for me, or someone else who knows the language. Would Ristolian mess with them with anything dangerous? Probably not, and if he had an emergency stop, he would label it as such. I would, at least. Wait, maybe he liked that list of rules for evil overlords . . . Fuck. Okay, best guess." I mumbled to myself for a few minutes, but we'd run out of time eventually, and the entry of our forces would be coming soon.

I punched the button alleging to stop the machine, and I waited. There was no instant attack on me, nor the sound of metal men approaching, looking to kill. That was good, so I slinked back to the office and knocked on the door.

It took a few moments, but soon the door opened, revealing my smiling, and slightly confused looking, companions.

"You found a way to turn it off?" Dras asked.

"Fun fact—our predecessor had the same feeling about fail-safes that the old Elven king had. Probably just so he didn't have that thing lose it on him or anyone else."

"Makes sense," Ulanion said. "So, are we getting out of here?"

"Still haven't found the shutoff for the wards," I explained.

"How'd you escape from the bathroom anyway?" Dras asked as we continued down the hall.

"Add a reminder to check that our plumbing is warded," I replied.

After a quick and very unproductive search of the office, we made our way to the largest and most heavily fortified door in the hall and began picking apart the protections. If there was going to be a way to turn the protections off, or cut off their power, it would be in there.

Dras and I were both experts when it came to things like this, and the door's protections were already beginning to fail. The building wards were, too, having not been maintained as they should have, but enough still worked to be an issue. This door, however, we could force, even if it took time. It wasn't like we were doing anything else until we figured it out or got help.

An hour of work later, Dras began ripping the whole thing out. Even without the magic in it, the door was still a formidable physical defense. As the door fell, Dras and I smiled. Our years of work had paid off. The sight that graced us beyond the felled door made me freeze.

"Is it me, or is that thing . . ." Ulanion let the end of his question fall as he stood there, mouth open.

"That is eerily familiar," my old friend said, looking upon it.

"And it's certainly doing more than just making light," I added.

CHAPTER 22

✦

NOT A LAMP

Hovering in the center of the room was a sphere so perfect I struggled to look at it. Runes covered its surface as it gently spun. This sphere was the very center of the underground area's whole setup. I stopped, jaw clenching.

"It's like yours," Dras said, turning to me.

"The effect isn't as bad, not at all," I replied.

"Care to explain?" Ulanion interrupted.

"I made a lamp when we were in school that was too perfect; it hurt to look at, like this. Might also explain why this place is still functioning, because it was insanely efficient," I told him, walking around the small depression from which the sphere was hanging.

"So . . ."

"So, Ristolian made something similar," I said, gesturing to the sphere, "but this is no simple lamp. I never repeated the experiment because it was weird, but this . . . It's the power source for this whole area, and possibly even further than that.

There would be no telling what all was going on here until I got around to taking it apart. This thing could very well turn our current warding scheme on its head. The possibilities were staggering to consider.

"Dangerous?" Ulanion asked, keeping close.

"No, I don't think so, at least not in and of itself. The lamp I made was odd, and very mana efficient. Suppose that's why things are so stable with it."

"So, if it's a storage device, we might be looking at something that would hold for, well, at least centuries. I can think of a few uses for that,"

Dras said, appraisingly. "How much is it storing? And why didn't you ever peruse this?"

"How much? Who knows. As for why I never looked deeper into something like this, simple; I had other things on my mind. I did tell Mystien; maybe he did. He saw the lamp and all, but neither of us expected storage as an option." It would take me time, a lot of time, to decode this thing completely, assuming what I was looking for wasn't hidden, which was a distinct possibility. "All right, let's look for controls, standard issue ones for turning these wards on and off. Just find them for now, see what we got, and don't touch yet."

The room was large enough for the three of us to spread out, maybe twenty feet on each side. The sphere alone didn't need an area this big, and since the room was basically a vault, such a thing would be rather counter-productive. The center of the space had the object we were most concerned with, and it was taking up a fair amount of space, about five feet in circumference. All around it were various panels with readouts and controls. This was, after all, not a room one would mess with without reason.

I quickly found some books, which were in excellent condition for their age, and began to carefully flip through them. One thing about old ink and vellum was that it just lasted for centuries without any issues.

"Find something?" Dras asked, seeing that I'd acquired literature while he was checking out one of the panels.

"Yeah, I think these are the operations and maintenance manuals. Joker or not, this guy was organized, like, impressively organized." I waved my hand at some of the sheets hanging over the little case with the books. A quick glance told me they were the records for this room, dated with all problems listed out.

"I think this is the power control panel," Ulanion said, pointing. He wasn't a mage, but he was very used to dealing with magic.

I strolled over to his section, looking at the levers and indicators. "Yeah, looks like. One sec . . . What did he put it under? Power . . . not on/off . . . 'Shutdown procedures' it is."

After taking the time to do a once-over of the current state of things, I frowned. The wards here were quite good, and while I could see that they were registering an attack, they were also very capable of keeping themselves up for quite some time against it.

"You've got that look," my fiancé said.

"That look that says if we hadn't shut this down, we'd be stuck in here for almost a month? Because yeah, that's the look right now."

"There's no way that's right," Dras interjected.

"According to these and some rough division, it is," I said, turning. I didn't like it that he didn't trust me in this.

"All right, let me look," he said, joining us to do his own estimates. There were a series of murmured expletives. "Okay, well either his outputs are wrong, or something odd is going on here."

"His sequences must be way more efficient than ours, and with that thing," I said, pointing at the orb, "running it well."

"Right, so, turning it off?" Ulanion finally said, looking quite ready to go.

"Ah, yeah," I responded, turning to the correct section of the manual.

There was another big, friendly red button to shut things down, but I didn't want to test my luck. It would probably work, but with things as old as they were, it seemed wiser to go through the process of lowering the defenses slowly.

As I let my hands work over the proper levers and buttons, it occurred to me that this room must have been made possible to break into. Surely it could have been a tougher nut to crack, but maybe that in itself was a fail-safe? If things went wrong, it would be possible to turn it all off, even if it took a while. I briefly wondered if there were design notes or instructions around here somewhere, because I was very curious to see old Ristolian's theories on that.

When the rescue team finally arrived, it was clear they were in a state. "Ma'am, we've been trying to get to you, but couldn't. Are you okay?" their leader asked.

"I'm quite fine," I replied. "Please secure everything here. I know it will be a chore, but we'll need guards and some way to seal it that we control. There's also a skeleton in the other room; please secure that as well. He needs a burial." My orders given, I had a growing list of things to get into.

I wanted to dive into researching the work Ristolian had done, as we'd found a veritable treasure trove of materials down there. With some time, I might manage to have us pumping out some of the most advanced protections on the continent in the next year or two.

Sadly, I had some personal business to conduct first. Never had I met that particular world-hopper, but I knew he'd had at least one friend. Since there was literally nobody else, it seemed appropriate to contact said friend and see about giving the man a proper funeral.

The letter I made for Justin was formal, and in English. I told him we'd found Ristolian's body; though, there wasn't much left. Then, I asked him if he knew of any particular arrangements the wizard would have wanted.

It took a few days, but I got a response. Another note hefted through the portal Justin and I were using as a mailbox. It was short and to the point.

"I would like to speak to you at length; please bring the stone."

When I arrived, Justin was there, his face, skin, and build the same as always. His eyes, though, looked so old for a few moments. It passed, but in those seconds, I saw the weight of the ages pushing down on him. I couldn't imagine seeing everyone you cared for turn to dust.

"My condolences. We haven't buried him yet, if you want to be there," I began.

"Thank you. I do, I do, but he should be buried at his home, and that complicates things. Let us put that aside for the moment," he said, nodding to me, smiling gently.

"All right, then what should we discuss?"

"You have the stone?" he asked.

As soon as I produced it, he snapped his fingers, and the stone turned to dust in my hand. I glared at him and wiped my hand on one of his couches. Just because he *could* destroy it, didn't mean he had to be rude about it. His eyes shifted, and they were almost apologetic, realizing his misstep.

"Are you done?" I asked in an exasperated tone.

"No, I've got a new one for you. Please see to it that everyone uses it. This will put a few safety measures in place, and I've included a document in old Elven explaining it all." A stone similar to the one he'd just destroyed was set before me.

"Wow, an actual explanation with it, thank you." I wasn't even sarcastic. I really did appreciate it.

"I'd also like you to deliver a letter for me, to the head of the temples." He seemed almost nervous to ask. "I do not think it will go well, but I really do need to get eyes on that anomaly you made."

"What does that have to do with the orders?" I knew they didn't like him, but I didn't know the specifics.

"Old history, Alana, very old history. If I took any direct action on your continent without discussing it with them, or heaven forbid, went there, it might well become quite nasty."

After that, he told me about Ristolian. He'd never actually learned what the man had been called back on Earth, but it hardly mattered. The human man had come to visit him, always with new stories and jokes, always with a smile. I got the feeling that Justin didn't get to do this much. I let him go on until he finished getting it all out.

"Everything well?" Ulanion asked when I got home, his face concerned about how long it had taken.

"Fine, fine. I need to go to Linden though. Wanna come?"

"Oh, Alana, you still haven't realized it yet, have you?"

"Hmm?"

"That my favorite place to be tends to be wherever you are," he said, pulling me gently against his chest.

I kissed him, if only to make him stop spewing corny lines.

CHAPTER 23

✦

A LITTLE CHAT

It was hard to say if I really wanted to go back to Linden, but at least this time would be straightforward. Justin wasn't blaming me for the dangers of the portals, which I was thankful for. He was even helping me with my mission to fix them before something terrible happened. It seemed the least I could do was go and talk to the only other living trans-migrator for him, or deliver a letter, as it were.

Before I did that, though, I had a few meetings with my own people to deal with. The first was with those of us who'd activated the stone and gained the ability to make portals—my people and Dras's. We were all in a large room, which had been reserved just for us.

"Good afternoon everyone," I began. "I have good news, and bad news. Let's begin with the good. I've got some new built-in safeties for the portal network, which should solve some of the biggest dangers for us. We'll still need to be careful, but it should allow us to get back to expanding the network shortly." My declaration was met with a small cheer.

"Excellent, so what are they?" one of Dras's people asked.

"This stone will allow us to upgrade our cores in such a way as to allow it." I pulled out the new stone, showing it to everyone with a small smile. "Now for the bad news. Everyone here will be restricted from leaving the facility until they've upgraded their cores sufficiently."

There was an uproar.

"Where did you get that!?"

"Changing the core isn't something that anyone can do, ma'am. Can you!?"

"We can't leave?"

Eventually, I whistled a tune to silence the room.

"I know you all have questions, and I understand your concerns, but this is not a negotiation. The one who gave this to me has their reasons for doing so, and the ability to force the issue if needed. I would rather it not be needed. There are other questions that will be answered on a need-to-know basis, and I hate to say it, but most of you don't. Please understand that I'm doing this for all of our protection," I said, giving each person gathered a harsh look.

Everyone other than me, Dras, Selene, and the twins was dismissed. We needed to have this conversation, and they needed to know the truth of the matter.

Selene mostly kept to herself nowadays, but her glare at the stone in the middle of the desk was hard. "Where did you get it?" she asked.

"The same place I got the last one," I answered softly.

"I found the last one, not you, and it was in a desk."

"Where I planted it at the behest of the one who made it." That got eyes from all of them on me, everyone knew how serious this was.

"That Elven mage we met, the one who knew you?" Dras asked.

"That was Justin, the former Elven king; the one who made the cores, and the one who's now demanding we do this. I'm going to be honest here. I went to him seeking help, and this is what I got in return. I also got a not-so-thinly-veiled threat about what would happen if we refused."

The bomb quietly dropped, and everyone stood there in stunned silence. Many looked several shades of unhappy, and I was prepared to deal with that. I'd already put fail-safes in place, and anyone who tried to flee with what they currently had would be dealt with swiftly. This was just too important, even if I hated it.

Leah blinked several times. "He'd have to be thousands of years old though?"

"He is," I agreed.

"And not dead?"

"Elves don't age like us. My understanding is that the full-blooded ones don't really age at all past a point," I explained. This was rumored already, but there were so few of them still around that it was considered unconfirmed.

"Can I talk to him? I mean, the light he could shed on any field of research . . ." the excitable researcher began.

"I'll tell him you want to, but he doesn't like most people. Far as I can tell, he tolerates me, but that's about as far as it goes," I said, trying to placate Leah before she did anything extreme.

"You know, Alana, I'm really beginning to dislike you and your secrets," Selene said tiredly. "Even if I understand why you keep them."

"Will you continue to keep them?" I asked, hoping she'd say yes.

"Yes, I owe you that much. For a while, I blamed you for what those bastards did to me, but they would have done it anyway for the portals. Could I blame you for that mission? Maybe, but we'd have gone anyway, and without you, perhaps we wouldn't have made it back. Just don't expect me to help you with missions like that in the future."

I looked at Selene with pain in my heart. Ever since our kidnapping, we weren't friends. She knew about me, about my past life—she was one of only a handful. Now she was here, broken, and her frizzy hair was wilder, her eyes more sunken than when we'd first met. She was harder, less bubbly, and it made sense.

"I won't; thank you for everything."

She left us, and Leah made sure I would request a meeting with Justin for her. Her brother looked more sedate, concerned, a good reaction to the information they'd all just received. They, too, soon left, leaving only me and Dras. My oldest friend was giving me long consideration before he spoke.

"Secrets, plural. Any you'd share with me?" he finally asked.

"I have a few more, Dras, but nothing that would change anything. I would still be me, and you would still be you. Please, let it be," I replied.

"Okay," he said easily. At my raised eyebrow, he smiled and continued, "Alana, I hope one day you'll tell me, but if you don't, you're still the same girl who found me and made sure I was trained properly, still the same girl who saved my life, well, how many times are we on now? Just tell me though. Is it something bad?"

"Not really, just something that would cause me a lot of awkwardness and pain."

"Then keep it. I've got lots to do right now, though, so if you don't mind." He rose and headed for the door.

"Thank you, Dras," I muttered as he left, trying to keep all the ups and downs of this particular meeting contained.

Over the next couple of days I was tense. Letters had to be sent, travel arrangements made. The city of Linden needed me to send a request for a meeting, and they needed to agree, all of which took time. The entire time I worried that my people might rebel against me, but they didn't. They accepted my judgment that the new update was needed, and everyone worked on it.

Ulanion joined me as I made my way to the portal room, satisfied that I could be missed for a few days without issue. That was a good thing, as there were times when I would need to be gone for extended periods. The guards there waited with us as the connection was established, and I stepped through. It wouldn't take too much time to go through the stop-over, at least. We'd need one due to the lack of a direct link.

"Hello, dear," my father greeted me as I stepped through, Mystien by his side. "We need to have a little chat."

I tensed. They weren't alone. There were over half a dozen others with my father and Mystien. Those two alone were enough to deal with the few people I'd brought along.

"No need to be afraid, Alana. We just want to speak with you about some of our concerns," Father began, his eyes watching both Ulanion and myself sharply.

My former mentor said nothing, just looked on. I could feel the magic he was holding in place, ready in case we did something.

"All right . . . Mind if we go somewhere private then?" I asked.

We were quickly shown to a room.

"I'd rather we do this privately too," Dad said to Ulanion.

Ulanion made a face, but then left quietly. We quickly threw up a number of privacy wards.

Mystien began. He looked quite unhappy. "Let us start with the basics. Why exactly did you destroy our one means of making new portals and place new restrictions on those who could make them? We've discussed this and were already having less made, and with more protections."

"I had to consult with an expert about the issues surrounding the portals to try and find a long-term solution. He is the one who put the new measures in place. I think the larger question is how you know about all of this?" I replied, more snappily than I would have liked.

"Alana, we have an intelligence wing. You know this," Dad said, sighing.

Mystien gave me a probing look. "Alana, you are the resident expert in portal technology, perhaps the best in the world right now." At my raised eyebrow he searched his memories. "The elf."

Dad quirked his own eyebrow, so I opted to explain. "We ran into an archmage of extreme power over in the Elven lands. He's very private, but agreed to look into this. He's the one who provided the new additions we're using to stop another disaster like Silversprings, or worse, which he agrees is possible. Good news though. It means we can restart adding gates when we've got that done."

"Who is this man? How are you contacting him?" Dad asked in rapid succession.

"An old gate left behind, and as for his name, well, I suppose I'll need Mystien's help with him soon. Most people just call him the Elven king."

Dad didn't understand, but Mystien let out a solid stream of expletives.

"Which king? Atal's?" Dad asked, his confusion quite visible. He knew a lot about politics, but only on our continent.

"The elves only have one king, Verren," Mystien said to my dad and then turned back to me. "They only ever had one king. He's supposed to be dead." The old spellcaster was finally speaking something other than curses.

"The rumors are exaggerated."

"The last time he showed his face he almost took over two continents!" It seemed my feelings on the matter didn't calm Mystien at all. "It took the literal formation of the orders to stop him, and even then it was said to be a close call! If word of his return gets out, the elves will go to fucking war! A war we cannot afford, and one that would put us on the front line."

"I'm glad you're up to date on your history. More good news, he's uninterested in that. What he is interested in is my project because it relates to his own." I stared them down, dad confused and Mystien looking like he wanted to throttle someone.

"Explain," Dad said, eyes furrowing.

"He's doing some work with the same kind of thing that goes into the portals. I saw his papers once, and if I'm being honest, it's all nonsense to me, but he gets it. The price for my consult was nothing bad. We got new safety measures, what we needed to know, and a friendly connection that may one day prove useful. Bad news is more information about the distortions is needed right now." I started listing other things we'd gained.

"Why didn't you tell me about any of this?" Dad asked, looking frustrated.

"Why haven't I seen you in months? And don't tell me it's because you're busy. You pass through the portal network all the time, which I know because I see the logs. Yet, not once have you come to see me, or even the woman who will soon birth your grandchild. You don't get to complain to me that I'm not telling you things when you're never around to chat." It was my turn to be mad. He'd been avoiding me. All I ever got was formal letters with instructions and requests for magical items.

We sat in silence for a few minutes. Mystien could see this was a family issue and kept his distance. My father and I just stared at each other.

"Your mother . . ." he began, trailing off.

"You think I don't know!? I was there. She died because I wasn't strong enough." He raised his hand to stop me from speaking for a moment.

"It wasn't your fault. You didn't hurt her, and nobody could have stopped her from stabbing that woman. It's that you look just like her when she was your age. I can't look at you and not see her, and I can't fight this war and be distracted too." He looked hurt, and tired, and his age began to show even through all of his strength.

"Oh." It was all I could say. I'd clearly not known his own issues.

I placed a hand on his and held it there. Dad needed time to grieve, and everything was preventing that. It hurt to think about, but he couldn't now, not if he wanted us to be able to see tomorrow.

"I'll try to come see you when I can, but there are things we still need to be kept in the loop on. Like why you're going to Linden," he said, finally going back to the point of their waylaying me.

"Because one old and powerful archmage wants to meet with another old and powerful archmage, and apparently, I'm now the delivery girl for them both. I'm hoping this will be enough to sate the elf and get him working on what I need, so I can spend more time on advancing our wards. I'm hoping Mystien will be there in case something goes wrong." I said with a shrug.

"You are a very frustrating girl who became a very frustrating woman," Mystien said.

"Thank you."

"Not a compliment."

"Yes, it was." I let it drop when I saw his eyebrow begin to twitch.

"When will this be?" he asked after a few moments.

"I don't even know *where* it will be yet. Working on finding all of that out now."

"I'd offer to send more guards with you," Dad said, "but from my reports, the people of Linden seem to be against the idea of a repeat performance of the last time you were there. If someone attacks you, I don't actually have much better than the priests they're sending. So, be careful."

"Keep us informed," Mystien added. "I *will* be coming by to see you soon. I'd like to see some of your new work, too, if you don't mind."

"I don't, but you will not interfere with my facility," I said, matter-of-factly.

"Are you satisfied?" Dad asked his companion.

"For now."

"Good, because I need to get back to the front. We're still unable to locate some of General Ozen's forces. I expect an attack on the eastern side of the country at any moment." Dad rose and left, giving some signal to the men outside. They fell in line, so I supposed that was good for us.

Union sent me a questioning glance, and I just shook my head. "Misunderstanding."

CHAPTER 25

✦

IRRITATING OLD MEN

"You're a problem, do you know that?" a particular old priest asked me from his desk.

His room was simple, so very simple, but it had a home-like quality to it. This was a place someone could relax and do whatever it was they found relaxing for untold years, and he had done just that. The only contrasting element was his desk, hectic and piled high with papers.

"I'm getting told that a lot recently, yes," I replied truthfully. "But not all problems are bad."

"I do not want, and will not allow, him here," he said waving the note. "Not within a thousand miles of here if we're being precise. To even suggest such a meeting is some kind of insane insult to order itself, and I will not have it."

"Aaron, I can call you Aaron right?" At his hand wave I continued. "I know things went poorly in the past."

"You do not."

"I do, but I have other concerns. If you had been there, if you had seen and felt what I saw and what I felt, you would too."

"You're convinced that this danger you encountered is what, some kind of otherworldly horror waiting to consume this world?" he asked.

"Maybe, maybe something else. I don't know."

"And yet you continue to use the very magic that you say nearly brought it into this world. How responsible," he quipped, clearly unhappy.

I leaned forward, locking eyes with him. "The cat is out of the bag, old man. Too many people now know about the portals; too many are already interested in the possibility of teleportation to just ignore it, or hide it. We didn't know about the threat at the time, or things might have been different, but they are as they are. What I am doing is trying to prevent any damage from happening, and to find ways for that to not happen again."

"Care to explain what you mean?"

"Bards. We're capable of fixing the little distortions caused by this sort of magic, if imperfectly. I figured it out years ago when trying to clean up after myself and am training others to do just that. That and working on items, some of the aid for which has been provided by the one you're maligning so harshly. I went to get his aid because he's the best with this kind of magic." I was already tired of this argument.

"What makes you think that?" the old priest asked.

"Because I've seen his work." I could see in his eyes that he wanted me to expand on what exactly the man he hated so viciously was working on, but he was out of luck. "Which you're free to ask him about if you agree to a meeting."

"Even if I wanted to meet with him, it would be impossible. I'm not going to where he is, or sending any of my people that could speak to him about this, and he is certainly *not* coming here."

"You can use my place; it's as neutral as anywhere could be," I offered.

"If I find that you've brought that man onto this landmass, we are going to have problems," he said, his voice low and dangerous as he loosed his aura, the power flooding the room. "Are we clear?"

"Crystal," I said weakly. He was trying to intimidate me, and it was working.

"Good."

Slowly he pulled his power back down. Over the years it seemed every stupidly powerful magic user seemed to gain both intuitive and perfect control of their aura. I wasn't quite there yet, but I was far better than most, and I was able to hide it when I wanted to. Many a caster always leaked some amount of it into the air, and I briefly wondered if that training made someone stronger or something.

"Teleconference," I said after thinking in silence for a few moments.

"What?" the ancient man replied.

"We have working radios. With some extra effort, we could easily set up a teleconference, or something similar. Either here or at the old fortress. He wouldn't need to be nearby, and you could actually talk rather than just having issues at continental distances," I suggested, hoping for some agreement.

"Our 'issues at continental distances' are unlikely to be resolved, but the idea is at least tolerable."

He sat back in his chair, tapping his fingers on his desk repeatedly for several moments. I might have him here. There were only so many objections someone could raise to accepting a phone call about potentially world-ending problems, and we both knew it. Heck, if he didn't, I'd probably find some way to get Justin what he wanted anyway, consultation or not.

"I'll consider it and get back to you later," he finally answered. "Part of the problem is you as well. You're associating with a known mass murderer, and if reports are to be believed, you nearly single-handedly wiped out everyone in a succession line in one swoop."

"Not how I wanted things to go. Lief needed to die for what he did to Durin, what he did to our country, and what he would have done had I not stopped him. I know reports were made on Ice's End, on what happened with those children." Intimidated or not, I spat venom at him now. He had no right to question me or berate me for doing what was right.

"And the children, what of them?"

"I did not kill any children," I said, gritting my teeth.

"No, you did not," he said with the calm truth of someone letting you in on their secret. "We have ways of tracking bloodlines you know? When the bishop in Lithere found what he did, he was most confused. Sent one particular little one to us to make sure. Your portal network helped bring her here."

"She has no family left, and if you tell anyone, that kid will either be assassinated or become a political pawn, perhaps both. She deserves a chance at a decent life." I locked eyes with him.

He knew these things already. Was he threatening to bring her forward? Did he think that having her here would make her a pawn, for him? I didn't know, but I'd done what I could to see to it that little girl would get a chance, and I would do so again if needed.

"Is that why you did it?" he asked.

"I didn't know she existed, and I didn't want to hurt her mother. They didn't need to die. As far as I know, they didn't ever do anything wrong. The mother didn't kill anyone, and the child is just a child. The question is, what do you plan to do?"

"Nothing." At my raised eyebrow he continued. "We're politically neutral on most things; we will do nothing. There are no parents to claim her, or even proof that she's the legitimate heir to anything, and exposing her to danger would be cruel. So, we'll do what we do with every orphan; we will raise her."

"Theodore?" I asked, wanting to know what the bishop might be thinking.

"Suspected she was a bastard. You wouldn't believe how many of those are floating around. I was hoping you might confirm my suspicions either way, though, I would advise you to watch for that in the future."

He had me there, even if it pissed me off. I could have just denied everything or stayed silent. Next time.

"Advice noted. I'm off to set things up so you or your representative can have that meeting. Kindly send them to the fortress as soon as reasonably possible."

"I didn't agree," he pointed out as I rose to leave.

"You will anyway," I replied as I left, closing the door behind me. I could hear the guffaw, but I was right.

CHAPTER 26

✦

SUMMIT PREPARATIONS

Unfortunately, the leadership of the various orders had decided to take their sweet time sending a representative. Normally this would be an issue, but I had so much work to do that it really wasn't. If anything, I was grateful for the extra time to get ready.

The main thing I was doing now was overhauling the wards for the fortress, again. Many of my workers were downright tired of me doing it, but with the current civil war, they all knew how important it was. Today, I even had a bit of help with installation.

"You know, I didn't come here to help you with your chores," Mystien chided as he floated several large pieces into place.

"You're here, and taking up my time, so you are in fact here to help me with my chores. By the way, did you happen to tell anyone the secret of that lamp I made?" I asked.

"The weird one? No, we studied it for a while, but I never could figure out why it was so weird. Is it important?"

"Sort of. The last piece is in the box over there," I said, pointing at a crate, which had recently been moved from my lab—the final piece to this ward. "Then I'll send you off with a few little toys that I'd like someone to test in the field."

The sphere was, much like its predecessor, really weird to look at. It was just so perfect, so oddly ideal, that it didn't properly fit in with what it should be. I'd been studying the setup Ristolian had used for the past few weeks and was now confident that it would fit in well with my newest updates.

"Interesting, and you took the time to hide what it's doing," he commented as he moved the final piece of the contraption into place.

"I did."

"What is it doing?" he asked.

"Oh, it moves some rocks in case we get attacked, nothing too bad," I teased.

"And the shape?"

"Increases efficiency and mana retention exponentially. We found one like it in Ristolian's old personal office that was still charged up centuries after being left there, with no external source. This one is the core of our new defense." I had no problem sharing those facts with him. From what he was seeing here, he probably already suspected. "I'll send you some of the results we got."

"I'd like to see the actual site," he grumbled.

"Denied."

"Denied? I think you forget who's funding this little operation of yours, Alana," he said.

"I am. I'm currently the only provider of portals and sky-metal, and the best provider of half of the magical items your strongest forces use." I didn't even have to exaggerate; it was all true.

"About the sky-metal, I'm hoping you might be convinced to spare some more. The meager amounts you're sending us are hardly enough for our needs right now."

Sky-metal, or aluminum in my previous world's language, was a premium material for many magical uses. I'd figured out the trick to making it back in school, but others had a difficult time making it at all. The fact that aluminum was practically everywhere in rocks helped, but without knowledge of atomic theory, wizards would struggle, and without proper visualization, bards would fail. I was the only real supplier.

For whatever reason, aluminum was highly conductive, magically speaking, and therefore, ideal for a number of purposes. It made workable parts for armor, but it was too soft for weapons. It was also excellent for static magical structures, with only a few materials gathered from magical beasts to really make it work well. Silver and copper were also extraordinarily good, but each had their own problems that aluminum lacked.

"When I get the time I'll be happy to," I replied.

"You know, telling me that you'll do it in your free time is rude. You could just tell me no."

He looked at me, and I just couldn't keep the smirk off my face. Both of us were swamped with the war going on. Sadly there didn't seem to be much of an end in sight.

I wasn't privy to all of the details, as those were for people who needed to know, but I knew a few things. Our faction had started off strong, with Father and Mystien and control of the portals, we had the best infrastructure of any of the various inheritors of the empire. We also had some of the best of the special troops. Sadly, we had access to fewer troops than a number of the other generals, and while we'd taken most of the former Bergond, we certainly didn't have it completely under control.

Other generals had the bulk of the army under their commands, and they'd been far to the east when things had gone wrong. There was also a breakaway faction in the southern sections of the two former kingdoms, trying to establish rule over lands that were difficult to take for one reason or another. The lines were blurry, with skirmishes nearly constant. The alliances also seemed to shift on a daily basis due to politics that were well outside my level. The only real solid fact for me was that one of the generals, a man named Ozen, had set himself firmly against our group. I knew nothing about him, save for the fact that everyone took him seriously.

"I hope that doesn't mean you're backing out of joining my summit," I commented with a grin, watching his face crease with displeasure.

"That I can't afford to do. Even if your 'friends' weren't too powerful for us to let wander around, I rarely get a chance to talk to people more powerful than myself. Their off-the-cuff insights could be world-changing."

"Good, but for now," I said, leading him to a small crate, "these are just preliminary, for testing. If they work as well as I hope, we can make more." I passed him one of the small boxes from the crate, knowing that the perfectly circular core inside it was the real prize. "Shielding arrays, mobile."

"Instructions?" he asked, only to see my finger pointing to the booklet in the box. "I swear you get cheekier by the day. Fine, I'll have my people look them over."

It was several weeks later when the envoy from the orders finally arrived, and it wasn't quite who I was hoping for. It began with a few guards emerging from the portal to do a security sweep, before the envoy herself made her way out.

My self-image instantly took a hit when the jaw-dropping Elven woman stepped through the portal. She looked, in a word, perfect. Her body curved in all the right places, and the guards I'd brought were clearly distracted as she sauntered through the opening and began looking around. Her snow-white hair fell into the cleavage of her simple robe as she studied the room, eyes eventually falling on me.

My eyes, of course, snapped to Ulanion who, to my satisfaction, was looking everywhere except at the beauty who'd just entered my home. If he'd been ogling her like some of the other soldiers, I'd have had a conversation with him.

"Ah, you must be Alana," the woman said with a smile as she approached. "I've heard so much about you, and about this little meeting we're supposed to have."

I knew the signs. I'd heard rumors of them, and seen them firsthand. The way her ears were so long and the color of her hair. This woman wasn't just an elf—she was an old elf, a pure elf. What I didn't know was why they'd sent her.

"Indeed, a pleasure to meet you. Unfortunately, I wasn't informed of who exactly was coming?" I queried, hoping to learn what I could.

"Oh? My apologies then. I'm from the Lovers. A pleasure to meet you. Do we have time before the meeting begins?" she asked, moving beside me and hooking her arm through mine.

"Yes . . ." I said, only barely registering that she'd not given her name.

"Good, good. I was hoping we might have a little chat, girl to girl. I'm oh so curious as to your relationship with Justin. Won't you tell me all about it?"

CHAPTER 27

✦

THE PRIESTESS

I was cornered, trapped by the priestess. Well, sort of. Somehow we'd managed to find our way to one of the many meeting rooms. Since the fortress had served as both a central location for a rebellion and an emperor's personal residence, meeting rooms were not in short supply. We sat across from one another, engaged in what some might call a chat but what others would clearly recognize as an interrogation.

"So, how exactly do you know Justin?" she inquired, leaning forward. We were alone now, separated from our various guards.

"We met while I was looking into the portals. I stumbled into his workshop and drank his tea."

She laughed and it sounded like wind chimes, and she leaned backward. "Oh, I would have loved to see that."

"How exactly do you know him? Or do you?" I asked, trying to parse who exactly I was dealing with here.

"Oh, we have history going back a long, long way, but that's not important right now. What's important is why he's coming here? Or wants to." Suddenly her face hardened, eyelids slipping down as she stared at me. "I won't lie; nobody is happy about this situation, but I want to know the basics of the situation."

"The math is beyond me, if I'm being honest," I began, and she nodded. Nobody really needed the physics details from a bard. "But, we managed to find that the portals are causing a number of anomalies in the world. The portals themselves are not the only way for variances to form, so getting rid of them would only be a stopgap. My hope is to figure out what the danger is, and find a way to mitigate it."

"Have you had any success in that endeavor so far?" All of the bubbly flirtatiousness was gone. We were alone now, and while this woman might have otherwise been well disposed toward me, I was after something her whole organization decidedly didn't want.

"Some, as I explained to the shield elder. My apprentices are being trained to do the best we can, and we know that with time, it all cleans itself up, eventually."

She seemed to still be quite unhappy, but she nodded. "Before coming here, I made inquiries among our staff and reviewed records. I hate to admit it, but this line of research is poorly understood. Your group might well be the best educated on the continent about it."

"I mean, it decidedly isn't priest magic," I pointed out.

"No, well, not really. At a certain level of power you can start to do some very interesting things that others might not expect, but that's beside the point. We also have more than a few wizards working for us and have had some powerhouses over the years."

"You also have methods of making items that don't really translate to the rest of us."

She raised an eyebrow at that comment.

"The marks," I clarified.

"Oh, yes, well, sort of. That magic is kept secret to prevent it from being abused, but it's more of a prototype, comparable to the common item creation. It just releases magic at a timed interval; the real magic is in the ink. There were older ones you know."

"I did not . . ."

"Tattoo type magic was somewhat of a fad for a time, but it fell from favor."

It was now my chance to lean in, as this was information I'd never heard, and was unlikely to hear from any other source.

"Why?" I asked.

"A couple of reasons. One, it's horribly inefficient compared to magical items; and two, the uses are limited to special inks. The effect of the Lovers' Marks was so slight and subtle that it became the most widely used. In fact so much that it still persists for common people. We're getting off subject again."

"Right, what else do you need to know?" I asked.

"The reports I have say you felt . . . something, looking at our world. Could you clarify? Can we fight it? Do we need to?" she asked.

"I don't know how familiar you are with the idea of this universe . . ."

"I'm aware of the very basics, and that there are travelers like yourself from other worlds." She frowned as she said that. "You all seem to cause big changes, for good or ill."

"Well, again, some of the deeper parts are beyond me, but there is a place outside of . . . reality, and there is something out there. Justin doesn't think there should be, and there were stories back on our world about that sort of thing, all generally bad. As for fighting whatever it is? From what I felt, I can't imagine it." I felt my own eyes slip off into the distance as I tried to picture combating something that made me terrified by its very existence. All I could imagine coming from it would be horror and pain.

"Stories?" she said, an eyebrow quirking.

"Lovecraftian was the term used, but I'll freely admit I didn't really read Lovecraft. Just knew the genre, and that they tended to have things that shouldn't be." I'd said the name in English.

"Love-craft? That sounds like something I'd be doing, though, doesn't it? Not some horror." That was enough to confirm she spoke my lingo; though, that shouldn't have really surprised me.

"Er, I think it was a writer's name," I explained.

"What an odd name." She leaned back and sighed. "Very well, when is the other party arriving? We'll need to get this over with."

"Tomorrow," I replied. "I do hope that's all right?"

"Of course, do we have rooms?"

"Yes, near our current resident priestess. I'm sure she'll be happy to have you around."

As we rose and moved to the door, she fell away from the hard, unhappy, businesswoman attitude and back into her previous, jovial persona. Our arms were interlinked by the time I got the doors open, and as I led her and her retinue to their rooms, I heard at least one of my men trip and stumble.

Kala looked over the moon when I introduced her to the Elven priestess. She was biting her lip, seemingly without thinking about it. I let Kala take over, the still nameless priestess moving to her side and lightly discussing the work around the fortress.

"Don't fall for it." Ulanion had appeared at my side once I was far enough away.

"Care to clarify?" I asked.

"That woman may not be evil, but she's dangerous. I've seen her kind before, like a flower with a poisonous scent. Within seconds she was pumping Kala for information on us; didn't you see?"

"I did, and she's certainly not a friend, but you think she's an enemy?" I asked, looking at him.

"I don't know, but what I do know is that she was sent here for a reason. I'd guess at least part of that reason is to get intel from us."

I sighed deeply, already tired from this politicking. "I'll need to warn our researchers to keep away from her and to watch what they say. Luckily, Kala's not too involved in politics. We probably can't keep her from spilling any and all important information on injuries, but luckily most of that shouldn't reveal anything of note." I stopped for a second and looked at him. "I do hope you're not worried that I've shared anything untoward."

"You tend to, but I'll trust your judgment. Did you tell her anything important?"

I ran over the conversation in my head. "Nothing vital that she didn't already know. Oh, we also need to add magical tattoos to the list of topics to look into."

"Never heard of anything other than the Lovers' Marks, but isn't the list already long enough? You've just taken a few things off, haven't you?"

"Aww, Ulanion, that's the thing about lists. The harder you work to shorten them, the longer they tend to end up."

He chuckled as we strolled off together to warn some of the staff—me the researchers, and he the guards. The latter definitely needed to be straightened out in short order.

CHAPTER 28

✦

NEGOTIATIONS BEGIN

I sat at the meeting table waiting, across from me the woman who I was fairly convinced had founded the Lovers. She sat there playing with her hair as I ran through my paperwork, looking over reports that had just arrived this morning. The scouts had noticed some of the local monsters were acting strangely, either missing or riled up. There were a few ways that might have happened, the most likely being that some other, bigger beast had moved into the area, but this issue was still far enough away that it wasn't an immediate danger.

Our table divided into thirds, Mystien was at my side. He was comporting himself better than most, involved in his own work and interested in meeting our final guest.

There were a few guards here, and they were all currently behaving themselves, Ulanion having given them a firm beating into shape. Though he was elsewhere. We had other concerns where senior staff was needed.

I thought back on my conversation with Kala this morning. She absolutely gushed about our guest, and knowing her, I was well aware how the two of them had likely spent their evening. The shade of red she turned when I asked her the woman's name and she failed to answer was both confirmation and a reminder that our Elven 'friend' liked her games.

The final third of our circular table sat before a portal, recently moved from my personal lab. As the time for our meeting finally arrived, it charged up, flaring to life.

The first one to step through was a rather familiar looking golem dog. It surveyed the area briefly before the figure of the ancient Elven king stepped through. His eyes swept the room before landing on the priestess. His face fell, shoulders lowering briefly and eyes taking on the look of age.

"Naturally they'd send you. I am at least glad to see you well, Adia." Now I had a name at least.

"Let's get this over with. You want to research this anomaly at Silversprings, yes? I'm willing to listen to the proposal, but we want guarantees that you'll do nothing else," Adia said.

"Not even a hello? After all this time, can you not at least forgive me?"

"I was satisfied with your punishment, which was never to trod these lands again, and yet here you stand." The priestess released her aura like an angry wave, undulating pink like a tide pushing across the room.

Mystien drew back in near panic at the amount of power she displayed, but I was less impressed, having seen such displays before. She was strong, sure, very strong, but this wasn't controlled. She'd actually lost her cool. A look revealed that Justin, too, was unimpressed, merely keeping a small bubble of bubbles around himself.

I flared my power as well. It was meager compared to the titans around me, but there was a point to be made that we wouldn't be bullied. As soon as he recovered, our archmage joined me with a display of his own.

"I believe we all agreed there would be no fighting here," I said with as much steel in my voice as I could muster.

In an instant the aggression fell away, returning things to their former state.

"My apologies," Adia said.

"We are satisfied to allow access to our lands," Mystien declared. "Though we do want the results of the investigation to provoke further disasters." While I might be in charge of this facility, he was the one who could authorize work at other places. "I'd also like to speak with you at length another time, as I feel it might be enlightening," he said to Justin.

"That is not enough for us," the priestess said, crossing her arms. "We want a guarantee."

"Of what kind?" I asked, hoping to solve this problem.

"That is the problem, isn't it? We have few who exist at the level of magic needed to combat him, and I doubt you lot could stop him from making a portal and marching an army through it," she argued. She was right.

"I no longer command armies, Adia, and haven't in a long time."

"Oh? And how many golems like that one do you have?" Justin's face was telling, and she snorted. "That's what I thought."

When I looked between the two, I could see there was history here, a lot of it, but neither seemed interested in getting into it. There was a deep-seated desire in me to know what happened between the two of them, but if I pried, one or both might spill the details of who I was to Mystien or the others, something I decidedly didn't want.

"If I wanted to do that, I simply would," Justin argued. "It isn't like there's anyone here who could do much about it. If an army of automatons to conquer land was what I desired to release, I would just release them. Clearly, though, you want something, so why don't you tell me what it is?"

There was a slight smile on Adia's face. "Alana, can you construct another of those explosive devices, like the one whose results he wishes to look into?"

"Not with the new restrictions on the portals, no."

"Convenient, but you *can*?"

"Yes?" I said, curious as to where she was going with this.

"Then why didn't you send one over to the other continent and repeat the experiment there? The mess would have been reproduced, and he could have studied it," she pointed out.

"One, because that's insane, and two, because I don't want something bad to happen there either."

It was clear where she was trying to go with this. *Why didn't you just do it there?* Nonsense. I wanted none of it. I'd dumped too much time and effort into seeing that particular mistake never repeated to just casually set off destruction elsewhere.

"I've told you the details of what happened, and if you're unaware of why I wouldn't do such a thing again, then you're too stupid to even have a seat here. Just say what you actually want and stop playing games," I said, already unhappy with the way this was going.

The only upside to this whole debacle, and this world in general, was that politicians tended to be mages as well, and therefore knew they had better things to do than dick around once their games had been found out. Sure, some of the more entrenched factions would play games with each other, but when it came to groups like ours, and any who had powerful enough individuals, it stopped. If you really were strong, you never needed to go around shouting to the sky about how awesome you were.

"Access to a number of golem designs, as well as some of the weapons and weapon platforms produced in the last war between our factions. Added to that, we want full access to the portal technology so that we might build and maintain our own network," Adia said, finally giving a list of demands.

"No," Justin said simply. "I'm not giving you all of that."

Now the real haggling began, and I felt myself smile when the old Elven king continued, declaring that I was Ristolian's inheritor and therefore the one who should own the rights to the portal technology as far as he was concerned. I knew it was a lie, that he'd still do with it what he wanted, but this ensured we still had a seat at the table. It did make my mentor give me the strangest look though.

The back and forth was intense, but there was some wiggle room. Justin was an absolute monster when it came to design, and the orders knew it, therefore they wanted some of his older ones. Both Mystien and myself heavily objected to this once we learned what exactly they were after.

In the past there had been a few ship designs that had allowed the elves to cross the ocean with ease. Both sides were vague about exactly what was going on with them, but apparently when it came to war, they were unparalleled. They'd also been built and maintained by a corps of elves led by our elderly king himself, one that had been lost to the ages. These matched with some of the magically powered boats I'd seen on their continent but had been of a different scale, one not seen since.

There were also magical weapons and golems that the old man had designed over the years that could work as a force multiplier. Adia wanted those, too, since there were very few who could design a working golem of any real ability. Ristolian's assistant was a good example—they had to be complex or they would get locked into circular paths of action, unable to escape.

Limited versions were eventually agreed upon, but then the priestess turned to me.

"Portals. We want to be able to make and maintain our own," she declared, like it was already agreed upon.

"Absolutely not," I responded. "I've done too much work trying to keep that technology contained to hand it over." I was slightly offended that she'd make such a request after our talks.

"We do not want you to have a pure monopoly on portal travel. It would allow us to move priests where they needed to be when we needed them to be there."

"Mind if I propose a compromise?" I offered.

She raised an eyebrow, but nodded. "You may."

"I can provide you with a limited number of portals for your people to place where they please. We can hash out the exact number, and where they would be delivered, but they would be yours, not ours. It would also allow me to keep the creation of those dangerous objects controlled for now."

"How many?" Adia asked, smirking. This may have been what she was hoping to get in the first place.

The next round of negotiations began. Mystien had things he wanted as well—the sharing of the plans for the portals, which we got, and the slower delivery of portal pairs than the priests wanted. While we could understand that they desired actions over promises, we were still in the midst of war and in need of all the infrastructure we could get.

A deal was eventually struck, with Adia securing the next five portal pairs we made, and then one additional for every five we made until we'd delivered twenty to the orders. It would be a hassle, but one we could deal with in both the short and long term.

As for the teleportation technology out there floating around, I wasn't too worried. I hadn't revealed to them that I had a way to track those, because why would I? If they decided to become a real thorn in our side, we could have personal visits to wherever they decided to stick their portals, and repossess them with vigor.

Once we had all of our agreements in place, we took a break so a scribe could put it all in proper legalese for us. These wouldn't be public record, but everyone liked having a receipt for their deals.

"Then we're all satisfied?" Justin asked tiredly.

"No, but we can live with it," Adia answered, tapping her fingers on the desk.

"I do hate to impose while in your home, miss Alana," said Justin, "but might my counterpart and I have a few moments of privacy?"

Mystien and I went for lunch while the two elves set up a barrier and began to chat. I didn't know what they were talking about, and while I could have planted bugs in the room, that had seemed in bad taste. I'd also hate to be found out for doing such a thing, and the many issues it might cause, potentially even the failure of these negotiations.

They joined us some time later, both looking rather drained from whatever had transpired between them. A few minutes into what should have been a cordial chat, Ulanion appeared.

"We have a slight issue," he said, leaning into me.

"What?" I asked.

He went over to the window and pointed at the horizon. I could see little more than a small blur. With a few small movements, I set up one of my lenses, expanding the view to cover what had him worried.

There was an army. Not the largest collection of men I'd ever seen, but one clearly well arrayed to assault us. They marched forward in rank after rank. Within their formation were carts and items held aloft. I recognized some of my own designs, older ones for warding and protection. There seemed to be mages, as well, outriders putting up spells and wards to stop anything we might throw at them.

"I suppose that answers what happened to Ozen's forces. He must have tried to bring them here without us noticing," Mystien opined. "Not sure we can fight that many on our own."

"You are absolutely forbidden from joining in this conflict," Adia said from behind, voice hard as she addressed Justin.

"Do not worry, my dear," the white-haired magus answered. "I wasn't planning on it."

"He won't be needed," I said with a smile. "Though Mystien, remind me to thank Ozen should we see him. I've been itching to try out some of my new protective schemes." I turned to my fiancé. "Have you already initiated the emergency protocols?"

"Of course," he chuckled. "We've called for reinforcement, and all of the gate rooms are on alert."

"Great, let's send out the Hall Monitor."

"The Hall Monitor?" Adia asked, her voice showing her confusion.

"Something an old friend left behind."

General Ozen

General Ozen stood among his men, staring at the captured fortress. This had been Durin's home, and the murderous little wretch and her ilk had taken it for themselves. There was no way some two-bit princeling had killed his lord, only to fall to that girl, and he would prove it, after he retook the empire.

With a wave the bombardment began. The shields were no surprise, as his enemy was well known for their defensive structures, but shields could, and would, be broken. It might be kind of a push to do it, and he had no doubt that some or all of the portals would fall before he could conquer this bastion, but that was fine. Doing it would still cripple his enemies, robbing them of one of their greatest assets.

Long range ballistae and magics bounced off a hard shell, the dome appearing only as the impacts fell, shattering and splattering across the surface of the protections. It was like trying to crack a turtle's shell, each impact one more blow against them.

And then the wind died.

Ozen looked toward one of his advisors, a specialized battle-mage. The man turned to the sky, eyes flicking as he pulled out observational tools.

"Shield, secondary and around us. Not too strong, I think, probably so their men don't have to deal with the cold as we fight them," the advisor said, shrugging. "Not a threat to us."

As they continued pounding against the dome surrounding the castle, a single figure emerged, pulling behind it a sled. At first, Ozen thought it a man in armor, but soon it became clear that it was too large for that.

"You are a threat to the academy. The headmistress has commanded that you be detained and handed over to the proper authorities," the golem declared, raising its arm.

Ozen's men answered without order, some turning their attention to the metal man. It became clear that the sled was some form of shield, as well, protecting the thing from harm. That said, it didn't actually do any-thing but glow.

"That is why you never use a golem," his advisor said with a chuckle. "They tend to get weird on the battlefield."

General Ozen snorted, sharing the humor. Several of his men were beginning to laugh at the failure of the hideously complex construct.

CHAPTER 30

✦

BATTLE OF THE NORTH

I watched from above as the hall monitor began his work. It took time for the gas to spread, and it wasn't fatal, but it didn't need to be. He was just the first wave, the first of many. These soldiers really should have known better than to do as they did. I understood it, but they were good and truly screwed now.

It didn't take long for the soldiers to realize that the golem was up to no good. The first few ranks were distracted by his emissions and started pounding him with spell after spell, but that was okay. It had been expected. I wanted them looking at him, attacking his defenses, not at other things.

Justin and Adia looked on as we were joined on the ramparts by a number of our support staff, and I began to sing. We sang about the wind and the rain, and while I didn't want the former quite yet, the latter was decidedly something we did.

Mystien had already left my side. He, Dras, and several of the other wizards were going to be busy adding layers to our defenses and bolstering the wards while we bards began to deal with the enemy. Our positions would eventually switch, but if we could cause problems using less mana, it made sense to do so.

It's something that had always kind of irked me—bards were considered useless. Alone, a bard might not be able to do much, but nobody really thought about the amount of trouble that a proper band of bards could really cause. We'd be changing that today.

The rain began to fall on the opposing army. Not snow, or sleet, or even the freezing rain that sometimes fell at this high latitude. No, it was hot, steaming. It landed just as the wizards aiding our enemy broke the outer shield and let the wind back in. It would hamstring the golem, but it would do so much worse to them.

The upside to laughing gas was that it was safe and effective; the downside was that it wore off very quickly. As soon as the fresh air was let into the equation, Ozen's men began to recover, but that was when part two began to take effect.

His soldiers had taken to wearing heavy coats and warm clothing, important with the ice and snow, but now their clothing was soaked in warm water. Now that they had conjured the wind, I sang a new tune. It was time to bring in a cold, cold wind.

"Hot water and steam? Oh, haha," Justin said, realizing what was going on.

"Oh, that's mean," Adia commented, right as the wind kicked up flecks of snow.

She was right; it was. We were going to distract them, spike up their body temperatures, and then drop them like a stone. This was a battle of attrition, not of strength, and I would take apart his army like I was ripping down a castle one brick at a time.

Ozen's mages were now struggling to both dry and warm his army— just another distraction. Doing this wasn't free for us, but it was cheap. Fixing it was painful for him, and pulled the legs out from under his assault on our shields.

There were only a few bards here to join me in the current section of the defense, but all had their place. Those that could add to the weather effects did, and those who couldn't waited for their chance to wreak havoc on our opponent.

Their chance came when Ozen's wizards became frustrated with the current plan and began lighting big fires to keep the cold and wet at bay. Those fires grew and grew in intensity, subtle songs adding fuel to the flames. It wasn't immediate, but in moments the fires powered by magic had the opposing army under a veritable heat wave.

It took almost fifteen minutes for Ozen to get tired of our shenanigans and renew his assault on the fortress. That was the right move, if a costly one. Letting his men go from sweating to freezing and back again like a yo-yo was already wearing on the soldiers, or at least the non-magical ones. He had to stop us.

"Time to switch," I declared, leading the way down to where the wards were fed.

Justin and Adia followed, content to watch for the time being. This wasn't their home, and they wouldn't act to defend it.

"You're up," I said to the wizards as I entered their section, placing a hand forward and beginning to feed the wards. They should still have plenty of power, but better safe than sorry.

My part in the battle was done, and now I got to sit back and wait.

"I've never seen anyone use bardic magic like that," Adia said. "Most people just use it for food generation during sieges."

"Oh, we'll use it for that, too, if we need to, but there's so much more we can do. How hard was it for us to cause them problems? Not very, I assure you. How much did they have to do to try and fix those issues? Far more. Even if he brought a mass of men, I don't have to kill them; I only need to make them stop."

"Could you have defeated them in open combat?" Adia questioned.

"With Mystien already here, along with his support people? Absolutely."

They asked questions about the wards that I was using, along with a few of the intricacies of the battle tactics we chose to employ. I answered some of those. I suspected that Justin knew of the perfect sphere trick, but he might not. If he didn't, I certainly wasn't sharing. Most of the rest of the wards were rather straightforward.

"I don't suppose you'll share that golem design? We could perhaps come to an arrangement on it," Adia said sweetly.

"Since I'm not the original designer, I think that I shall not." There was no need to tell her that I couldn't even if I wanted to, that I only managed to take control of the thing, not create my own.

I waited, and waited. I wasn't on the front line, so there was nothing else for me to do. In time, I began to worry about my friends and closest confidantes. Ulanion had gone to reinforce the gates, and Dras had joined Mystien in the magical assault. Even the students had their place, doing the damage they could.

It was hours before this battle was over, and though we'd won, it wasn't an absolute victory. Men had died. Twenty-three of our weaker wizards and knights had fallen, including two of Dras's assistants. Eventually we received backup, but this attack had been happening at the same time as several others. Ozen, it would seem, had been using the radios I'd provided to coordinate.

General Ozen

I groaned as they dragged me into the fortress. The irony wasn't lost on me that I was being pulled into the very place I'd fought so hard to enter. At this point it was clear we'd lost. My army, five-thousand of my best men, was shattered, though perhaps a few units had fled before the final blow.

My own fall had come at the hands of a fiery young mage whom I would have loved to have for myself. He'd wielded fire with aplomb, and if I was to fall, it seemed better to lose to an up-and-coming opponent.

At least I'd fared better than the bulk of my war mages, who'd been slaughtered at the hands of the old archmage who'd once served under Durin. Jets of water and waves of power had broken their ranks. Had I known he would be present, well, I would have waited for the assault.

Now though I was bound hand and foot in enchanted chains and floated through the gates to whatever fate awaited me. Any hope of a dignified demise was lost when I saw the young blonde woman marching toward me.

"Ah, and the demon shows herself. Well, if you're going to kill me, I'd prefer if you cut my head off like you did Durin rather than cook me," I said, blood dripping down my lower lip.

"I didn't kill Durin, and your fate is out of my hands. I don't suppose I can convince you to give an official surrender?"

"Why? You've already beaten us."

"Because," she sighed, "if you tell your men to stand down, I'll have less problems holding them until reinforcements arrive."

That was odd. Many of my people were strong enough that holding them would hardly be an option unless they surrendered. They'd just be killed, and if they did give up, maybe even be executed, if they were men at least.

"My soldiers, you'll spare them?" I questioned, raising an eyebrow.

"If you order them to stand down and they swear before a priest that they shall behave, I won't need to kill them, now will I?" she asked with a small smile. Anyone who betrayed such an oath would expect to die, and rightly so.

"I suppose you have witnesses and paperwork?"

"Naturally, paperwork makes the world go round."

It hurt to chuckle, but chuckle I did at that one.

CHAPTER 31

✦

CLEANUP

My father literally couldn't stop laughing. It was refreshing to see him in such a good mood since he was far more dour than I'd preferred since Mother's death. On the other hand, it was getting a tad frustrating to deal with.

"That he actually came here to lay siege . . ." he began before giggles overtook him again.

"Honestly, it's like he never even looked at the defenses on the place," my brother added.

"It wouldn't have been as clean if Mystien hadn't been around, but yes, I can't imagine what he was thinking," I agreed.

While I wasn't known as the most aggressive of sorts, I'd always been heavy into the magical items, and anyone who'd even bothered to read over my history would know that I had a knack for coming out unscathed. Then again, without any real military experience, I supposed that perhaps he'd thought it would be an easy win, even with the known defenses of the fortress.

"Well, I suppose I should go and get them all," Dad said. Anything else that needs my attention?"

"I passed over the papers indicating General Ozen's surrender and that of his army. I really didn't have enough room for them all here. The cleanup alone was more than my current staff was prepared for. We'd manage; it would just be a pain.

"So, with Ozen out of it, think things will go on much longer?" I asked.

"He may be out, but not all of his men will be. Some of his territory will accept our rule, but we need to be prepared for the same thing that happened with Durin. Some of the sub-commanders will split off, claiming they're now in charge. Some may even become bandits or some other large-scale issue. There's also the fact that there are still other claimants to the imperial legacy that may absorb parts of Ozen's land and will definitely keep opposing us," Dad answered, no longer laughing.

"Boo," I said, quite wisely, in my opinion.

"Civil wars are nasty, little sister," John said with a smile. "We'll get back to normal, one day."

I was glad both of them were here. They'd not managed to come immediately when we called for help because of the other attacks, but those proved minor. It looked like I'd been the real target, the others just distractions to keep aid away. Since this was the largest portal nexus we had, it made sense. The smaller one would have been useful for them, but this would have been the real prize.

I gave John an appraising look. Some days he still seemed an idiot, but even now I had to admit that he'd become quite the leader. When our father stepped down, I thought he might one day step into his shoes.

"I sure hope so, John. Well, if that's all then, I have guests that I need to attend to," I said, leaving them.

The two elves had been more than patient with me, leaving them for so long. I briefly wondered if it was because living for so long just made you patient. Or, maybe they saw that it was a genuine emergency. In the end, it didn't really matter, as I soon made my way back to the meeting.

It turned out I was wrong. My guests were sitting at the table staring at each other. Walking in on them like this felt rather odd, like I was walking in on someone's therapy session.

"Sorry for the rude interruption," I said, nodding at them.

"I actually found it rather interesting. What exactly did you have that golem doing, if you don't mind sharing?" Justin asked, one eyebrow quirked.

"Laughing gas, something Ristolian left behind," I answered with a shrug. "Hilariously effective."

He snorted at that. "That does seem his style."

"Laughing gas?" Adia asked.

"Nitrous oxide, a temporary, if effective, painkiller," I told her. "Causes feelings of joy, happiness, things like that, also makes it hard to function due to dizziness."

She made a face. "A poison then? I can't say I approve."

"Everything is poison in the correct amounts, but this is fairly benign. Frankly, the temperature see-saw was a lot meaner than that," I argued. Poisons weren't banned by any of the orders, but they weren't well liked either.

"I personally thought that was rather inspired too. Seldom do I get to see bardic magic abused in war so thoroughly, and never in that manner, which is saying something. I've seen a lot of magic over the years," Justin said.

"There have been a few similar uses, but few," Adia answered, tapping her chin. "Mostly those involved making it cold and wet rather than hot and cold."

"Well, thank you for the compliments. Mystien should be here to rejoin us soon, but I think we're pretty much done anyway. Justin, when exactly would you like to go and see the site?"

"It will take me a few days to get my side of things put together. A week then?"

"Sounds good to me. Miss Adia, I'll discuss portal deliveries with you later. So, unless either of you have anything else, I have somewhat of a mess on my doorstep."

"Would you mind if we had the room for a little while longer? There are some things I'd like to continue to discuss with Adia," Justin said, getting a quirked brow from the other elder.

"No problem, please excuse me."

I met Mystien in the hall. It looked like he'd just finished up some of his own tasks and was indeed coming to rejoin us. After a brief greeting, we went back down to my lab.

"Alana, you know I feel like we have the same conversation again and again," he said.

"What about?" I asked.

"Secrets. I'm not stupid, and while you may have met Justin on that little trip of yours, there's certainly more to it. Any fool can see that. I cannot say that I would give the same concessions as he did to someone I'd met only a few times. Oh, as well as the fact that the collective orders were willing to send what is very clearly a senior priestess to this meeting."

"I have more and more as time goes on," I answered, and it was the truth. "I think I've shared more than enough of them with you, even when I didn't want to."

"True, true you have given me far more than I could ever have asked for from an apprentice." I raised my eyebrows. "Don't look at me like that.

While I may not have been responsible for all of your education, you are certainly one of my students. There's one more question that I really would like answered though."

"And what is that?"

"Your aura," he said. "Why is it the same as Justin's?"

CHAPTER 32

◆

HALFWAY

Mystien allowed me to lead him to my office. If we were going to have such a serious conversation, the hall wasn't the place for it.

"Well?" he asked.

"Well, obviously I still have secrets," I responded, slightly unhappy he'd noticed.

"Clearly, but before I go and talk to a mage that could quite easily turn me into a fine red mist if I irritate him, I would like to know what exactly I'm dealing with."

I sat in my chair, contemplating what to tell him, how to tell him. I could reveal everything, but that seemed to generate even more issues. A truth would be the best way, but a partial one, one he might understand.

"Justin and I are different," I explained. "As was Ristolian, the maker of this fortress, and the leader of the orders."

"Different? Different how? Because you're no wizard and no priest, and I remember your birth, young lady, so you're certainly not as ancient as that man out there."

"Knowledge, knowledge of places, and people, and things our eyes have never seen. I think it's different for each of us, and I won't go into the specifics, but all of us were born aware of who we were, and knowing things that others didn't." I paused, considering how to continue. "I can't explain how, or why, as I simply don't know. I think Justin is working on that—something to do with space magic and the like, but his work is beyond me."

I could see Mystien's gears turning as he, too, took a seat, staring off. He sat like that for a long time, fingers tapping on the armrest of his seat.

It looked like he was going over things one by one, trying to piece things together.

"Your insights into the nature of water, or the rearing of bees, or Pi," he said still focusing on the wall.

"Yes," I confirmed.

"How much more do you know? I've seen so much already."

"That's difficult to put into words. I know quite a lot, and a lot of what I know I don't realize I know. Like how you could probably identify a lot more areas when you see them, rather than if you just tried to list them out or something. There's a lot, though, some of which I won't share with you."

"You won't?"

I sighed. "Mystien, I don't need to be the one to explain to you that some knowledge is dangerous, do I? Even with what I have shared, look at the damage that has come from some of it, and what could have happened if it were in the wrong hands." I contemplated how to put it best. "You know, Justin said that he did some bad things in the past, and I don't want to get caught up in the kind of pain he's in, or that he seems to have caused. Ristolian was also known as terrifyingly powerful, wasn't he? And I can assure you that the others have been a danger too."

He looked at me, and I could see worry in his eyes. "You were born with this?"

"Yes."

"Your maturity as a child, the control you always had. It was like you were an adult, never throwing tantrums, never losing your focus. Because you were? You were actually born old, and knowledgeable weren't you?"

I nodded. "Again, I can't explain why or how, but that is how it is."

"Yet you've always cared about your family and your friends."

I was somewhat offended at that. "Of course I loved my family. Why wouldn't I? They showed me love before I could speak. Before I could ask for help, they helped me, were there for me. The same with you, and Dras, and everyone else. I care for you because it's the right thing. I may know things I shouldn't be able to, but I'm not some monster."

That made him blink, eyes losing some of their focus. "Oh, I see."

"I didn't want to talk about this because it's weird, and I know it's weird, and I know the kind of trouble it could cause. Other than you, only a few people have ever found out, and I wasn't happy about letting them know. So, I would appreciate it if you dropped it and never spoke of this again."

"Your family?" he asked, and my face must have betrayed me. "Alana, they'd understand, you know that, right?"

"Mystien, it would cause problems, too many problems. I obviously can't stop you from telling my father and brother what you know, but I would appreciate it if you didn't."

"You should tell them," he said.

"Maybe, but that is between me and them. Kindly stay out of it."

"Very well. What sort of knowledge is Justin likely to have?"

"What? Isn't that obvious? He knows more than I do, and some of that's experience, but you should expect him, at his age, to be able to change the form of the world around him mostly at will. He knows how things are bound together, for sure, how to make them change and become new things, has deeper understandings of things like fire, and water, and how things move or whatever. He probably also knows more about lightning than anyone else alive. Basically anything, or at least as far as I would guess." I leaned back. "He knows how the portals work better than I do, how the core works better than I do, because he made it. I've seen him teleport, and we both know he can make complex magical items."

"So, basically I should assume that if he wants to do something, he can?"

"Maybe? There are limits on magic, so he probably can't just destroy everything, but within reason and how wizard magic works, I'd say he can pretty much do as he pleases." I really didn't know how to word that any better.

"Any insights as to what he wants?" my mentor inquired, maybe looking for something he could offer.

"He's interested in the portals, in space magic. That's why he's here, but as for the reason he's interested, that's his business, and not my place to tell you. I don't think we've got much on that account to offer him other than access to Silversprings."

"Why do you think that?" he asked.

"Because I've personally seen some of his notes from when we were on the Elven continent. Let me tell you that we're nowhere near it. The only thing I could make heads or tails of was his tea set." I laughed internally at the idea that I'd sat there drinking the man's tea, confused about all of his work.

"Helpful," Mystien deadpanned.

"I mean, we know what our opposites want; that makes negotiation easy."

"I suppose. I'll go and have that chat with our guest. When are we good to take him to the disaster site?"

That was an easy question. "Soon as everyone is ready. There's not much I need on my end."

"Good, that at least is simple."

CHAPTER 33

RETURN TO SILVERSPRINGS

Justin and I meandered along the road to Silversprings. He'd brought a fair quantity of equipment so he could stop at various places along our route just to check on the area's space. When we arrived at the town proper, it would be so he could get some extra readings.

Technically, I didn't need to be here, but I'd come for a few reasons. The first was that we didn't want him getting into any trouble, and somehow I was supposed to aid in that endeavor. I was also deeply curious about what all he would be doing, and if I could learn anything from him. It was also of note that I would be useful in closing up any issues he might accidentally stumble upon or open in the local space. Truthfully, though, the most important reason was that I wanted to get out, and Silversprings was kind of nice.

My travel companion was currently playing with a small item that looked suspiciously like a tablet, humming and hawing about what all was going on.

"You know, things seem oddly normal here. I can detect that there are some subtle changes due to the presence of the portal and 'something' over that way." He pointed toward the giant hole I'd made. "But it is overall far more in line with what I'd expect."

"I'm glad that I did a passable job cleaning things up then," I remarked dryly.

"More than; the town itself looks almost normal."

He currently looked like little more than a normal human researcher bent over the small device. It was a small spell of my own, designed to keep us lower in profile than we'd otherwise be, so we didn't alert everyone to the presence of an elf in their midst. It was more than a good enough use of magic for me.

"I'm sure the new mayor will be thrilled that there aren't any underlying issues," I said.

I wasn't sure what had happened to Mallowsweet, but given that I'd pretty thoroughly burned my bridges with him, it didn't really matter. The new guy was polite, if a smidge distant, and appeared to be mostly trying to stay out of our way. That really was the best thing I could have asked for, since someone underfoot during this particular operation wouldn't help at all. He'd even managed to get the new mine closed for us, something I was quite thankful for.

As a point of fact, most people seemed to be trying to stay out of our way. On the whole, the citizens of Silversprings were taking one look and quickly ducking away as fast as they could, with only a few exceptions—a few people giving us the stink eye or looking on curiously as we passed.

"Something bothering you?" Justin asked as we left.

"People were friendlier last time I was here," I said.

"Hmm, since you did seem to blow something up the last time you wandered through town, they may well be worried that you'll do so again," he said. "Though, if we're being honest here, I'm probably not the best person in the world to take advice on working with others. I'm out of practice, you see."

That got a good chuckle out of me. "Really, you hardly seem out of practice."

"Well, I might be rusty, but I've been the source of this kind of animosity before. Some things stick with you, and that is one of them. Now, let's get to this disturbance of yours."

We chatted for a little bit, mostly on lighter subjects, as we rode out to the new mine. I was of two minds about going back, and the fact that it was so very far from the city gave me plenty of time to consider all that had happened here.

As we rode up, I began to note the changes since I'd last been to the site. The spot had been developed into a proper mine, with a ramp into the crater and small dams blocking off the water sources that had fed into it. Overall, it looked like time had repaired the worst of the damage I'd caused to the local bodies of water, rain filling the lakes and ponds back up, which had drained into the ground. It was now a source of wealth for the locals.

My companion whistled. "I know craters, and that is some crater there, Alana. The size of the explosion must have been . . ." He tapped his fingers as he mentally did the math. "Not bad at all. You're lucky you survived."

"I'm aware," I said dryly. I had been there after all.

He began his work, this time with far, far more interest than he'd had at other points during our journey, measuring and observing things. At one point he even floated himself into the middle of the crater and took some numbers from the space there.

After a time, I came up with a question and decided to ask. "So, we're on a planet, yeah?"

"Yes, though the local solar system isn't much like that back home from what I've seen," Justin said.

"Right, but it's moving? Like around the sun."

"Mmmhmm."

"Which is also ostensibly moving."

"I would guess, though, I've never measured it."

"So, why does space seem to stay in the same place?" I asked.

The elf put down his tools and looked at me for a time. "That is an interesting question. Let me follow it up with one of my own. Where is the center of the universe?"

"Um . . . I don't know," I answered.

"As far as magic seems to be concerned, the center of the universe is wherever that reading is being taken. It makes sense enough, if you ask me, as anywhere can be the center, but that's how it is. The reason things like this, and your portals, and everything else doesn't just fly off at some insane speed is that as far as magic knows, their perspective, and yours, is the truest one. The planet is stationary, with everything else moving around it. One of the odder quirks about the world, but a useful one, huh?"

"So if we sent something into space?" I began.

"Been done, though never too far from the world. Things seem to be the same up there, too, regarding their own location as the true one."

I had an odd feeling that I should write this down somewhere, so future generations wouldn't need to work it out again; but I was unsure who to tell. It was a great insight into the world at large. I also didn't know how we would ever use it, except in situations like this one.

"Huh," I observed, tapping my chin.

After several more hours of work, the fallen king looked over at me. "I think I understand some of what happened here, but I do have a concern. It will need to be looked into before we're fully finished here."

"What's that?" I asked.

"This area is full of silver and silver-based magical beasts, if I'm not mistaken." At my nod of agreement he continued. "As you certainly know, silver is rather magically reactive. I don't think it had an effect, but we need to be sure."

"Makes sense."

"Good, then would you like to join me in taking some readings underground? It's been far too long since I delved into something like this, and I'll admit that I'm pretty excited at the idea." He smiled as he spoke, like he was offering me some adventure.

"Fuck no."

"Sorry? There's no need to worry about the monsters, Alana. I'm more than capable—"

"Nope, I am absolutely not going down there," I said, cutting him off.

"Why?" the ancient mage asked.

"Allow me to share one of my own insights about magic." I had his attention, eyes sparkling as he believed I was going to give him some deep insight, which I was. "Every time I end up underground—every single time—everything goes to shit. If I go down in that mine, something, somewhere, will collapse, and someone will almost certainly suffer or die. It is a rule and promise of this world, that for me, underneath the soil is a bad place. Always has been, and always will be."

Justin looked at me for a solid ten seconds in silence, then he began to laugh. "You know, if you have a phobia of tunnels . . ."

"Nope, nothing like that, just a real understanding of how the world works," I said, standing my ground.

"Fine, fine, I'll go on my own then," he declared, slowly descending into the hole.

Twenty minutes passed, and there was a deep rumble in the ground, followed by a burst of dust coming from the mine entrance. Nearby, one of the small barriers holding back the water began to break, and I took time to fix it, keeping the whole place from flooding.

Eventually Justin returned, looking a little winded, which was saying something, considering how powerful he was.

"Alana, did you know there was another chamber down below the mine?" he asked.

"No, but I should have suspected it."

"Indeed, full of those snake creatures, hundreds of them."

"Mmmhmm."

"There was a small collapse. Don't worry, I fixed it and dealt with the creatures. I don't think there will be any further issues." I pointed to the damaged dam and watched him consider the implications. "Had that failed, it would have been highly inconvenient," he observed.

"Sure would have. Learn anything of note?" I replied.

"Won't know until I run the numbers." With that statement, he turned to leave, and I just followed, shaking my head. Perhaps one day he would understand the deep truth that I had laid upon him. Then again, maybe not. Perhaps there were just some things that worked for bards and didn't for wizards.

CHAPTER 34

✦

PLANS

I sighed and sat down, leaning up against Ulanion on the couch. Immediately, I found myself wrapped in his arms, as he properly understood that I wanted cuddles. After letting me bury my face in his freshly showered chest for a few minutes, he spoke.

"Things that bad?" he asked, rubbing my back.

"Not bad, but not good."

"Are we in a solutions or listening sort of situation here?" he asked, making me smile.

"Well, there's no good solution. Ozen was our biggest opponent, and with him gone we're retaking most of the territory, at least according to my father's letters."

"Most."

"Most, in some places, people are turtling up and fighting, and some are devolving into small-time warlords, as if we didn't have enough of those already."

"My understanding was that there were several suits for peace?" he replied.

"Sure, but it seems like every time something changes, the lands just split again. That and Dad's not Durin. We now have almost a dozen different nations and city-states all vying to gain land or keep what they have. It feels like the war will never end."

He stayed silent for some time, contemplating. "Alana, did you know that in all of Elven history there has only been one period where we were at actual peace?"

"Let me guess," I began.

"You hardly have to. Even then, though, we were expansionists. Once all of our own warring nations were brought together, we came to the human lands and began expanding again. So there was never really true peace, and as far as I know, humans are the same way. Kingdoms rise and fall, and split and join, but the fighting never really stops."

"We had peace," I complained.

"Did you?"

I had to sit and think on that one, and I quickly began to understand what he meant. While where I lived might have been peaceful, the empire certainly wasn't. There were constant struggles to suppress the former leaders, or to take new lands.

"I guess not," I pouted.

"Why does it bother you?" he inquired.

"Guess it doesn't."

"Alana, if you don't care to tell me, that's fine, but I would prefer it if you didn't just lie like that." There was a slight edge to his voice, but the hand rubbing my back never stopped, so he couldn't be too angry.

Playing with one of his buttons, I considered my answer. It wasn't like I didn't know what I wanted, but it was just weird to say it.

"Neither of us are getting younger," I complained. "And I told you we'd marry after the war was over."

He laughed, and I was overtaken by a strong urge to punch him. Sadly, I had neither the muscle mass nor training to make that a viable option against a normal guy, much less the superhuman sitting next to me. Instead, I just glared, letting him dig deeper and deeper.

"Well, love," he said when he'd finally stopped laughing, seeing how much it annoyed me. "I suppose that once, and just this once, there's no need for me to hold you to your word."

For a moment I stopped and just looked at him. "Kala insists we have a ceremony," I declared.

"While her opinion might not be that important to me, mine is, and I find myself in agreement. There are important reasons for it," he said.

"Someone will interrupt and attack, like every big party I've ever been to," I argued, frowning.

"Now that's just not true at all. I've met your friends, and I understand that you've gone to and hosted a number of absolutely massive 'ragers' in your time." The logic was really getting on my nerves. "If it helps, I can ask everyone to come armed and armored to the teeth."

We went back and forth for a little longer, discussing arrangements and how many people needed to come. While I wanted a good wedding, I didn't want a lot of people. In the end we agreed to shortened list—a few of his friends and coworkers, some of mine, and nobody that neither of us particularly cared about. His family was gone, and mine was small after all the deaths, so it wasn't like there was too long a guest list anyway.

"Fine, I'll start on things tomorrow," I finally declared, "for tonight, I'm tired." I leaned into him and settled down. There were at least a few things I could look forward to, like cake.

Ulanion

I moved through Alana's lab, on a mission. Currently she was out and about, putting together details and deciding on exactly what she wanted. The first real issue was the venue. If we held it in the fortress, we would have a repeat of Durin's wedding. There were a few other locations in mind throughout the empire, but each had issues, so she was having somewhat of a fit.

The portal shimmered briefly as I stepped through. My coming today was prearranged, as was all travel through this gate. After some time in the blank room, I was teleported to Justin's office, the man himself sitting at a desk.

"Well, this is a bit of a surprise," he declared and blinked owlishly at me. "Something come up?"

"I've been asked to personally deliver an invitation to you," I said, holding out the small envelope.

He took his time reading the missive, painstakingly written by my fiancée, in what I was told was her best calligraphy from her previous life. She'd frowned a lot trying to get it right, but eventually came up with something she could accept. It was the only invitation in that particular language, and both of us felt her penmanship was far, far better in either the common human tongue or Atal.

"Oh, congratulations. Sadly, if it isn't held on this continent, I'm afraid I won't be able to attend, and holding it here would cause its own host of issues," he said, setting the paper to the side.

"We both thought that might be the case, but it seemed proper to extend the invitation anyway. There's . . . actually something else as well." I hesitated to ask. "Traditions. I know Alana likes some of them, but I don't know if I'm missing any."

"There were a number of them, most rather silly in my opinion, but only a few were vital. A cake, a white dress, and rings are the big ones," he said, listing off things that were a little odd to me. Well, some of them.

"She's already declared that there will be cake and is currently fighting every cook she knows to get the one she wants."

"And I imagine she'll take care of her clothing too," he said.

"What about a ring though?" I asked, a little nervous.

"Oh, yes, that's a big one. Actually, I can help with that. Consider it a gift, since I won't be able to attend." He rose and moved to a door, and I, of course, followed.

We passed through a small hall and into what was clearly a workshop. The tools were largely different from those in common use, but a few of them were familiar. Moving to one of the desks, he produced a small bag and opened a drawer.

"Now, diamond is the traditional center stone, but in my time, there'd been some move away from it. Smaller versions of the same, or rubies, emeralds, and sapphires are good for additional decoration, with the whole thing set in either silver, or gold, preferably the latter." As he spoke, he picked up and inserted a mixture of gems, each at least as thick as my thumb, into the pouch.

"Those must cost a fortune," I said.

"Hmm? Not really, no. These are synthetic, a tad gauche, but they'll look great, and I've got tons of them laying around. They are integral in some of my golem designs; one of the reasons I don't overly mind handing some of them over."

"Syn . . ."

"It means I made them myself," he explained, passing over the bag. "But I'm no jeweler. You'll need to handle that part yourself."

"Thank you," I said with a slight bow. "This is quite generous."

"Your girl has given me a few good laughs with her antics, and those are worth far more to me than a few shiny rocks. Now, I'm sure you're busy, and I know I am, so I'll leave you to it."

As I passed back through the portal, I began making a list of people to talk to. If a ring was the right thing for me to give her, then I'd be seeing she got the best one in the country.

CHAPTER 35

✦

TYING THE KNOT

My morning had been hectic—hair, makeup, and all the other little things that added up to me being very tired already. As I looked in the mirror, though, it all seemed to fall away. My reflection certainly wasn't what most girls on Earth dreamed of for their wedding day, but it suited me well. Today would be a mixture of traditions, some from this world, and some from my last.

The dress, rather than white, was a cool velvet blue, its fabric punctuated by tiny flecks of the glowing thread that was becoming increasingly scarce. Nestled in my hair was a small, decorated comb that my father had given me, something of Mom's to wear on this day. Kala, who still was one of my best friends, hooked a thin silver chain around my waist. In this world, it was a symbol of binding two lives together, marked in silver, a metal indicative of purity.

"So, is everything in place?" I asked Kala, since she was taking care of things while I got ready.

"It's fine, Alana. Everyone is here, and they're all very aware of your opinion on interruptions, and the protections are in place," she said, sighing.

"It's not an opinion," I said. "It's a fact, and the fact is that if anyone interrupts my wedding, I will kill them horribly."

"So you've stated," she griped.

"And I mean it," I replied.

"Everyone is on their best behavior, and I assure you, nobody who isn't here knows we are here."

I'd needed somewhere proper and spent quite some time trying to find the perfect venue. Most were out since it would become a spectacle, and that I didn't want. That left me with smaller places. I looked everywhere near a gate so we could use them to be better organized. I'd popped in and out near all the locations I'd had good times in over the years, and even to places that people had suggested to me, but none of them felt quite right.

Then I came up with a better idea. I needed somewhere important to me, but where nobody would go, and there was one place that fit my preference perfectly. For that reason, I went home. I didn't go to my home in Lithere, or my home in the fortress. Nor did I go to the orphanage I'd spent a winter in, calling it home. No, I went to my first home.

When I got there, the village was abandoned, with almost nothing left of its former self. The houses were gone, the walls gone, and what hadn't been consumed by the fire that had destroyed it had rotted in the many years since. Even the roads were completely overgrown, nobody having wanted to settle back into this area.

Dras had agreed to help me with setting up the venue, a small building made of local stones melded together by his magic. While he'd done that, I'd taken seeds from the gardens of the fortress and sewn them all around. I'd never tried growing things with my magic before, and it was somewhat of a struggle, but they didn't need to be huge or anything—just some flowers for decoration. The soil being very rich and having lain fallow for years helped.

Our little structure used many of the techniques Dras had worked on when making the hot springs retreat everyone loved. While the stones were different, they were very similar in appearance and function, with a few small rooms and a larger open space for the ceremony itself. It stood close to where my first home in this world had been.

Mystien appeared beside me as the last touches were put on my appearance. "They're all ready for you whenever you're ready."

"Good to hear," I said with a smile.

"You should also know that I've already had to hear five different complaints about your abuse of the portal network," he added. "They've all been told to contact you no sooner than a week from now."

"They can all get stuffed," I replied cheerfully. "I made the gate on my own time with my own funds." Nobody could ruin my mood today with such trivial issues, particularly when I'd already thought of them.

"Hah! Like those are even concerns for you."

I shrugged. Being able to make valuable materials out of literal rocks meant that budgets didn't really apply if I didn't want them to. Well, at least for things of this level; larger projects still took time.

Kala left to take her place, and Mystien to take his. For a few moments, I was alone with a couple of the maids who's joined us, all carefully chosen. There were many forms of security, but the best, in my opinion, was simply not letting anyone know what was going on if they didn't need to. Heck, many of my guests didn't even know where exactly we were.

There was little time for reflection before the light sounds of music drifted to me, my signal to enter. I knew more than enough bards, so I found a few to play at my wedding. While none of them had heard "Canon in D" before, they learned it at impressive speed.

I registered that there were subtle magical effects going on all around me—decorations and the like that I'd probably spent too much time on—but none of it seemed to matter. The only place I could look was forward, to where Ulanion stood with the softest smile.

He stood there in a coat that matched my attire. The subtle shades of blue mixing well with his dark hair and the fabric fitting perfectly on his large frame. There was a twinkle in his eyes when he first saw me, and it lit up his entire face.

Kala officiated and read a speech she'd written for just this occasion, but I missed most of it. I was busy looking at and thinking about the man in front of me. It was quite embarrassing when she finished and told us to kiss. Since I missed the signal, I stumbled, but it was fine. We exchanged the customary three kisses before my now husband did something unexpected.

"Ah, I got you something," Ulanion said nervously, taking out a small box. "I do hope this is the right time."

The ring inside was a work of art, dainty and swirling. Gems of every color imaginable circled a massive clear stone in the center. Shaking, I extended my hand and he slipped it onto my finger. It was warm and comforting, and I wanted to cry as it slid into place. My desire to keep my face in order was the only thing stopping the tears that welled.

"Thank you," I whispered.

Time flew by quickly after that. There was a feast, albeit a small one, with drinking. Then it seemed that every bard in the building, save me, took a turn playing and singing so that people could dance. I had only two partners, my new husband and my father, the latter of whom made his way in for one of the slower dances.

"I never thought I'd return here," he said, and it was clear he was having a lot of feelings today.

"You don't mind do you? It seemed . . . right."

"There's never been a more perfect place for this, Alana. I never wanted you to suffer through the things I had. All I wished for you was a happy life with a man you loved, perhaps even staying in the village and away from all the madness in the world. Well, some of that seems to have happened at least."

"You were, and are, a wonderful father. I couldn't have asked for anyone better," I told him truthfully, bouncing up on my toes to kiss his cheek.

Several more dances were shared, and the crowd began to wind down. The food was gone, the drinks consumed, and it was time to go. At this point, Dad stepped back out before the crowd, making a brief call for attention.

"All right, everyone, now that everything else is done, it's time for the running to the chamber!" he exclaimed with vigor.

My brain made a brief skip as I tried to figure out what was going on. When it hit me, it was like a ton of rocks. Of all the many traditions, I'd forgotten this one. While last time I'd been unhappy about it, this time, well . . .

I made my way to the door with all the other girls and struggled to get my shoes off. In my head I cursed the fact that I'd gone with such complex straps as I pulled them away. They'd barely come off when the first signal went up and I bolted for the exit.

As a group, we flew across the small courtyard of flowers and to the portal. It was off, of course. I'd barely gotten the thing up and running before the second signal, calling for the men to give chase.

We all hurried, particularly those of us who'd been escorted by physical magic users. Nobody tried to beat me through the gateway, and unlike them, I knew my way around the fortress pretty well. Still, I was only reaching the end of the first hall away when the first giggling screams reached my ears.

I went invisible, and I began to use one of my other favorite magics. I teleported all around the halls, cutting distances by leaps and bounds, taking circuitous paths to throw off my pursuer, even though I'd not seen him, and moving as quickly as I could while not being too obvious.

I made it all the way to the last hall, teleporting into the junction and looking down. The floor felt strange. I had just enough time to register that someone had sprinkled powder on the floor before I was taken off my feet, arms like steel wrapped around me.

"Tsk, tsk," Ulanion said as I dropped the invisibility. "Even if I'd not prepared for you to be hiding, I would've seen the portal. You're getting predictable, my love, almost like you wanted to be caught."

"Boo!" I said between laughs, as I was lifted and carried to our room.

His hands were fast. He'd somehow managed to get my clothes off before we'd even properly entered the door. I was gently tossed to the bed, still laughing as he, too, began to quickly undress.

"Well, you've caught me. Now what?" I teased.

"Hmm . . . let's see," he said, as he was pretending to think. Then, he looked at me and froze, his eye settling on my thigh.

It was at that moment he realized that I'd let the magic run out on my Lovers' Mark. Our eyes locked onto each other's, and very quickly he joined me upon the bed.

CHAPTER 36

✦

HONEYMOON

I stumbled to the washroom, taking each step gingerly. Behind me my husband still lay in bed, soft snores coming from where he lay. We would need to have a talk at some point. He'd been overly excited, and while he might be inhumanly durable, I was not.

The large mirror in the room reflected a myriad of things. All along my hips, thighs, and backside, even going up to my stomach were bruises. Yellow and purpling marks in the shape of fingerprints and large handprints clung to me like some sort of odd body paint. While it hadn't been unpleasant at the time, it certainly was now, and it was something I needed to deal with promptly, along with other more private places.

The tub was powered by magical items, which both created and controlled temperature of the water. There were a number of features, mostly prototypes, that were built in.

I hummed a quick healing tune as I stepped in and sank into the water. It was the perfect temperature, with small bursts of heat whenever the water got even a little bit too cold. Those were one of my favorite additions to my personal tub, and I was thinking about releasing parts of the design to the public soon.

While I soaked, I thought about the future. There were so many small household items we could standardize. Sure, there weren't all that many mages, and for those who designed everything from the ground up, it was a pain. Maybe a book of sequences was in order, basic designs for myriad items. It might even be fun to publish.

There was also magic, and so many more places I could go. I liked growing plants, but it seemed rather inefficient to me. They were slow and sort of limited compared to what a priest could do, at least in my opinion.

Just thinking of priest magic pinged in my mind. There was something I'd been neglecting, making the mistake of thinking I had time. Sure, I might have some time, but we were all on a clock. Well, unless you were a pure-blooded elf or a powerful priest, but maybe we could change that.

I needed to get to work on extending my own life, and perhaps that of others. Where to start though. Could I work on mice, like I had for other things, or would I need to start with myself? I let my fingers lightly flick the water as I tried to come up with ideas, frowning the whole time.

"Good morning," said a voice from the door.

"Mmm, and you," I replied as Ulanion joined me, slipping into the water.

For the longest time we just laid there, soaking, something I had no objections to at all.

"Do we have anything pressing to do?" asked my husband.

"I don't, and I told everyone I was taking a week off, bar any emergencies. Didn't you do the same?"

"Of course, but I thought you might want to go Lithere or something, get away from the fortress."

While there wasn't much in the way of tourism in this world, there were a few places we technically could go. Some, like the hot springs retreat, were even pretty nice, but mostly because of their services. Once you'd seen them and experienced what they had, it was less enticing, particularly if you could perform the services yourself.

"Eh, maybe a visit or two, but I like it here, and I've got some things I want to try out," I replied.

"Oh, really?" he said with a smirk, turning so we were face to face and pulling me close. "And here I worried I might be the only one."

"On that note," I added, splashing his face with a handful of water.

"Ah, what's that about?" He looked genuinely confused at being rebuffed.

"Me having to *heal myself* this morning. You need to remember that I'm not made of iron."

I watched his face fall quickly in regret, an excellent response. "I didn't realize at all, why didn't you tell me? You know I'd have stopped."

"I was a little busy at the time," I answered, blushing. Really, neither of us had thought of it, but it was a concern.

That got me a laugh. "Well then, I'll be more gentle."

"Don't tell me," I said, wrapping him up in arms and legs. "Show me."

He proceeded to do exactly that, in a manner that left me with no complaints at all.

We spent most of the next several days lazing around our quarters and various workshops. I carefully avoided all "work," but there was always more research to read. There were a few notes from people doing truly interesting things with moss at the academy, and I began to write down some of the basic designs I would use for household magic. At least when I wasn't spending time with Ulanion.

He, of course, took breaks to do things like draw and write poems, one of the things I found quite endearing about him. He could rip a monster in two, then go home and sketch out pictures of flowers or compose a love sonnet without missing a beat.

Eventually, though, restlessness set in, and we headed to Lithere. A quick change of clothes and a hat to hide Ulanion's ears, and we slipped out into the lower city. I didn't care much for the richer districts; instead, I wanted to go and see some old friends.

Ulanion and I walked hand in hand as we strode through the back-roads and alleys, which I'd spent much of my youth traversing. I looked at the changes all around us, and there were so many. The roads were clean and far better maintained, with clear effort on someone's part to fix anything that reared its head. The buildings, too, were in better condition—more vibrant, more alive.

I watched as couple after couple passed us, and while many displayed the short stature of someone who'd not eaten too well in their childhood, there were no thin cheeks and no sad eyes of refugees. The people looked like they had hope, hope for the future and what was to come.

The Starlit Sky stood where it always had, and while a few of the changes to back streets had thrown me, we found it without too much trouble. There were some small signs of renovation—fresh plaster and newer signs—but the bulk of it remained as it had been. Inside, there was still a hustle and bustle, but the chatter soon faded.

The ceiling was an illusion today of gently swirling stars with a huge moon adding to the light in the tavern. Its source was obvious—the old bard sitting in a corner, feet propped up and mug at his side. I waited until his current number finished before I approached, fingers on the strings of his lute stopping as the song ended.

"Mind if we join you?" I asked Lucien, slipping into a seat before he could answer.

"Well, well, well, look who's here. If you're wondering, no, we don't have any rooms for rent," he said with a smile.

"All full up? It's not even winter, old man," I replied.

"Maybe not, but we are. All the traders coming into the city like places to stay."

"For someone whose business is booming, you sure seem relaxed," I pointed out as I leaned on the table, doing a double take as I looked at his cup. "Are you drinking tea!?"

"Two things, no, three. One, I handed over all the day-to-day operations to the lad a while back; two, I'll drink whatever I please; and three, had to lessen the ale. I got sick a while back, and the priest who fixed me up told me in no uncertain terms that if I kept drinking like I was, I'd be in my grave soon. Heck of a time cutting back though. That in itself nearly killed me." He leaned back and began strumming again, but much softer this time.

"All the operations? So, what do you do now?" I asked.

"Sit here, drink, and play music. Well, still do some magical item charging and the like, but not much more than that. Pretty good retirement, honestly. Oh, and your wedding was beautiful, by the way."

"Thank you," I said with a smile. "It's good to see you again."

"You too. By the way, what're the chances of me getting one of those gates to somewhere I can put another location, like an outdoor bar on a mountain somewhere?" he asked with a grin.

"Zero, I'm sad to say; though, that would be some attraction, wouldn't it?"

"Well, if you're sticking around and taking up space in my chairs, why don't we see if we can bring a little bit of that skyline here?" he said, eyebrows moving up and down at his request for an illusion. One of his hands went up briefly, signaling a waitress to bring us drinks before he started the lute up again, a song we both knew well.

CHAPTER 37

ONE YEAR LATER

I lay back in the slightly raised bed I'd finally been shown to, completely and utterly exhausted. Sweat was beginning to dry on my skin. At some point I would need to clean myself, but that wasn't important right now.

What was important was held against my chest, quietly feeding. Just looking at him was enough to make my heart flutter with joy and bring a smile to my face. He was there, my child, with a huge, adorable head, and the slightest points to his ears, almost imperceptible.

Kala removed her hand from my stomach, placing it on her own.

"Good as new, though, you'll still want to rest. There's no real way to cure bodily stress, and you've had quite a lot of it," she said kindly. "When he's done, I'd like to examine him if that's all right."

Just the thought of handing him over made my hackles rise briefly, but then I remembered who this was. Kala was still one of my oldest friends, and I knew she would treat my son as if he were her own. "Of course. Mind grabbing my husband?"

She nodded. "Of course, so long as he's calmed down."

Ulanion, for all his merits, was inexperienced with pregnancy and birth. I wasn't sure how he'd lived as long as he had and not managed to be present for a few. Over the last month or so, he'd become more and more stressed and protective, and tonight he had panicked over the pain I was going through, insisting that something was wrong.

Nothing had been wrong, of course. It was just how things were. Eventually, his continued interruptions had made Kala ask him to step into the hall until we were done. That had gone over about as well as a lead balloon, and shortly after, he'd been hit with a sedation spell by my irritated midwife and physically carried out of the room. I was glad she'd done it because I really didn't want to have to.

A few moments later, Ulanion appeared, fists clenched but otherwise outwardly in control. "How is he?" he asked as soon as he'd reached my side.

"Fine, he's fine. Now come here and let him meet you."

"Hello, little Rodrick. I'm your father," he uttered, the gentlest smile blooming on his face as our baby grabbed onto his finger and held tight.

It took time for our son to be given his first checkup and put to sleep, and by then, I was quite thoroughly exhausted. Like most babies, little Rodrick had decided to be born at an unreasonable hour and had taken his time. His father and our maids should be enough to deal with him for a little while.

Moving much hadn't been possible so far, and though it pained me to leave them, I did need to clean up. Walking to the washroom was . . . odd. In the last few hours I'd lost a ton of weight and my waistline had shrunk. Those two things were not doing my gait any favors. I would go back to normal soon enough, but the abrupt shift was throwing me off.

The real surprise came when I left my shower, though, because my image in the mirror did not look at all how it should. Magic could, and did do, magnificent things, and one of them was this. My skin was not loose or stretched. As a point of fact, I looked almost like I had the day I'd realized I was pregnant. Sure, I'd lost some muscle mass, and I'd gained a few pounds, but nothing a diet and exercise couldn't undo.

I might have stayed in the bathroom a little longer had I not heard commotion through the open door to the living quarters. I threw on a robe and headed out to see who was here. Everyone knew that I'd be out for a while, so there were only a few who might come calling. Of them, fewer still would be allowed into my rooms.

Father was knelt down beside the crib, opposite his son-in-law, and both of them were now wearing the same dopey grin. I had to hide my own silly grin at the sight of them. There were no magical cameras yet—though, not for lack of trying—so I'd be committing this to memory.

"Hi, Dad," I said when he looked up.

"I came as soon as I could," he said, rising to hug me. "Had to put a few things in place before leaving, but nothing your brother can't handle while I'm here." We headed for a nearby couch. "He said he'd come see you later."

"He's done more than enough already, and I can't help but notice some other things. You've been having him take more and more responsibility recently."

The first part was quite true, as John had managed to secure me a couple of the staff he'd had hired and trained for his firstborn. He and Etia had another on the way, and I was sure he'd want them back, but she was still early on, and the help for the next few months would be invaluable. Trustworthy people who were also well versed in the care of infants were few.

"Of course, he's my heir. Since you've made clear your opinion on ruling."

"One which hasn't changed."

"And one I respect, but he needs to learn some things before he takes over. I didn't get that, and the lessons are still coming to me. It's not something one can do easily without training," he concluded before hugging me tight.

Something drew my eyes. I'd noticed that Rodrick had woken up. He was still quiet; rather than crying or making other noises, he just moved around, enough to grab my attention, but not so much that he needed me right now.

"He's so small," I said quietly, watching him move his little legs.

"They all are," Father told me softly.

"I have no clue what I'm doing." It was something that itched at my mind more than I'd like to admit.

He chuckled deeply. "Nobody ever does, but you'll do fine, and you have help."

When my father left, I joined Ulanion down by the crib. I was determined to enjoy these moments as much as I could. I knew they wouldn't last forever. Children grew up; there was no getting around it. I could only hope that my father was right, and I would be okay, because nothing I'd done before had ever properly prepared me for this.

Before long, my child found his way back to the land of dreams, as newborns often did, and I soon joined him. It had been a long morning already, and I wanted my strength for what was to come.

CHAPTER 38

✦

FIVE YEARS LATER

The rain poured down over the city of Lithere. There was no thunder, no lightning, only the sky weeping over the city. It was appropriate, the right kind of day for it, the right time for such a storm.

At the foot of the statue, on a small dais stood my brother in mid-speech, the crown upon his head shedding water. The way the droplets flowed down both his face and the stone statue behind him made it seem as if both were weeping. It felt like both had tears pouring forth due to what had to be done today.

When the Empire of Shadows had finally stabilized, the name needed to change, for there were far too many people still claiming the empire. As we were no longer truly an empire, it was, at my suggestion, renamed the Penumbral Kingdom. Father had taken the name Penumbra as his sur-name, and regardless of the fact that I refused any other title, had heaved it upon me as well. Now John Penumbra, the second king, ruled, and none questioned him.

As John finished his speech, some unspoken signal was given, and the coffin erupted in flames. Magic was in use here, and through it, the body was soon reduced to nothing but ash. My heart sank, and though I'd already wept several times, once more I felt salty drops make their way down my face.

When the ceremony was over, I retreated to the palace, into one of sev-eral rooms set aside for us. Ulanion and Dras wouldn't be joining me for some time yet, as they'd both volunteered to help collect the bones once the fires were out.

"Have you been good?" I asked the children.

"Yes, is everything okay?" Rodrick asked. He was still too young to understand everything that was going on, but clearly he knew something had happened.

"It will be," I answered.

"Mommy, cousin Amara is fun," said his little sister, Illa. "We should come see her more often."

"We may do that," I told her, patting her head gently.

I looked at Omos and Amara, my niece and nephew and current prince and princess. They smiled, near the same ages as my own and both very well mannered, and offered me a greeting. Their parents had not raised them to be too proud or haughty.

The door opened, and I smiled at the echoing calls of "Grandpa Verren!" from the kids. Soon he was swarmed, and I got to watch as his face transformed from one of sadness to the kindest he could manage.

My father bent down low to the ground and embraced them all, leaning in conspiratorially. "Now, Grandpa has some people he needs to talk to, but you all behave, and I'll come play with you later." There was a chorus of agreements before my father motioned to me, and we moved to the other side of the room.

"How are you?" I asked once we were far enough away from the children.

"I've been better, but I should ask you the same, shouldn't I?"

Dad had aged. His hair now nearly solid grey, and his skin showed wrinkles on his forehead and around his mouth. Mom's death had taken a lot out of him. In the past few years he looked like he'd aged decades. Now he'd lost his oldest friend.

"I'll miss him. It's so odd, knowing that I'll never see Mystien again. He'll never tell me off again for something I did, or come to see what I've been working on," I said as I hugged my dad.

My first teacher was gone, fallen in battle against mankind's first enemy, age. He'd been ancient, and though magic could do much, he hadn't been able to fight off the specter of time. It had at least been fast. His wife woke up one morning to find that he was gone. We're all thankful it was not some drawn-out process.

"I think he'll rest well, knowing that there are plenty who can keep his legacy going." Dad rubbed my back, holding me close.

Father was right. Mystien may be gone, but he'd left behind some of the best trained mages in the world. Dras wasn't his equal, but among the wizards in our nation, he was sitting near the top. I was considered one of the best in the world when it came to magical item production, and bardic magic, some of my most recent creations being added to massive public works.

"Have there been any issues?" I asked, wanting information, but still enjoying the hug.

"A few people thought they might get clever, and they received what they should for it," Dad answered, a hard note in his voice.

Father had only taken the throne for a short time, setting things up as they should be before stepping down. It was a good plan and would likely save us problems in the future. The first few years were always the most delicate for any new nation. If power was not handed down properly, or if there was some confusion about who should take over . . . Well, we'd already lived through that, and nobody wanted it again.

Dad went to go play with the children. Nobody who had ever met him on the field would have believed how he acted with them—happy, childish, a little foolish sometimes, making silly faces and joining in whatever game they were trying to play with him. As a grandfather, he seemed determined to spoil them all with attention. He was also doing a wonderful job distracting them from all the sad adults, appropriate since we were all in a private room.

My brother joined me not long after. "Hello there, little sister," he said teasingly.

"How are things, 'your Majesty'?" I teased.

"Oh, they're as well as can be expected. At least none of the other powers have tried anything stupid."

"I think most of them are smarter than that," I said.

"Indeed. It's a shame there was no way to stop time for the old man. They told me stories about his youth earlier, and I'd have loved to see it."

"I've been experimenting with that, you know? Trying to reverse aging."

He looked at me and blinked, then really looked at me. "Does it work!?"

"Sort of. I can slow it down a bit, at least on myself. Maybe one day I'll manage it on others, but I've had issues since I'm not properly able to get the emotions right for others. It's weird," I explained, and it was true. I'd managed to slow my own aging process by a little, but even then not fully. "It's also extremely mana expensive."

"Could a priest?"

"Probably, but they all seem to have hangups about it, and that stops them from doing it properly. Well, almost all of them." I didn't elaborate. I knew one old man who definitely could.

"I'd like you to keep me informed on that." His voice took on a touch of the command he used in official functions.

"Giving me orders brother? Don't worry, if I find anything of use to others, you and dad are already at the top of the list. We've already lost enough family."

Etia soon joined us. "She's ready for you."

"How is Veska?" I asked. I didn't really know the woman well.

"Not well, nor is the daughter." That was unsurprising, and one of the reasons we were in separate rooms for now. Veska and Veska—yes they'd named the daughter the same as her mother—were still in mourning, whereas our kids weren't.

"All right, I'll see you soon," I said, turning to head toward their room with more than a few worries.

CHAPTER 39

◆

FIFTEEN YEARS LATER

I stood by my window, looking out upon the ice. In the reflected image I could see myself. I could still pass for somewhere in my mid to late twenties if I tried. Though, that was certainly no longer true in person. My work with age-controlling magic had generated results, but it was still decidedly imperfect. I was still aging, just at a snail's pace.

"You know, vanity is foolish," came the voice of perhaps my oldest friend.

"Maybe, but I can indulge sometimes. How are things going, Dras?" I turned to look at him.

Dras had fallen prey to the receding hairline a few years ago, and though he was still well, he looked quite distinguished now. No longer was he the slightly roguish young boy in a bar I'd met so long ago, but the smirking archmage of the kingdom.

"Most of my people and equipment are out. I can't believe you're actually doing this."

"It's what this place was supposed to be in the first place, and with our portal networks as they are now, we don't really need this hub. Regardless, no pouting. I've seen your new facility in the capital," I responded.

"Won't be the same without you," he quipped, and I could tell he was unhappy that I wasn't leaving.

"I'll be here if you want a consult on anything, but we haven't really needed me to butt in, in years. You sure I can't convince you to stay?"

"And do what?"

"Teach, of course. You know as much about magic as anyone, and more than almost anyone when it comes to fire magic," I replied.

"Maybe one day, but I like what I do," he said and shook his head.

"Fair enough. If you change your mind, you know where to find me."

He left, and I began to look around once more. There were expansions going up everywhere, and had been for years, all part of my evil plan to turn this research facility into a proper school. Over the past few years we'd run into problems, lots of problems.

The old academy in Lithere was wonderful, magnificent even, but it just wasn't big enough. It was made for a different time, and a different system than what the kingdom ran on, one where only the few could get a proper education. As we found, and tried to train more and more casters for our army, they just wouldn't fit because they'd never been meant to. It wasn't going anywhere for now, but rather being converted into something like a magical primary school, somewhere local students could begin their education, one we'd be finishing here.

There were other schools, of course, lesser ones, but those presented their own problems. They were small and normally in cities where they couldn't expand, and were often sub-par. It simply wouldn't do. These, too, were being consolidated into my school, brought into the fold as it were.

I turned my gaze from the grounds and began to delve deeper into the fortress, for a fortress it still was. There were halls and rooms, dorms and barracks. Even if we weren't going to be military anymore, we'd still have a few security people around, necessary for this part of the world, and in case someone decided to attack us. Ulanion was heading that group, and I'd be meeting up with him later. Now I was headed to see some other people.

As I closed the meeting-room door, I looked at the people gathered around, all of us bards. The twins, Leah and Robert, were there, along with Ian, one of my first students. Then there were Rena and Perry, who'd both assisted in my lab over the years and learned more than a little about portals from me. Finally, there was the aged Professor Magnolia, who'd been one of my schoolteachers and would be joining us not only at the new school but in this clandestine organization.

"Good evening, everyone, and welcome to our first official meeting. Since we're all here, let's begin discussions."

This was one of the problems I had. I needed more people I could trust. Things were still going well, or well enough for my liking, but problems would undoubtedly appear one day, and a new group was needed to deal with them.

"We need a name. The Order of Gatekeepers, maybe?" Leah said thoughtfully. "Or the Knights of the Doorway?"

"We're not priests, but bards. We need proper nomenclature, and a symbol," Magnolia said with a chuckle.

"Something we can put off for later. What we really need is more people, not a ton, but enough to keep things going even after we're gone. Call me crazy, but I think the world will need what we have to offer one day," I said, cutting through the jokes.

"Yes, you're right, those distortions are concerning, as are the reports I got on the 'incident' and what came after. To think they persist like that." It was Ian this time that chimed in, leaning back.

"Right, and while things are safe now, the world will continue to grow. If we can just have someone there to protect it when things go wrong, that will be worth our effort." Keeping them all on track was the hardest part of my job sometimes. "For now, though, just get settled in and make sure your lessons are ready for the next school year. We'll be keeping an eye out for talent then."

There was a chorus of nods, and some more discussion on names. Soon, we'd have to come up with something, or one of the members would just place one on us without asking me first. Secret societies always felt like they needed some kind of title, but I wondered if that was such a good idea. Names gave a sense of belonging and purpose, but they also made things much harder to keep hidden.

Everyone split, all heading to get their items ready. It would be a few months yet until classes actually began, but since this would be our first year, there was still a monumental amount of stuff to do. They needed their lessons planned, their classrooms laid out, their supplies in order. There was also all of the administrative work that landed on my desk. Luckily, I'd burned through most of that over the course of the last few weeks. Now I was just putting out fires and having meetings as needed.

My husband was waiting for me when I got back to our rooms. We'd been occupying these for quite some time now and were well and settled in.

"Hello, love. I see you've finished up for the day." He came close, wrapping his arms around me and kissing me like we were still newlyweds.

"I have indeed, and I have just enough time to spend with you before I head out in the morning. Still sure you don't want to join me? First chance to go home in a long time," I offered.

"Nothing back there for me. You sure you need to go?"

"Before classes are scheduled, I need to get a look at some of my students, see their measure."

"And I'm sure seeing the kids has nothing to do with it," he teased.

"Nothing at all. Though if they're not up to standard, I'll be putting them in 'remedial' classes over the break, taught by yours truly."

That got me a hearty laugh. "You've been teaching them magic since they first manifested it. I'm sure they're up to standard."

I ran a hand over his face. There were a few more grey hairs, one or two more wrinkles, but he'd changed as little as I had. "So, bedroom? Or elsewhere?" He laughed as he pulled me close, I loved my children, but having them out of the house was liberating.

CHAPTER 40

✦

FIELD TRIP BEGINS

The seat below me shifted only slightly as I looked up at the interim headmaster. My alma mater had lost the old one a few years ago, and since we were setting up a new academy that I was going to run, there had been no reason to replace him. This man was cheery and bright, and would be taking over here after the changeover. He'd been chosen specifically because he specialized in training younger mages, as had some of his staff.

"How have things been this year?" I asked pleasantly.

"Honestly? Kind of rough with all the new students. We were already bursting at the seams, and this most recent batch has us renting nearby buildings," Headmaster Gorin replied.

"Well, I'll be happy to take the lot off your hands then, and if you ever decide to move to older students . . ."

"I'll keep you in mind. I suppose you'll be visiting your children while you're here? Not often we get parents from so far away," he said.

"No, the kids don't know I'm coming, and aren't supposed to know that I'll be escorting them on their little field trip." I raised an eyebrow, and he indicated with a silent word that they didn't know. "Just want to see how they and the royals are doing. Is their Atali going well enough?"

"You've nothing to fear in that area. Both they and the royal children are doing magnificently, almost like they were taught it from the cradle," he said with a wry smile. "The four of them will be leading the first group, of course. Setting an example for everyone and all that."

We chatted a little longer, and then he handed over the list of students who would be going on the field trip. Most of them I knew nothing about, but some I did. Of course, I recognized my Rodrick and Illa, as well as my niece and nephew. The fact that Veska was coming was a little bit of a surprise, but quite welcome. The list in my hands covered all the students going, both from this academy and the knights' academy.

"Good mix," I noted.

"Our counterparts across the ocean have been absolutely over the moon about this. They offered several tutors on language and have assured me that more than a few of their own have also been picking up ours. I've even met with the ambassador a few times, which I may say is not something I'm really used to."

None of that was particularly surprising to me. I knew for a fact that the elves of Atal had been over the moon when they learned that our royal line was mingling with some of their people. It didn't really change much at first, but it had served as a point of pride for them.

Those friendly relations had led to the next step though—my brother suggesting intercontinental trade. Apparently, Etia sometimes complained about missing foods from her youth, and there were some things even money had trouble buying, like produce from the other side of the world. So, he'd come to Dras, who was running most of the portal network now. There'd been months of consults on security and design, but eventually we'd come up with an acceptable agreement for everyone.

Getting the portal across an ocean was no small feat. Though, I was told they ran into significantly fewer problems than my own passage had. Tomorrow it would have been two months since it had been set up, and the diplomacy had been nonstop. Messages and gifts flowed back and forth, and now a small group of about twenty students would be going over there to see the new continent themselves. It was a clear publicity stunt, and the public at large was eating it up. Both countries now had the honor of hosting the only intercontinental connection, and all the boons that came with it.

There was also the bonus that this served as both a sort of final feather in the cap of the old academy, and the first for mine. Most of these kids would be coming to me and after a summer break would be attending my school. About halfway through the week-long trip they would even be changing from the older black uniforms into the new deep blue and purple ones for my school.

For those reasons and many others, I would be serving as both chaperone and admin of this little trip. I'd be invisible the whole time, of course. They didn't know that I was coming, but if anything needed to be done, I'd take care of it. The fact that I was a member of the current ruling family was key here as well, since it meant that I had enough authority to deal with either the prince or princess if they became too big for their britches.

Gorin and I left the small back room together and headed for the portal room. The fortress we now occupied sat right in the middle of the city, and like all other portal locations, had a number of defenses pointed inward. The main hall had the only portal here for now. Before we arrived at our destination, I hummed a few words and disappeared like mist on a sunny day.

"It's spooky how you can do that," Gorin said.

The last thing he heard from me in response was a small echoing chuckle.

The main hall was packed with parents milling about on one side, and on the other side, diplomats from both nations. In the center were the students, two groups of ten each from both the knightly and mage academies.

Amara stood tall before the knights, her hair pulled back over her ceremonial armor, sword and buckler on her waist. She took after her mother in a lot of ways, with a dancer's body and bright eyes. I was told when it came to physical magic, the princess was no slouch either.

Opposite his sister was the crown prince, Omos. He was the spitting image of his father at his age, though not as muscular. His light robe and staff displayed the school he represented. All around him his aura blazed bright, flaming like both his father's and grandfather's, but in a cool blue color. I'd seen his grades, and he, too, was doing quite well.

As with any ceremony there were speeches. The headmasters of both the knight and mage academies felt the need to drone on for a small eternity about this and that. They were followed by representatives from each of the nations involved. The whole thing seemed to drag on, and by the end of it, the students looked like they were struggling to focus on being attentive.

My brother sat behind the podium, looking thoroughly interested. This was an act, of course, and I knew it, as he'd bemoaned longwindedness. Once speeches concluded, he rose, looking down at the gathered youths.

"You have all volunteered to serve as some of the first of our citizens to go through to Atal. For this you have my gratitude, so now go, go and show the greatness of our nation," he said, and once they'd all given him a proper salute, my brother returned to his seat with a smile, nodding to the youths.

The portal opposite the podium lit with a slight whooshing noise, and as one, the outgoing group turned, heading two by two through it. I, of course, slipped into their ranks, silent as a ghost.

CHAPTER 41

✦

ARRIVAL

When the children and their "official" chaperones had made it through the gate, I slipped in, moving behind them quietly. Well, pretty much everything I did was quietly, since there were spells in place canceling the noise of my feet and clothes, and making sure that there was no incidental noise heard from me.

Over the past several years, I'd steadily improved my spells, particularly when it came to stealth. After failing so many times and being spotted, I'd dedicated time to making sure it would never happen again. Stopping me would no longer be as simple as finding someone with the rare ability to physically manifest eye magic. My pupils, once a telltale sign, were now expertly concealed through illusions of light and perspective.

Sadly, on the other side, people were still shuffling around, everyone trying to get into position for the reception. Once or twice, I had to give the gentlest of nudges to let myself through. This spell was one that had taken me an embarrassingly long time to come up with. It was much like the spatial deformation used in portals but much more subtle. Rather than a proper gateway, the area just shifted slightly, turning inches into feet. Subtle or not, though, it wasn't perfectly invisible. Well-trained people who knew what to look for could still see it. There was also a practical limit. Pushing through an area a few inches wide was one thing, but trying to get under a door was another, and would basically just be a portal.

There were a few greetings by the staff and visitors on the far side, and one in particular stood out. This elf was clearly older and with slightly longer ears than was average around here.

"Welcome, welcome to the wonderful students of Penumbra. I am Headmaster Indir. Let me be the first to bid you good day. It brings my heart joy to see you all, and soon enough I'm sure we'll meet once more, but I understand you've been through several speeches already, so if you'll follow my assistants, they will show you to your rooms." The man in question spoke in Atali, with a slight accent which, if I was hearing it correctly, sounded very proper, similar to my old friend Justin.

A quick glance out the window confirmed what I already knew—that while we'd left in the early afternoon, it was still morning here, so far to the west. That change was being widely discussed in some circles, mostly by the students who didn't already know such things.

Almost everyone had gone to their rooms, with only Headmaster Indir and a few others remaining. One was an elf there with armor, her potent aura focused around her head like a fine mist. Another female elf moved up to Indir's side and looked around curiously.

"Sir, wasn't their headmistress supposed to—"

"Greetings," I said, letting my protections fade slowly and stepping forward.

The armored elf snapped her head in my direction, eyes bulging. "No sound, no smell, no visual cues, no aura? Ancestors above, I'd heard you were subtle, but that's something."

"Headmistress Alana, I presume? Lovely to make your acquaintance," my counterpart said with a smile.

"And yours, sir. I do hope we get the chance to work together in the future as well. I feel there is much progress that could be made through such cooperation." That was the official line.

"Indeed, though I know that our magical research is ahead of your nation's, I must say the mastery you've shown in this teleportation magic is not something even our people can yet produce reliably," Indir admitted with a small smile.

"I've long known the research team involved in it, and I would suggest the utmost care if you try to pursue it. There have been accidents, and they have been . . . catastrophic, even with controls in place. Though, if you want more of these portals, that might be something our governments can arrange," I replied.

"Advice I will take to heart. On a happier subject, let me welcome you. I know you're here to watch over your students, but I hope that during your stay, you'll get a chance to see our fair land for yourself," Indir said, opening his arms.

"That would be wonderful, Headmaster Indir. I traveled here long ago, but sadly I didn't get to see much of the city."

We talked as we walked, and I could tell that the elves were as proud as ever. In a sense, they had a right to be. When it came to magic and standards of living, they blew humanity out of the water. As such, they were ever eager to show me how magnificent their lands were, how nobody went hungry, and how housing was of the highest quality.

I smiled and nodded, but we both knew the truth—Elven culture was advanced, but clearly stagnant. They didn't innovate at the same rate as humanity, and they never tried to improve designs or materials. For so long, the elves had been leaps and bounds ahead of everyone else, but their leadership kept things from progressing.

The real benefits the elves had were that they were obsessive, perfecting things to a pristine degree. The few Elven magical items that had made their way across the seas and into my hands had never displayed anything unusual, but they'd all been pushed to the limits of their capabilities. The sequences and codes that governed each item were pristine, optimized as far as they could be. That and the fact that basically every elf had at least some mana, and it was hard to compete with them magically.

Elves had a much higher rate of mages than humans, even if their population was much lower. Even those who weren't mages were almost always what we would call "talents" back home. These were rare individuals who had magic, but only one ability, and could normally only use it once or twice at a time. These talents tended toward small things like being able to make a gallon of water or healing small wounds. They could even manifest as physical quirks that let a person greatly increase their abilities for a short time. Even though they weren't full mages, these people could still put their small quantity of mana in an item, allowing them use of the Elven infrastructure.

After our chat I was shown to my room. It was separate from the main dormitories, and rather nice. They'd even been so kind as to provide a schedule of all the planned events and maps before I could ask. There were a number of tours and meetings, meals with the staff and students, all rather regular activities.

"Well," I said with a sigh, "it looks like it's going to be a rather long trip." After setting down the few bags I'd brought with me, I turned and headed for the students' dorms. If they were going to make trouble, it might well be immediately.

CHAPTER 42

✦

SOME LOW-KEY RACISM

The first few days of the field trip were fairly boring. Mostly the students were shown around the school grounds and had some basic lessons. There were a few things I would need to address later, but nothing major. One of the boys was getting very touchy with an Elven girl, but she liked him, and they were quickly hiding in some lost corner of the school.

Atal had one of the best academies I'd ever seen. The whole place was a blend of boarding school and college campus. It was far more open and greener than either of our schools were or would be, but it also housed a lot more students. Elves had a much higher rate of mages, even with their low birth rate, and it showed. They also spent a lot longer in school, though that varied.

The school was divided into tiers, in a way that reeked of eugenics. The simple fact of the matter was that elves with less human blood just lived longer. They weren't immortal like pure-blooded elves, but they lived for ages. The slowdown began in late puberty, and it meant that some of these students would have much more time to study here, hence the tiers.

Students who had less Elven blood were on something of a 'rush' track. Everyone attended the same lessons and had the same general classes, but after that, these kids were pushed out the door and into their specialties. They didn't have the luxury of spending decades in academia, with lifetimes of only a couple of hundred years. Had my children been born in Atal, they would certainly be on that track.

Above that, there were two levels of medium tracks, each spending more time at the academy and gaining more specialties. Where a rush student might specialize in fire and related magic, with only general education in other specialties, the students in the medium tracks could take between three and five.

Finally, the longest tracked youths. These few could have almost every specialty there was, only missing one or two of the ten offered unless they really wanted to work hard. I spent some time near these young elves, listening to them, as well as my own students, after hearing a few things that concerned me. I had questions about some of their language, and lucky for me, I had someone to ask about it.

Headmaster Indir and I were having a nightly meeting after dinner to discuss what we'd seen throughout the day—problems to nip in the bud and places we could improve.

"Headmaster Indir," I began, "I have my suspicions I know what it means, but could you confirm the meaning of the word *thinnies* for me?"

My counterpart's jaw visibly tightened, and I noticed his hand clench, even though he tried to hide it.

"Where exactly did you hear that term? Not from any of my staff, I hope?" he said, displeasure hardly hidden.

"No, students. A few times from those on the longest and second longest tracks," I answered.

"I would like their names or seating locations and descriptions, as we don't tolerate that sort of language here." He sighed when I raised my eyebrows. "As you may have guessed, there are those who believe that over-mixing with humanity has been a bad thing. It's a small movement, but one that is considered both foolish in the extreme and a rampant danger. They would press it as being watchful over their lessers, but the term *thinnie* indicates that a person has thin blood, as opposed to a thickie, someone with more Elven blood. Used in such a manner, it is widely considered an epithet."

"You do separate them based on those criteria," I said, not trying to hide how I felt about it.

"Yes, but not because I like it. We simply have more time with some of our students than with others. If I could, I would give every one of them a full run of all our courses." That was a pretty good answer, and I even believed him.

"What about pure elves?" I asked. "Do they get involved in this nonsense?"

That got me a bark of laughter. "No, they have better things to do, and are rare enough that it's considered beneath them. During my tenure here, we've had not one such student. If one were to be born and attend our academy, it would be a whole ordeal."

"Really?"

"Mmm, yes, our culture loves children, as I'm sure you know, but there's more as well. Those that have time are expected, nay, required, to invest it wisely. A child who might live for millennia must be nurtured as well as possible, as they will, without doubt, one day become one of the councilors that rule our nation, or a ruler of one of the others nearby."

That made good enough sense. A mage who could just keep growing could surpass almost everyone with enough time. I'd seen such things myself a few times. I also didn't doubt that they'd be watched like a hawk to quickly correct any bad behavior.

"That I follow," I admitted.

"Have you met any of our esteemed councilors?" he inquired.

"No, I've not had that chance, but there are one or two others still bouncing around on the human continent."

That made his eyebrows rise. "Are you sure?"

"Yes, though that's all I'll say on the subject. I got the impression that privacy was of importance to certain people," I said firmly. There were some sleeping giants that were better off that way.

"I cannot dispute that statement," he said, chuckling.

"So tomorrow, what's on the schedule? Looks like you're taking everyone into the city proper to see some monuments?" I said, switching the topic to something else.

"Hmm, that's right, standard tourist type things. It'll be good for optics and something fun for the young ones. Couple of museums, His Majesty's palace, all the standard locations are on the list. It might be a bit much for one day, but at the end, we're going to a lovely restaurant that serves some of the best traditional foods." He flipped through the pages while speaking.

"Not sure I've ever had any traditional dishes," I admitted. Ulanion never really said much about those.

"If you can disguise yourself, you can join in?" he said.

"I could, but it would be a risk, one I'm unwilling to take," I said with a shrug.

"Well, at least allow me to have the cook put something together for you then. It's not a chance even I get often."

"Personally, I'm more excited about some of the other demonstrations you're pulling in over the next week. Some of these disciplines are not taught in our country." In particular, I was looking at the one on tattoo magic, something I'd gotten almost no information about from even our best institutions.

"Oh, good to hear! Tomorrow then?"

I nodded and left him, looking forward to getting to see more of the city than I had on my last visit.

CHAPTER 43

◆

MUSEUMS

The morning had begun with museums, then continued with much of the same. The elves took my foreign students through several different ones, all devoted to various parts of their culture. I watched from a distance as my charges marveled at the exhibits.

The first of them was by far my favorite. This museum had a zoo, displaying various animals, both magical and non-magical, which were found throughout the Atali lands. There were cats of all sizes, various deer and their equivalents, along with a large rodent that I swore looked like a capybara but had the ability to spit acid.

Beyond these creatures were displays of some of the more dangerous, and some extinct, animals of the region. Stuffed bears covered in spikes, a large cat that could supposedly shoot lightning and make magnets, and a very familiar mock-up of a pitch-dark wolf. These were artificial but had info on what they were like, how to fight them if you encountered them, habitat and diet, and all other useful info. I was already thinking of how useful such a display would be for the populace at large back home, and I was taking notes.

After the lesson on biology, we went through one of the historical museums, displaying the greatness of Atal's past, and the Elven past in general. It was much smaller than I would have thought. The exhibits were just like any other.

The thing that struck me most was how fast the rise happened. Justin hadn't been born into a medieval world like I had, but a far, far more primitive one. From there he'd sped them through several eras of historical development, not quite to where they were now, but quite close.

Heck, some of the things built during his reign were still in use. Nothing had come to be that could yet compare to the personal work of someone trained on Earth.

This meant that the elves missed . . . a lot. They'd skipped whole technical sections that would seem normal. It even looked like they'd gone straight from stones to steel in under a century. Therefore, there were huge gaps they were still filling in for industries that they'd never developed. It was like a society that had skyscrapers and planes without mastering the steam engine first.

"This is it, right? The last place for today?" I heard my son whispering to his sister as they entered the old palace.

"Dinner after this, but yeah. Would've been nice to have more time here, you know?" she replied, stretching her shoulders.

The palace was much as I'd remembered it, huge imposing stones filled with relics. I stayed near enough to my own children to hear their opinions while still keeping an eye on the rest of the students. There was a trick to being unnoticed while invisible, and that was to stay out of the path of people. More than once I'd been found snooping simply because someone had bumped into me. That couldn't happen today; it would ruin half of my purpose here.

We finally arrived at the giant flaming letters, and once again I shook my head. It was anything but subtle. The tour guide gave the standard explanation that nobody knew what they were, the same thing I'd been told all those years ago. Maybe they kept the same script year after year. There were questions, but few answers, though one comment drew my ear.

"Hey, isn't that the script mom uses in her notes?" Rodrick asked Illa.

I snapped to attention, eyes bulging. I'd given both of my children a proper education on programming and magic before they set foot in their school, but never on actual English; it was too dangerous, too much of an identifier for transmigrators.

"What!? When did mom let you see her personal notes? That's so unfair. She only ever let me see things she prepared," my daughter said with a pout.

"Um . . . well once or twice I might've . . ."

"You broke into her office? Without me? You little turd. I can't believe you." Illa punched him, and frankly, I wanted to beat them both, but this was not the place for that conversation. "So what's it say?"

"I dunno," he said with a shrug. "Never learned to read it. Can you?"

"Obviously not, but here, I'll write it down and we can ask her later." She sketched the letters, and I wanted to puke. There would be a reckoning regarding my son breaking into my personal effects, and then improved security, again.

I let the tour group pull ahead so I could have a moment to collect my thoughts. Mostly I sat there beating my fists against my head, hoping that nobody had heard that particular exchange. Stupid. The boy was stupid; he should have known that sharing any information about a mystery language was a terrible idea. He would need to be corrected as soon as possible.

"Now that was one of the more interesting conversations I've heard in a while. How about you?"

My eyes led the way to the sound, turning to see an elf leaning against the wall near me. He looked young, almost boyish. Starting at the ground and going up, I could see his clothes, all well made and tailored to fit. His suit was loose, almost like a robe, and dark gray. There was a vest over his shirt, and he had on a long jacket. He looked like the prototypical con-man, all the way to eyes that sparkled, speaking to how he'd seen every trick, several times, and was oft unimpressed.

Above them was short, wild, white hair and long ears. "I can see you, you know. Mind dropping the illusion?"

"Who are you?" I asked, after doing as he had requested. The students were gone by now.

"A friend of a friend, I suspect. Mind joining me for a chat?" He didn't wait for a response before turning down one of the side halls, one that was roped off, and strolling forward.

"All right, how did you see me?" I inquired.

"Oh, there are ways. I've got to admit, you're one of the better ones I've seen over the years, but you still give off heat, even if you don't release it. There are other things, but I think I'll leave those out for now. Let's just say you're not the first invisible girl I've encountered. Shall we? I also might have known roughly where you would be." There was a smile in his voice, sheer amusement.

We turned a few times before coming to a set of doors.

"Where are we goi—" I tried to ask.

"Madam, I'm afraid this is a restricted area! You can't be here." One of the workers had spotted me and rushed down the hall. Only then did I notice that my companion had angled himself so he wouldn't be seen.

As soon as the woman approached, she could see my escort, and things began to register. "Um, sir, this is not a public area of the palace," she said, her tone instantly settling.

"Councilor, actually, and I'm quite explicitly allowed here." He waved his hand over a section of wall near a door, and it lit up with various symbols before popping open with a click. "See? Now, if you'll excuse us."

I watched as her skin paled and eyes grew to the size of dinner plates. "Um, yes, sir. Uh, I mean Councilor, please . . ." she sputtered.

The Councilors were the rulers of Atal, all old, all powerful. I didn't know the specifics, but based on her reaction I didn't need to.

After a quick wave at the interruption, I was pulled into the room, the door shut behind us.

CHAPTER 44

✦

OLD FRIEND

Why don't you take a seat?" my new companion said, pointing to one of several chairs around a large table.

We were in some kind of meeting room, and a look around told me that we were in one of the unused sections of the palace, and an older one. Oddly, it had the same feel as Justin's lab, something about the magic that seemed to be constantly cleaning it along with other background enchantments. Something about the way he had flippantly opened the door had alarmed that woman, but I didn't have the full context quite yet.

"Aren't these replicas of ancient furniture?" I asked as he helped himself to one of the chairs.

"Hmm?" He spent a second looking at his own chair. "No, I'm fairly sure these are the originals, but what is the purpose of such things if not to be used?"

"What if I should damage a valuable historical artifact though?" I teased.

That got me a laugh. "These are chairs, not something important, and I assure you they can be remade. It's not like we don't have plenty of them anyway."

I picked one and settled down. Ancient or not, it was intensely comfortable. It was being maintained, either by magic or hard work, though, I couldn't tell which.

"So, what do you want to talk to me about?" I asked politely.

"Is that a real question? Clearly, I was listening to the conversation between your children; clearly, I know who you are; and clearly, I recognize your mana, no? Add to that the fact that in living memory only His

Majesty and that old bastard of a priest have ever been known to use that language . . ."

"Perhaps I was unclear. What do you want?"

I half expected him to flex his power like old mages were often prone to do when challenged, but no. He merely smiled.

"To know what it says? No, no I already have a pretty good idea of that. Perhaps you think I want to win you over to my side? Why though?" he rattled off reasons that seemed normal for people. "What I want is to know first what your intentions are, and if you're a threat to my people."

"My intentions? To build my school to be better than anywhere else, and protect people as best I can." I didn't get why people had a hard time understanding that.

"Really? You expect me to believe that?" he asked as one eyebrow raised.

"Why do so many people have trouble believing that?" I asked.

"Because too many people become obsessed with power, and you have a reputation."

"A reputation I gained by protecting people I cared about. I'm not sure how much of some of the events of my past have been reported to you, but I'm not particularly inclined to fight unless I need to." I snapped. I didn't need to be told that in some countries back home I was still vilified, even after all these years.

We spent several minutes looking at each other over the table. After a time, he even began to tap his fingers. One problem with dealing with some folks was how patient they were, letting things hang in the air.

"Either you're a very good liar, or you're telling the truth," he finally said. "Let's put that aside for now, as I have other questions."

"Go ahead," I said tiredly.

"The last time you came here, one of our people sent someone to follow you and your team." He didn't seem to be too concerned, just stating a fact.

I blinked at that. "What?"

"Come now, it shouldn't be that odd, should it? You, without knowing it, spoke a name you shouldn't have known, that even most of our younger generations seldom learn. Certainly you understood that would garner attention. Lady Mistan sent someone to follow you, and . . ." He let his sentence hang.

"Look, I didn't know someone was following us. If he died, it was probably the Umbral Wolves. Nasty bastards." Just thinking back on their den sent a shiver up my spine.

"Oh, we got him back, eventually. We also learned about the monsters. Thank you for cleaning those up, by the way. No, my question is about the individual who sent him back to us."

I tried to school my face, showing nothing. "Oh?"

"See, that's what people look like when they're hiding things." He laughed.

"I didn't even know someone was following me, much less who sent them off." True, but I could guess.

"I think you do. I've only one more subject to ask upon. Is he well?" For the first time in this conversation the man's smile dropped, and he showed genuine concern.

"No clue who you're talking about," I lied.

"I'm sure," he deadpanned.

"But if you were to have old friends somewhere, and you were concerned about them, you might try visiting," I suggested.

"Not sure I'd be entirely welcome . . ." I knew that there were a lot of old people here, and that some of them really didn't like each other, but he did seem to be truthful. He also was dancing around exactly who we were talking about, which was a good start.

"I find that time helps with old wounds, but maybe not; your choice. Now, if you don't mind, I really do need to get back to my students. Call it intuition, but I feel leaving them unattended is a bad idea." I shrugged, not wanting to get involved with something that really wasn't my business.

"Can't say I disagree with that. Well, I'll leave you to it then," he said as he rose and let me out of the room.

The worker we'd left earlier was still there, and still seemingly surprised. As the Elven man turned and headed back down the hall, I looked to her.

"Excuse me, don't suppose you could point me in the direction of the tour groups?" I asked sweetly.

I didn't manage to make my way back to the students until they were nearly at the end of the tour. A quick count of heads told me that nobody was missing, and since no alarms had gone off, it didn't seem that anyone had done anything else extreme.

The only hiccup was that I nearly forgot to re-cloak myself as I approached, realizing at the last minute. I even made it a step into the hall, quickly stopping and singing a few notes. Luckily, it appeared nobody had noticed. My little disturbance had thrown me so far off that I was making amateur mistakes. No good, no good at all.

At least the restaurant wasn't far. They didn't even bother using the carriages to get everyone there. Instead, everyone walked. As the sun dipped behind the city's spires, casting long shadows over Atal, the sky ignited with hues of gold and blood red.

CHAPTER 45

EVENING OUT

The restaurant was wonderful. It was clear the elves were really try-ing their hardest to show off. Everything from the tablecloths to the aromas wafting from the kitchen, a mixture of sweet and meaty scents.

I skirted along the edge of the room quietly as my students began to take their seats, watching them all like a hawk. To my relief, it seemed that all of them had been taught manners. Each was polite to the staff and chatted lightly among themselves and with the official guides the school had assigned.

There were no menus. This particular establishment did not need such things. The students were offered a few choices of specials and would then get whatever else the chef made. A good way of doing business, in my opinion, forcing them to try new things while also making sure they would get at least one dish they liked.

As soon as I was satisfied, I slipped back into the kitchen with the staff. When I passed the door, I promised myself not to worry too much. If they caused some kind of trouble, I'd be right here.

The kitchen was clean and highly active. It was also quiet when I com-pared it to what things were like in my old world. Even in this world, the kitchens on the human continent were often quite hectic, but this one ran like a well-oiled machine. Each of the people cooking had assigned jobs they knew well and could do without any outside input, including the head chef, who was quickly putting plates together and checking over every dish before it went out.

It was surprising that for all their boasting, there were hardly any magical items at all. I spotted a couple—what appeared to be a freezer and something that I got the impression was helping dampen the sounds of cooking, but little else. All the stoves were powered by wood, much as they would be back home. The head chef was the only worker who had a real aura, the rest merely had talents, as almost every elf did.

Seafood was on the menu tonight. There were fish and shellfish, all prepared with few, if any, spices and no herbs that I could see. An odd choice, but one that made sense if this was supposed to be historical Elven food. Side dishes included some form of tuber and sliced fruits, all grilled to seeming perfection. It was simple fare, but I could tell the cooks took great pride in their work.

"Good evening," I said as I let the illusions that hid me melt away.

The chef's head turned toward me with a brief look of surprise. "Ah, you must be the chaperone Headmaster Indir told us about. Welcome to my kitchen. I'm Corina."

"Alana; a pleasure."

"And you. Don't suppose you know what you'd like?" she asked, not looking up from her work.

"The fish, if you don't mind. It looks lovely." The dish in question was straightforward enough—grilled filets of some local variety, nearly two inches thick and a brilliant golden color, served with a citrus fruit that looked rather like a lemon.

"Good choice," she said. "Make sure to squeeze the fruit over it before eating for the full experience."

"I was told these were all old recipes. Do you get requests like this often?" I asked as I waited for my plate.

"More often than you'd think. The classics are classic for a reason, and while some of the ingredients are hard to attain, we get a lot of clients that are older. I've even had a few councilors come in, hoping to get food from their youth," she bragged.

"Oh really?"

"Sadly, the plants have just changed. Some of the flavors, particularly the astringent ones, are just gone now. The fruits and vegetables taste better, but breeding has made it so that they're just not the same. The cultivated ones even affect their wild brothers and sisters, sadly—seeds spreading and all that." She personally showed me to a small table off the kitchen where I could eat.

The food was good, wildly different from what I was used to, but good. The starchiest food was a local fruit that resembled a sweetened bread when roasted, but other than that, it was simple, well-made food.

I kept out of the way as much as possible, finally giving Corina my compliments before going back to join my students. They kept up much as they had, without a care in the world, as they enjoyed a good meal after a long day. It was nice watching them enjoy themselves; my children, and those of my brother not knowing the starvation or strife we had as youths, something I wouldn't wish upon any child.

As we left, we were met with a cadre of carriages, all bearing the insignia of the local academy. Above us, the clear evening sky had grown cloudy, with a few drops falling from the billowing clouds. That wasn't unusual. With the humidity in Atal, evening storms were expected, but the sound of distant bells was coming from the harbor, if I wasn't mistaken.

By the time we returned to the school, the rain was in full force, pounding on the rooftops. While the children went off to bed, I went to my evening meeting with Indir. Most of what we talked about was rather mundane. There hadn't been any large issues throughout the day that he needed to know about, and I was keeping my earlier meeting to myself. He, too, was quite happy with the proceedings.

"Oh, one more thing, the bells?" I asked.

"Those are for the harbor, not something we'll need to worry about this far in, just an indication for the vessels there to take shelter," he answered.

"Is there a storm or something?" I inquired, not quite satisfied.

"I'm honestly unsure. Storms this time of year are not uncommon, but it would definitely put a damper on things. It could also be some monster has been sighted in the area, and ships will need to stay moored while the military sorts it out."

"I once fought a Hurricane Whale, you know. One of those would be a true disaster if it came near," I said, already well versed in the danger of some of the mega-fauna that lived in our oceans.

"Oh, those don't come near shore. The shoals are too shallow for them, and the mana not nearly dense enough. Do you get them over in your lands?" he inquired, seemingly truly curious.

"No, thankfully not," I answered with a laugh.

"The worst it could be is likely one of the species of magical shark or cephalopod. Nasty business, but not a real threat."

✦

CHAPTER 46

STORM AND SEA

The storms continued through the night and well into the morning. By the time everyone began eating breakfast, it was clear that the demonstrations for the day, which had been planned for one of the outdoor areas, would need to be moved inside. That was a shame, as the winding brick paths and large grassy centerpieces were relaxing.

Like the magical academies back home, this one also had an arena, something I'd not properly instituted in my own setup yet, but clearly I would need to. These were used for testing, magical combat practice, and exhibitions against any captured monsters for both the staff and interested parties to observe. This one was also covered, which made it perfect for the various individuals showing off their tattoo magic to display their skills.

I walked out after the groups of students, watching as they went between the stations. Mostly I kept near the royal children and my own, keen to keep an eye on them, but I got around to each and every one of the presenters by the end.

Sadly, there were very few actual forms of this magic still in use. There were a series of men displaying markings that allowed them to harden their skin into steel or strike with incredible force. These were the bulk of the users, simple physical expansions, and I had to admit that even I was tempted by some of these. Having that extra oomph would be nice in some situations, but at this point in my life, I could at least mimic most of what they could do.

Other than the power enhancements, there were some of note though. There was a man showing a tattoo form that allowed him to heal himself of injuries. He explained that it was really inefficient but something he'd gotten in his youth while hunting magical beasts. Mages were very common at this academy, but it didn't mean they were always available in the type you needed when you needed them.

My favorite presenter was a woman covered in silvery lines. Her particular markings allowed her to go without breathing at the cost of mana. I gathered that she was a bard and the silvery tattoos allowed her to do swimming dances, which she spent much of the time doing. I was not the only one interested, either, as many of the male students were enamored with the lithe woman, who was wearing a rather revealing bathing suit. It reminded me of a one-piece from Earth, but here the women wore dresses that reached at least the knees, so this bathing suit was likely considered scandalous.

The elves had a penchant for that. In my youth, the dance costumes for a lot of their traditional work had caused somewhat of a ruckus. It still did amongst the more prudish parts of society. These young men who'd come to Atal before were probably more accustomed to it than others, having at least some exposure to the Elven language and society.

There was nothing like the Lovers' Marks here. I didn't know if they had the right methods for such magic or if it was just uncommon here. Elves were well known for their poor birthrates, so I imagined that lowering them further was probably not desirable to most of them. Then again, there were plenty of reasons for not wanting a child, so who knew.

I managed to learn that a lot of the formulas depended on either magical beast or plant parts and were extremely old. There was little research on developing new ones, though every now and then, it seemed that the old formulas would be improved. The bases for them were all similar though, and while not all of the ingredients were available in the human lands, it seemed probable that with some reference material, we could replicate some of these. I'd ask if we could trade for them, and enlist some help when I got home.

The storms seemed to continue through the day but didn't worsen at least. The rain was falling in sheets, turning the ground into a muddy mess, but nothing worse than a simple thunderstorm. Hopefully, these would all end soon. It was getting old.

We all headed for the dinner hall, hoping to dry off soon and make it to bed. Hiding in the rain was more difficult than using my illusion on a normal day, so I held back when the students, went inside. As I stood under an overhang, whittling time away, I saw several red lights fly up from the east, flares blaring brightly in the sky, even through the downpour.

A Certain Councilor

The doors opened of their own accord, and I marched forward, heels clicking against the shining tile surface of the meeting room. It was uncommon that I ended up called to the military's headquarters, and it always meant trouble. Not from our neighbors, no, Atal may not control all of the former empire, but we still outclassed our fellows to the point that nobody sought war with us. Often the enemy came from the depths.

The windows across the room looked out upon the city and the port. It was difficult to see through them because of the heavy rains. There were enchantments that could aid with visibility, if needed, but they were currently deactivated. The problem was still far enough away that there was no need to waste mana on that.

Rain like this was clearly unnatural to those who'd seen it so many times before. The season was too early for such storms, and there was a tang of mana to it. It wasn't some kind of focused ability, or a controlled one, just the product of a lot of power being used, most of it geared toward water. That alone, though, didn't constitute any sort of emergency, as such things could happen either naturally or from creatures that didn't care about us.

"Greetings. Status?" I inquired as I sat down, rather shortly perhaps, but I'd been deep in consideration of some important matters before the message arrived, and woe to whatever fool had done the calling if this was a waste of my time.

"Glad you could finally join us," one of my juniors said in a rather snarky manner.

I turned and glared at her, and the woman shrunk back quickly. She was a councilor, as well, but there was a ranking system among us, and she was far, far below me. It was a simple fact of the matter that almost everyone became crotchety and set in their ways after a millennium or so. It's one of the reasons we seldom met. Such meetings, if not properly managed, often turned to bloodshed.

There was one other councilor beside her—a man, and the youngest of us, he was quiet but he seemed to be well liked for his more controlled attitude. At least I wouldn't have to worry about him trying to provoke me. There were also several higher ministers in attendance, ones who were not quite as powerful as us yet, or who may never reach our levels. That meant the three of us were the only members of the council currently in Atal, and that boded poorly for whatever the emergency was.

"Please, we didn't come here to argue," the third councilor said. "As for the situation, we've lost three of our larger warships. Something followed a merchant back to port from the deeper waters and seems keen to enter our bay."

"Identification?" I asked, and all heads turned to the man in charge of the local fleet.

"None as of yet, sir. Visibility being what it is, we can't get a good look at it, but I can tell you it's unreasonably big, and advancing. We deployed a few of the old weapons, but that seemed to do little more than stymie it," he told me, looking worried.

"Flares!" someone declared with urgency, but not panic, their training taking over.

Before I'd even turned fully, one of the assistants had enchanted the window, letting us have a full view of the city. Red dots shone as they climbed higher and higher over the skyline, originating from the port, the port that was quickly emptying.

The sea was pulling back, back, back, sand and shells exposed as a veritable mountain of water retreated. Ships fell to the exposed bottom, or were held in place to piers by their moorings, hanging exposed in air. There was a beat of silence as a claw the size of a city block was revealed by the fleeing water, followed by a chitinous leg.

Alarm after alarm sounded, and the city's wards sprang to life as the creature surfaced. From here, it looked like a normal crab, distance robbing our perception of its true size. Normally such things stayed in the ocean, but a quick glance revealed why it had come ashore, back to where more like it could be found. Below the beast was an egg sac, full to bursting.

"Well," I said as the water returned in the form of a tidal wave, carrying a monster straight at our docks, "time to get to work."

CHAPTER 47

RUN FOR THE DOOR

The ground flowed under me at speed as I ran toward the dinner building, throwing my protections and stealth back up. If I was spotted, so be it. I needed to get to my students, and I needed to be there now. I briefly considered teleporting but held back for now. The mana cost on those might well be spent elsewhere.

The flares had clearly been some form of warning, and they had lit up the city like a bulb. Something had struck the city wards hard enough for all of them to go off at once, and whatever it was would soon be upon us.

As I made it to the doors, there was a roaring sound, deafening, powerful. The school was outside the city proper, so it wasn't protected by the same warding as Atal, but it possessed protections of its own. Now those were lit up, seeming to brighten the sky as they defended against whatever was hitting us. The danger soon became apparent as a wall of water flowed up the protective bubble.

My first mentor had been a wizard specializing in the use of water, and I would be a fool if I didn't know the danger here. If nothing else, there was a mountain's worth of mass bludgeoning us, trying to sweep this place away. Those outside the protections were likely dead, or soon would be.

The lights inside had already changed, several of the small illuminations changing to a deep red and bathing the building in the color of blood. There was also a chiming sound, another warning that something had gone wrong. People were rushing for the inner sections of the building, but a few were coming out.

I noted that the Elven headmaster was no coward, leading a cadre of their teachers toward the doors, magic spinning around him as he moved.

All of them seemed nervous, but it was also clear that they were all ready to face whatever was out there, regardless.

"It's a tsunami," I said, having not gotten my sound wards up quite yet. Both Indir and his staff turned in my general direction, some of the latter looking slightly alarmed.

"Our visitors' chaperone," he hastily informed his subordinates. "How bad?"

"Quite, it struck the city too. It would be best if we got our students out of the way while it is dealt with." I didn't want to abandon him, but with both the royal children and mine here, I had other priorities. Once they were safe, I could stay behind and aid where I could; but until then, I wanted them far from this disaster.

Indir turned to one of his fellows, a lithe woman with a tightly coiled bun. "Please take the visiting students back to the portal and begin evacuating them. I hate to cut the visit short, but it appears there's an emergency."

Internally, I made a note that I owed him. The man could have been angry that I was prioritizing my students over his, but he'd understood, and quickly took the necessary steps. Once I got back home, I'd need to immediately approach my brother to get together what we could for aid, should the elves need it.

The other teacher didn't miss a beat, heading back inside and quickly rounding up the human students before leading them back to the room where the gateway awaited. I held back, eyes keen to make sure none got separated from the group as they moved.

The campus was in full emergency mode, few leaving any of the other buildings as the cadre of humans passed, everyone knowing that they needed to seek shelter. As the youths entered the building of their destination, there was a second wave, and the same roaring sound accompanied it as it washed into the school wards. The wards began to crack ominously, the protections simply not meant for this level of abuse.

As the last of the kids disappeared inside the building, I mounted the steps. This particular part of the school was slightly higher than the rest of it, situated on a small hill overlooking dorms and various classroom buildings. I gave one last turn to look back toward the city, if for nothing else than to see how it fared. I was shocked at what I saw.

Over the tops of the buildings, I could see the source of the disaster. It appeared to be a fairly normal crab, save for the size, its shell a mixture of mottled red and deep blue. The monster was attempting to climb atop the city's warding shield, smacking away at the dome and trying its hardest to break it open like an egg.

Figures darted around it and spells flew out from the city's defenders, laying claim to its massive size. It was bigger than some buildings. A massive crustacean that looked ready to roll into Tokyo and pick a fight with everyone's favorite giant lizard. Most of the spells bouncing off of it looked like little more than angry threads.

Another wave of water struck the enormous crab, and all around it were small orangish spheres, catching in the water and spreading like a wave of pollen in a high wind. Perhaps those were the nodes for the water control, or some side effect. It was hard to tell what the specifics were from this distance.

Seeing the oncoming wave, I bolted into the building. There were layers of security that had to be passed, layers of protections that I should have needed to run through. A series of quick gates bypassed most of that, the protections the elves had set up not prepped for someone who could bend space.

There was a brief moment of pride as I arrived in the departure room. Rather than putting themselves first, the prince and princess had taken last place, making sure all of their fellow classmates escaped first. Beside them were my Rodrick and Illa, unwilling to leave their cousins until the last moment and helping as they could. While clearly rushed, everything was running smoothly, and almost everyone was through. There were only a dozen or so left.

I nearly sighed relief until I heard a sound like steel being ripped, and the hissing roar reminiscent of a waterfall. The sound of water cascading toward us echoed through the walls. The children ran, trying to reach the portal as the building shook and cracked, bits of the ceiling beginning to fall as behind me a jet of seawater slammed through the doors.

CHAPTER 48

✦

SHELTER IN THE STORM

Crown Prince Omos

As I was thrown, tossed around the room like a ragdoll, my world was filled with dark blues and greens. Some last-ditch ward had managed to redirect most of the water's momentum that would have surely killed me. The water was still here, though, and still trying to fill the room.

Almost as quickly as it had come, the wave receded. A brief pull toward the exit door sent everyone, and all the furniture, back in toward the entrance before dumping us unceremoniously on the ground, and then the lights went out.

"Amara, you okay?" I sputtered, sending a light up.

"Yeah, I'm here. Where's the portal?" she said, pulling herself off the ground.

It didn't take us long to find it, or the teacher who'd been sent with us. The Elven woman had apparently dived for the exit at the last second, something even those only barely familiar with portals knew was a bad idea, and she was now a demonstration as to why that was. Much of her torso and a large part of her head were gone, pulled through when the connection broke. On the only part of her face visible was a single eye, seeming to radiate pain and terror.

As for the portal, it was smashed, some piece of rubble having destroyed the gateway. In its place now stood an undulating hole in the world, not large, but giving off a palpable wrongness. As I rose, I looked toward it, almost taken in by the oddness.

"We need to go, now," said my cousin as he pulled his girlfriend up from the ground. He thought he'd been sly, hiding who he was dating, but more than a few of us knew. "That is dangerous. Mom always told us we needed to get away from any of that kind of thing."

"Little help here, brother," came my other cousin's voice through gritted teeth.

None of us had had time to register it yet, but Illa was leaning against a wall, a spar of wood, perhaps two inches thick protruding from her gut. As soon as she spoke, we all looked and saw blood dripping from the corner of her lip and mixing with the seawater. It looked like she'd landed on a chair or table leg or something.

"Shit, shit, shit," I said as I tried to rush over to her, only to be beaten by the last person in the room.

The last of our little group was a blonde. I didn't know her, having only seen her around school. She was one of the older students, and I was pretty sure she was in her final year, but that was about all I knew. Without hesitation, she rose, wet hair falling down her back, and ripped the shard of wood from Illa's stomach with a sickening squelch.

"You're going to be fine," she said to the now screaming Illa, reaching out one hand and letting a golden glow flow forth, closing the wound near instantly. "I'll check on you again later, but for now, we need to move."

"Right, after me, we need to get to high ground!" I declared. If tidal waves were the problem, we needed to be as high up as possible. I grabbed my staff from where it'd fallen and looked back.

Amara had our injured cousin, as she was the strongest physically of us all. Without hesitation, the rest fell in line, and I led us back to the door. It didn't take us long to find our way back into the overcast light, the evening sun fighting to illuminate the world through the thick clouds.

"The city? They have skyscrapers," said Rodrick.

As one, we turned toward the nearby settlement and saw the battle commencing there. The wards were by some miracle still up, but the clash between some giant monster and the defenders was visible, even from here. Before I even had the chance to comment, a large spell was launched, followed a second or two later by an ear-shattering "*BOOM*."

"Yeah, I don't think they're gonna let us in right now," my sister said.

I let my eyes sweep around quickly before pointing. "That way. There's a slope upward. It may not be much, but it's what we've got."

As a group, we ran for the best place we could find. All around us were shattered buildings and rubble, trees that had been knocked down, and a few dazed people pulling themselves from wherever they'd ended up. There were also bodies, a lot of them—those who'd not been fortunate enough to survive. The blonde girl, clearly a priestess, pointed at a few, seeming to try and check for signs of life, but with everyone not already moving she only commented that they were dead.

The rather odd things I noticed were large orangish spheres, which had seemed to lodge themselves in nooks and crannies all over the place. Every minute or two we seemed to pass another, sometimes in groups of two or three. They were each about as tall as me, and clearly unusual, so we just gave them a wide berth.

After ten minutes of running, I heard Amara shout "Incoming, two minutes tops!" from behind me.

We all started looking for the highest spot, and it was Rodrick this time who yelled "There!" and gestured.

The hill he'd found wasn't steep, but it was large, so we all ran as fast as we could, pushing ourselves for the high ground, and hopefully safety. As we neared the top, I saw small bushes and weeds, undisturbed by either of the former two waves, and sighed. This was a good spot.

No sooner had we reached the apex than the water came, this time much lower. It spun around the bottom of our safety net, loud and fast, but not high enough to come even close to us. When it became clear we were safe, I nearly collapsed, spent and coming down from the rush of excitement.

"So, stay here for the night? See what we can do in the morning?" I suggested. There were no objections.

With the number of spellcasters we had, making a shelter was painfully simple. The walls were dirt, and the ceiling some form of local bush our priestess grew into place, but it would keep the rain off. We even broke it into sections so there'd be some privacy while drying clothes and cleaning ourselves up.

Once we all met back up in the little front room, Rodrick requested some bowls. Those were easy enough to make with magic from the local clay and stone. Once he had what he needed, he began filling each bowl with warm pasta in some kind of creamy sauce.

"You know, I always thought mom was paranoid, insisting I learn to make food, but she may have had a point," he said.

"Well, at least you don't do plain bread like she does," his sister said, laughing. She took her food and began to eat.

It seemed all the girls knew each other, each settling somewhere they felt comfortable. For Rodrick's girlfriend, Veska, that was right up against him. She was older than him. Nonetheless, the redhead was one of the better-looking girls I'd ever met. I looked to the only person in the room I didn't know personally.

"Sorry for the delay, but it seems I've forgotten my manners. I'm Omos; pleased to meet you," I said to her.

"Lena, your highness. A pleasure to meet you," the priestess said with a small bow. Her voice was polite, but it was clear that she wasn't wowed or anything, which was refreshing.

"Name's Rodrick. Pasta?" the only other male in the room said, proffering a bowl. My cousin was a good enough guy, but not what one might call cultured.

"Well met, and absolutely," she said, taking it from him.

We were all tired, and the food was hot. Sure, we had to eat with belt knives and sticks with the bark shaved away, but it was good. The little chunks of not-mushroom and not-meat were perfect with the meal.

A rotation of watch was quickly agreed upon, but before we lay down, a pair of Elven women approached, shivering and looking scared.

"Um . . . is there any chance we can get out of the rain? Our house is gone and everything's a mess," the taller of the two hesitantly asked in our language, her accent quite heavy.

Over the course of the night, we got little sleep, as group after group of those seeking some form of shelter joined us. Some were injured, and they all appreciated warm meals and a place to get out of the rain. A few gave us odd looks, as we were clearly foreign, but most were just too exhausted.

CHAPTER 49

✦

A NEW PLAN

Crown Prince Omos

The sun dawned on a new day, which would have been magnificently fresh if not for the small rock hut full of refugees I found myself crawling out of. I was tired, physically, mentally, and magically, and quite ready to get home. That, of course, wouldn't be nearly as easy as I'd hoped.

Our portal was gone, and that was not a small issue. Without it the only way home would be by ship—a long, arduous, and dangerous journey. That was if we could even find a ship with the current state of things.

Atal was a mess, and while a quick look toward the sea confirmed the city was still standing, I could also see flames. That wasn't even mentioning the countryside, which the rising sun revealed to be wrecked beyond compare. Other than a few small hills like ours, there was bare dirt everywhere, strewn with wreckage.

Lena soon emerged beside me, hair a mess and looking roughly how I felt. "How are things?" she asked.

By way of answer I just motioned. There wasn't much for me to add, and I was sure that things were, in fact, far, far worse than I could guess.

"Think we should head back to the academy or no? Honestly, that place is bound to be in a panic with all the destruction," I said, for once unsure of my course forward.

"Too bad we can't get a better look at things," she said with a frown.

"Actually, we can." I took a moment to reach out and begin shifting the world, using the air like a magnifying glass. For a few seconds there was a considerable blur, but soon enough the world came into clear resolution, giving a magnified view of the city.

"Neat trick," the priestess said.

"My aunt showed it to me, said it helped her a few times," I replied.

"Well, see if you can figure anything out. One of the people who joined us last night had some fruit, so I'm going to go plant these. I like pasta, but only so much." she said, holding up some seeds. Priests really could do a lot with those.

She moved away from the door, not out of sight or sound, only enough to give everyone some room. While she did so, I began to scan the city, looking for the monster from the night before.

It was good to report that the large legs pointing to the sky indicated that the defenders of Atal had won their battle. Though, a quick look revealed that at some point the crab, or whatever it was, had in fact breached their wards. Several buildings were torn up, with chunks missing from buildings. There was also something odd, but I couldn't quite put my finger on it.

As I was playing with the magnification, trying to get a better look, I heard another joining me from the shelter.

"Oi, Omos," I heard Rodrick say sleepily. "Not spying on the girl's dorms again are you?" he added with a chiding laugh.

I turned to tell him off, only to see the displeased gaze of Lena in the background, eyes narrowed as she judged me. It was more than a little shameful, but true that in my younger and more curious days I may, or may not, have engaged in just the slightest bit of peeping. That, of course, had come to an abrupt end when none other than my cousin had stumbled in on me in a rather compromising situation. Though, after some ribbing and blackmail, he'd agreed to keep quiet about it.

"Shut up, Rodrick," I said through gritted teeth.

He sensed the reason for my annoyance and turned, spotting Lena behind him.

"Haha, just an old joke . . ." he said.

"Shut up, Rodrick," she replied.

The other girls soon joined us as I kept trying to get a good image of the town. Under ideal conditions, it wouldn't be a problem, but between the still-growing sunlight and the distance, it was taking time. Soon enough, I had slightly better resolution, and I could see something odd going on.

"Movement," my sister said.

"Yeah, on the sides of some of the buildings," I said thoughtfully.

"No, at the bottom of the hill," she replied, pulling her blade.

That got everyone's attention quick, as did the small orange blur racing up the side of the rise we were on. Cousin Illa was the first to act, hands shooting forth a shimmering barrier that the assailant slammed into at speed.

My first good look at the creature revealed that it was a crab. Legs and all, it was roughly the size of a horse but much faster than one, as it scurried sideways toward us. The wall Illa had thrown forward made it tip ever so slightly to reveal its oval-shaped top to us.

Veska and I followed up her move with bolts of cold blue frost and pure force, respectively. While neither seemed to do much damage, the area around it was now rimmed with ice.

While Rodrick began singing more barriers into place, Lena threw a bolt at the beast, the black energy sizzling as it soared through the air. The leg it impacted shriveled, but that was clearly less than she'd anticipated. Everyone knew priest magic could be nasty on living flesh, but the thing was somehow resistant.

As the monster shattered Illa's shield, Amara stepped forward, sword gleaming as it traveled in a wide arc, landing where the priestess's spell had and severing the creature's appendage. There was a shriek as the oversized scavenger tried to pull back and retreat, but it was outnumbered and outclassed. We piled on spells, one after the other, as it tried to run, unable to move as cold seeped into its flesh and injuries piled up.

"Well that was a bit much," Rodrick said, huffing. His spells had been mostly defensive in nature but had worked well to aid my sister when they'd finally come up.

"More resistant than I'd like to see," Veska said with a frown.

"All right, I need to get eyes on the city, and then we can decide what to do," I said, gritting my teeth.

A few minutes later, I got the view I wanted, but it was not what I'd hoped to see. Atal's capital was in chaos. There were groups of elves on the roads fighting the crab monsters one by one, but there were quite a lot of them.

The academy was worse. Some of the buildings remained standing, but they were clearly in a defensive battle, waiting for aid. It also pained me to see places where the crab monsters were eating people.

"I think going back to the city is out," I said, noticing a few of the elves who'd joined us now emerging and looking shocked at the dead creature where it lay near the bottom of the hill.

"Well, we need to get home," Amara said, "and a boat is our only option with the portal down."

"What about the other one?" Rodrick asked.

"What other one?" several of us inquired, looking at him.

"The one my mom and them took back? She told us the story when we were young," he said.

"Maybe, but who would remember where it was? We haven't heard those stories since we were like five," his sister said sarcastically.

"Eratol, it was called Eratol, in the ruins there." There were some raised eyebrows. Rodrick could be somewhat of a joker at times, but I didn't doubt his memory, and he loved stories.

"All right then, since staying near the coast is out, let's head there," I declared. Even if it failed, it would still get us out of danger for the time being.

Alana

I sat atop their building, listening as the kids decided where to go. It had been difficult for me not to step in during their little fight, but they needed to learn to fly on their own. Of course, that didn't mean I was going to throw them from the nest unaided, but maybe I'd let them struggle a little.

It was odd, watching them talk and act amongst themselves. There was so much I didn't know, so much hidden or that was just never brought up in front of me. Kids could be like that, so different when they didn't think any of the adults were watching. It was nice, seeing sides of them I had never seen before.

On the other hand, they really needed to set up a better watch at night. They'd not noticed that that wasn't the first, but rather the third, crab to try its luck, the others sent off with a few stay bolts of lightning to find easier prey.

As they turned to consult with some of the people they'd taken in, I leaned back. Hopefully my old friend wouldn't mind helping me get this lot home.

CHAPTER 50

✦

HELLO AGAIN

Rodrick Penumbra

Stop fucking getting in front of Amara! If you die, I can't heal you!" screamed the angry priestess from the back. She really was a ray of sunshine, that one.

I kept channeling, kept pouring mana into my spells. One thing about being a bard, it was slow, but if you could get things going . . . well, then it really did get going. Earlier in the day, I'd been going for defensive measures, but when it became clear that it was going to be a lot of fighting I'd changed over to offenses.

As my feet moved and my singing voice peaked, I saw the streams of water being pulled from the giant crab's carapace, a steady flow from all of its joints and onto the ground below. Perhaps I lacked the explosive capacity of my comrades, but how much water did any animal need to lose to just die? Not much, that was certain, and aquatic animals were no less sensitive to it. I'd killed my fair share of these already, and this one was slowing down even as I watched.

Beside me, Veska, my dear Veska, was grabbing up that water and turning it into deadly projectiles of ice. Her hair blew in the wind, and I was very nearly distracted as she turned briefly to smile at me. Maybe she didn't speak about it most of the time, but I could see from the fire in her eyes, matching the tone of her blazing hair, that she lived for this.

Our enemy wasn't going down easy, though, bobbing and weaving from side to side as it tried to pick apart the front-line fighters with its claws. Amara was supposed to be on point, keeping the creature's attention, but every now and then, one of the refugees would decide they wanted to take a shot at a chink in the shell. This was a source of great frustration for our healer.

I couldn't do much as one of the men thrust forward, makeshift spear aiming for a softer looking part of the belly. With a flash of movement a claw zipped outward, snapping shut and sending a spurt of blood into the air. The Elven man went down screaming, his arm held in the grasping appendage of the magical beast.

A cursing Lena sent forward a spell, sealing up the wound on the elf's arm as one of his fellows tried to pull him away. He wasn't the first to get hurt, or the fifth; though, he was probably the worst injured. Mostly people had been struck and sent flying, but if things continued like this, they might well start to die.

Regardless, Amara didn't let the monster's momentary distraction go to waste, her sword zipping forward in a beautiful arc and separating both of the monster's eyes from its head. From that point forward, it wasn't much of a fight, with everyone backing off and letting the ranged attackers finish it up.

Our knight was nearby huffing as she tried to catch her breath. "What was that, fourteen?" she asked when we finished up with the beast.

"Fifteen," her brother answered.

"At least a lot of them seem sick," Illa said, and I nodded in agreement.

"Yeah, but sick from what? We don't know anything about these things. Maybe some are just born weak, or maybe something's getting to them," I added.

Of all the crabs that we fought, maybe a third were sluggish, slow, weak. It made them really easy to dispatch, but caused other problems.

"Hey, Lena, can you check one of those after you're done? See if there's something wrong with it? We need to know if there's some disease or something we should be worried about," I requested of the healer, who was still stabilizing the guy who'd now be left-handed.

She gave me a look that could have cut glass, but did as I asked.

"Nothing's wrong with it. Well, actually it looks like it was suffocating or drowning. Maybe they need water to breathe?" she said with a shrug.

"Then we need to keep heading inland, away from the bulk of them and where they'll have a harder time," Omos declared.

Our brave leader could be a bit of a jerk sometimes, and really couldn't take a joke, but he was right. Not that we hadn't been headed inland anyway, but he was right. Unfortunately, the sheer number of these beasts was causing problems, as was the size of our group.

Our classmates were quick, and we were trained, and we were also stronger than most. The many elves we'd come to take under our banner weren't. Many of them were young, or old, or just injured from the tidal waves, and it was slowing them down. Between that, the monsters, and the destruction blocking or destroying paths, we were going at a snail's pace.

"We need a clearer path," I told Omos. "It's almost noon, and we've made it what, five miles? Heck, you float me up a little, and I could probably still see that hill we stayed on last night."

"Suggestions?" he asked. Sadly, I had none.

"There's a road that shouldn't be too far," one of the elves pointed out, indicating a slight northerly direction.

"Is it higher or lower than the ground around it?" Amara asked.

"Um . . ." the woman considered for a moment, clearly thinking about the road itself.

"Not high, but it runs along a river, which would probably make it lower," another of the refugees answered.

"That way then," Omos declared, leading us forward.

It was about another mile before we made it to the road. It did look to be mostly clear, save one little problem. The road we were trying to get to was on the other side of the river. Our side was nowhere near as clear, but at least it was better, so we began following the water. The river looped north and west, away from the coast. Traveling here was faster, though not by much.

As the afternoon wore on, we saw our first group of other people. They shouted and waved but were opposite us, across the river on the road we'd been hoping for. Projecting my voice was part of my repertoire, so I became our communicator.

"Hey," I said into my spell, letting the sound flow across the river. "Do you know of anywhere we could cross?"

"Ahead! Two miles, there's a big bridge that might have survived!" their representative yelled.

The bridge had in fact survived, and so there we crossed. Our side of the river was a little lower, so it had taken more damage, but the far side had a few trees left standing and looked that much nicer. That evening we all gathered together with the refugees, setting a much stricter watch before trying to get some rest.

We sat around the fire that night, exhausted but alive. Over her pasta, Lena kept looking at me curled up where I was with Veska.

"Food's not that bad is it?" I teased.

"No . . . You're the new headmistress's kids, right?" she asked, looking between me and Illa.

"Yeah, why?" I responded with a quirked brow.

"What's she like?" the priestess asked, nervous.

"Mom? Hmm, nice, bit moody sometimes, why?"

"Well, during the fall of the old kingdom, she saved me," Lena said, blushing slightly.

"Really?" Illa asked. She looked surprised.

"Mhmm, those monsters took me from my family in Ice's End. The Shield told us they were planning to keep us all as servants or whatever, make us their slaves. I found out later she's the one that led the assault against their keep. I was a baby then, of course, so I don't remember it, but she and her men rushed in and saved us all. So, I'd like to thank her at some point."

"Shit, seriously?" I asked. Mom didn't really talk too much about the fighting. I got the feeling that for her it was more sad than heroic. "Was your family all right?"

"Never found them. I did get magic, though, so at least I can join the Shield and try to make sure something like that never happens again." She laughed briefly. "The others in the orphanage were always so jealous, but at least they understood what I wanted, to keep more like us from being made."

"That's a noble goal," cousin Omos said with a soft smile.

There was a crash somewhere in the brush. Before any of us could think, Amara was on the job, blade out. She scanned the area briefly before frowning.

"Broken branch; nothing here," she called back.

As the surprise wore off, I turned back to Lena. "Yeah, Omos is right. We'll introduce you. I'm sure she'll be thrilled to see you're doing well."

CHAPTER 51

✦

WORRIES

I was ready to curse, having just barely evaded discovery. The girl had caught me completely off guard, but I knew she was out there somewhere. With my luck, I should have guessed that I would be meeting her sooner or later. It's just that here was rather unexpected.

I'd left the princess with the Order of the Shield years ago and intentionally avoided contact. When I later found out that they knew who she was, that was a surprise, but I'd still kept my distance. Many times over the years I'd thought about going and trying to see her, to check on her, but I hadn't. I'd told myself at the time that I didn't want to jeopardize her, even a little, but the truth was that I wasn't sure if I could deal with it if she was doing poorly.

What could I do if the child I'd orphaned turned out to be miserable there, unable to get what she needed? What if she pined for parents that she'd never seen, parents that I'd killed? Could I live with that? Could I look upon her and know that I'd caused her suffering? I knew it would cause me pain, so I'd avoided it.

Perhaps the only thing that would have caused me more trouble than her being sad or lonely was if she'd been a bad egg. If I'd released another havoc-causing royal onto the world, I wasn't sure I'd be able to live with myself. Luckily, it seemed that while she was somewhat easy to tick off, she was at least dedicated to the ideas of the Shield. Perhaps she'd been unhappy with people getting hurt, but she was working hard to help them.

I gave their camp another quiet once-over before pulling back. They'd chosen an excellent spot and used debris from the disaster to form a wall around themselves. None of that would stop one of the giant crabs, but it would certainly slow them down. I could pull back, leaving them alone for a while; it was something I needed to do. The day had been long, and I was exhausted. Soon I would need to rest, but there were a few other things I needed to do beforehand. First, I found the highest point nearby and pushed on my left earring. This was a variant of one of my oldest magical items, one much improved from the original version.

"Hello, hello, hello, can anyone hear me?" I said as the magic activated.

I repeated my message three times, frowning but unsurprised. I knew that it was technically possible for radio waves to bounce off the atmosphere and reach truly epic distances, but I also knew that I'd not made these communication devices quite well enough to do so. Back on Earth I'd not known enough about them, and while I was confident that this little one would reach someone if we were anywhere near our homeland, we were very far away.

"Ulanion is never going to let me live this one down," I pouted.

My husband had suggested several times, that I bring a small portal with me, just in case. Something a few inches wide might not have seemed like a big deal, but with it we could easily have sized up in a hurry and gotten the kids out of here. Making a lot of those and carrying them around grated on me, though, so I'd refused. Had I not, we might have the kids home by now.

"Shit, John is never going to let me live this down," I added. His kids were here, too, and I could only imagine what he'd be like right now, hearing the reports of what had attacked us. He might even be sending some military vessels.

Well, I'd try to establish contact if I could, but if I couldn't, I'd just deal with things as they came. For the moment, that was my only real option, so I began taking stock. One by one, I went over my magical items and tools, hoping to find something that I'd missed, some extra trick I could use.

My earring was already being used, and it was straightforward enough. It was an amazingly potent transmitter and receiver, and even had a small storage function built in. There were flaws, and it had never been tested for what I was using it for now, but if someone did manage to get a strong enough signal out, it should notify me, and it would save the message. Until then I'd only have to try and keep establishing contact.

Next was my anklet. When I was young, I'd made one of these that had saved me once or twice, but the one I had now made that one look like a cute little trinket in comparison. The shielding and ability to redirect force contained in that piece of jewelry could be staggering, but it was nearly empty. Using it along with my own spells had been enough to redirect most of the water that would have killed us. I supposed that in that way it'd done its job well.

My belt didn't do much, but functioned to make a small shelter where I could rest anywhere, and with a built-in alarm. The bubble it could project around me would shield me from casual observation, weather, and light attacks, but little else. I activated it, giving myself eight hours; that would be enough to wake me well before dawn.

Finally, I had a bracelet. It, too, did far more than it looked like it should. This last item was something that I didn't need time to charge up to fire. It could shoot projected lances of kinetic energy, either many very small ones, or one, really, really large one. I'd never used it in combat before and really hoped I wouldn't need to any time soon.

One thing that my few items all shared was optimization. I didn't carry many, but each one did its job well. I'd spent a lot of time getting the features I wanted put into the most straightforward form possible, molding them and readying them for use. Then I'd pushed them all to the very limits of what they could achieve, the edge of what a magical item of that size could manage to hold and project.

As I settled down to sleep, I hoped that tomorrow would be just a little easier than today had been.

Veska

I stood at the edge of camp, eyes scanning. We needed to get moving soon, but unless we were willing to abandon the elves we'd joined up with, mornings would take time. That many people always took time.

Lena came to join me, looking for any approaching enemies. She held out a fruit for me, one of the local ones. They were all so sweet, the flavors so floral and magnificent. I moaned lightly as I took it and bit into the soft flesh.

"We need these back home," I said.

"Agreed. Anything happening?" she asked.

"No, but I can't shake the feeling that I'm being watched," I answered.

"Something bad?"

"Who knows? Those stupid crabs don't watch, but we don't know all the animals around here. Could be we're being followed by a scavenger, or could be someone from the city. Then again, maybe I'm just paranoid." I couldn't do anything but shrug. "How about you?"

"Honestly? I'm a little frazzled. The new group is worse off than ours was. They're all stable, but they need proper medical attention as soon as they can get it. No real healers among them and no good casters means the crabs they met did quite a number on them, and frankly I don't have the facilities or the mana to do much more than get some of them walking." Even in the short time I'd known her, I could tell she cared.

"We should find more people soon, more help," I reassured her with a small smile.

"Sure, but what if we can't get back home? What if we're stuck in this disaster for who knows how long?" she asked, admitting her real worries.

"If Rodrick says there's a portal at that village, there's a portal there," I answered with a shake of my head.

"Rodrick is kind of an idiot; even I can see that. I know you like him, for some unknowable reason, but that's not enough."

Now I got a real laugh. This was something I'd heard before. "He looks that way, doesn't he?"

"Seriously, other than the pedigree, what do you see there?" she inquired.

"Our families have known each other for years, if in passing, but I never really spoke to him until his first year at school. We met in one of the combat training sessions. Did you know that?" I asked, and she shook her head. She wasn't in those classes. "I thought I was hot shit, with my parents, and my grades, and the way I dominated our spars in class."

"Okay?" she said, clearly confused as to where I was going with this.

"When I went up against him, I planned to do the same, but I've never been so thoroughly dominated in combat in my life."

She blinked. "What?"

"Sort of my reaction, too, as I lay there in the sand. You know what he told me when I asked how he'd done it? That he'd only let me in on the secret if I let him take me on a date." I giggled. It was a funny memory, in retrospect. It had also been a pretty good date.

"And?" the impatient priestess demanded.

"He'd watched all my fights, everyone's fights. My Rodrick might look like a fool, but he's got a mind like steel. If he sees or hears something, he remembers it. If he sees a tactic, he comes up with a counter. He'd seen my spells, and how I fought, so he knew how to beat me. That's why I'm sure it's there. He wouldn't forget such a key detail like that." I stood confidently, knowing things would work out.

"So he's actually a really good fighter?" she said in disbelief.

"Eh, sort of? The next time we went up against each other, I changed things up and wiped the floor with him. We spar a lot, and I'll tell you, the same thing almost never works twice." I left out that he also wasn't too bad on the eyes. She could already see that if she wasn't blind. Just his ass alone . . .

"You're all weird," she finally said after mulling things over for a while.

"And you're not? I may not know a lot of priests, but I'm pretty sure most would wash your mouth out with soap if they heard how you talk while fighting." She blushed and turned away. "Oh-ho! Hit that right on, didn't I?"

There was a sound from camp as someone tripped while putting on their makeshift bag. "Looks like we're heading out," Lena said, seemingly happy to have been interrupted.

"Let's get going then. We've got lots of ground to cover," I said as we rejoined the others.

CHAPTER 52

✦

BESIEGED

Amara

The day we met up with the second group of refugees, we'd walked down the road for hours. There should be more people—way more people—than we'd seen. I wasn't sure the others realized it quite yet, but the roads were too empty. Only one answer presented itself to me—that this disaster had been on a scale the world had seldom seen. The reason nobody was around was because they were hiding or dead. I realized that nearly all of the missing people likely belonged to the latter category; everyone would seek help after a tidal wave like that unless they were under siege.

The crabs had at least thinned out. By noon we'd only killed five or so of them, their carcasses left in our wake. It almost seemed like a joke, celebrating because I'd *only* had to fight five magical beasts by lunch. I nearly laughed. Even with our larger group, the additional people weren't too much help, worn down and beaten by their own experiences.

I hoped that the city was faring better, that it was just the outlying areas that were so wrecked, but I honestly didn't know. It had seemed during our tour that almost everything was in the city proper, with few outside of its walls, but it wasn't like I'd done a census. That, of course, wasn't altogether odd, as most people, when able, moved into protected areas, the simple existence of monsters in the world encouraging it.

My ears perked as we reached a bend in the road. There were sounds before us, the sounds of battle.

"Eyes up!" I called back. "Something's going on up ahead."

As we ran forward and cleared the corner, what I saw both warmed my heart and caused it to sink. We weren't the only ones who'd been busy, it seemed, as someone had used magic to raise a small palisade. Atop the walls were dozens of men and women, some in uniforms, some not, with banners hung nearby. I didn't know the local symbology for such things, but this was clearly meant to be a refuge, a camp raised to save all they could.

What chilled me, though, was the assault taking place. I could personally see no less than ten of the nascent monstrosities besieging the wall, and I couldn't see the whole area from my vantage point. The defenders were putting up a fight, with spears and spells raining down on the enemies, intermixed with arrows. However, it was clear that the crabs were outmatching the elves here.

"They need relief. Start bombardment! Fighters front, and cast!" my brother yelled from behind me, stirring our stunned companions from their daze.

I smiled. I might be able to take Omos in a fight, but he could get people moving in ways I never could. He didn't even seem to try sometimes. I knew for a fact that over previous generations, many royal siblings had fought each other endlessly over the throne, but not us. Never had I wanted to rule. It just seemed like too much trouble. Brother had looked that trouble in the eye and smiled, though, taking the duty of his birth without complaint.

There was no time to think about it now, though, as the first volley from our casters flew forward, slamming into the backs of the enemies. The defenders and their little fort hadn't even noticed us, but they looked up now as a wave of spells washed forward, crashing against the wall of chitin that was trying to destroy them.

On day one, we'd worked out our method. The casters would aim at the fringes, while I held the center, pushing back with all I had to give them the time they needed. It worked. Crabs weren't all that smart, after all, and had no tactics to speak of, other than 'run at enemy, crush.'

The enemy didn't seem to realize our presence fast enough, either, losing several of their number, and even more legs, before the first of them even turned to us. Cold magic prevailed well, and the priestess' bolts turned whole sections of legs into little more than blackened twigs. It all needed time though.

The first of the crabs reached me and gave a quick, but clumsy swipe with its claw. It had taken me a long time to adjust to these things, their movements strange and limbs even stranger to fight, but adapt I had. I ducked under the appendage, the shell on it whizzing inches above my head.

Like fully armored knights, these things were hard to damage, the thick shell equal to enchanted steel. However, like a fully armored knight, there were weak points. On the first day, I'd had difficulty cutting into the joints of their limbs, the odd angles required for a clean slice that was foreign to me. Today, however, I sent a thrust up into the place where the claw intersected the thorax, slicing deep and sending out a spray of blood as it went limp.

There was a scream, and I could tell one of the elves had fallen. We were going to lose a few; there was little I could do about that other than hurry. The other front liners weren't like me, their bodies not so enhanced by mana that they could move and think with the same speed I could. Attacks that would be minor injuries to me would kill them; therefore, I needed to be their protector, their shield, as much as I could.

I bobbed and weaved under the crab, striking and slicing. Even giving my best, it still took me nearly a minute to dispatch the thing. It had become more cautious after my first strike. I was methodical, perfect blows topped fast ones in situations like these, and there was no room for error.

The second crab that I fought fell much faster though. It had been busy looking at two of the men who'd joined us when I hit it from the side, slicing both eyes off. If they had a weakness anywhere, it was the eyes, the viewing organs sitting on little stalks above their . . . heads? Thorax? Whatever. If only they weren't so good at keeping a claw ready to defend against strikes, we'd have no issues at all.

Once we'd killed our group of enemies, I looked up. The elves manning the wall were shouting, some motioning toward a small gate. One of our cadre surged toward the opening, now that a path toward relative safety was open. I let them pass me, determined to be the rear guard should any more monsters make their way to us.

As I made it through the gate, I took quick stock. Our side of the fort hadn't been the only one under attack. On the far side, even as I watched, a monster pulled itself up the fifteen-foot-high wall, bringing it into view.

I felt a surge of power in me and I *moved*, charging across the open space in the middle like a loosed arrow, the ground blurring under my feet.

"No, no, no, no!" screamed an Elven soldier, terrified and panicking as he brought his spear forward again and again uselessly, the monster cutting it in half with a single movement of its claw.

With a single push upward, I bounded up. My sword led me, the lightly enchanted weapon finding purchase where a leg met body. My boots landed against the thorax of the beast, pushing hard and sending it back over the side. To bleed off the last of my momentum, I turned in the air, my golden hair flying in an arc behind me before I landed by the man, who now looked up at me with an odd combination of fear and awe.

"Don't worry," I told him. "We're here to help."

CHAPTER 53

MOVING FORWARD

Lena

I swore under my breath as I tried to patch up some of the injured elves. My group was strong, but they acted as if they were immortal, diving in with no real plan, no idea what they were going to do. The worst were the elves desperate to prove their worth, always in places they shouldn't be and doing things that got them killed.

My mana wasn't infinite, and I'd been running through it fast over the past few days, never getting a chance to fully recharge, never getting enough rest to recharge. If we didn't change things up, and soon, there would be injuries that I wouldn't be able to heal. Surely the others were as tired as I was; they had to know that.

At least we were in a place now with more of us. There were a few useful talents in this little compound, ramshackle as it was, and one exhausted mage.

"Where in the world is your army?" I asked one of the soldiers lying down nearby. His wounds weren't that serious compared to the man I was aiding.

"Everyone's been rushing to the city. Reports are sparse, but it looks like most of the survivors went to hide there. But even with the extra people, there are a lot of these damn things. They're swarming every large group," he replied.

"So, you're what, splitting into smaller units?" I asked.

"Yes," the wizard who'd put the walls up interjected, limping her way over. "We were only about twenty when we got here. Some of the local authorities had armed themselves and gathered what survivors they could. It looks like all of their casters went to the city to get aid and never returned."

"Then you guys came in from outside . . ." I began.

"And found nearly a hundred helpless civilians under siege from those things. I barely got the walls up in time," she replied. "Thank you, by the way."

After we'd shown up and taken down the current wave of hostiles, there'd been an eerie calm. The defenders had been under attack from multiple waves, it seemed, whittling down their defenses. The soldiers had numbered twenty, according to the wizard who was now resting, but numbers didn't lie. There were only around seventy people left, just over half of the original number.

That night Omos called a meeting between our group and the leaders of the soldiers here. He was the nominal leader for us, and though a lot of what he decided seemed obvious, he'd actually stepped forward to do it. Making a decision in a pinch was needed, so without someone to do it, we'd probably all still be sitting back on that hill from the first day getting swarmed.

He began by looking at the Elven wizard, who seemed to also be their commanding officer. "We need to discuss what we'll do," he declared.

"Since you lot all appear to be students, we'll wait here for backup," the woman replied.

"That doesn't seem viable. These monsters are getting more aggressive, not less, and with the number of people here, I have to consider other options." Omos sighed, tired.

"We must protect the people here, regardless. It is our duty as elves of power to secure the lands," she responded. "Surely you know this?"

I was glad to see Omos clench his jaw, not giving an inch. One had to have their ideals, after all. "My companions and I are not from Atal. While I'm sympathetic to your current plight, and more than willing to aid where I can, my duty is to them, not the people of Atal."

"We cannot abandon these people. It wouldn't be right." As I spoke, it stuck to me, stuck into my magic. I knew that if I tried, my spells would begin to fail, start to wither and die as I betrayed myself. That was the weakness of any priest, but also our strength.

Both sets of eyes settled on me, blooming in understanding. The others in the room held back for now, watching to see what would happen. The commander looked triumphant, but Omos was the first to speak.

"I don't suggest we abandon anyone, but rather evacuate them. We get the people we can to safety, and then my friends and I continue on. If

I return home, I will petition my father to send all the aid he can, and it will be easier for him to do so if we succeed. I know him, and he won't let people die like this if it can be helped."

"My orders," the woman told us, "are to move toward the city. I merely got delayed here."

"Your orders," Omos replied, "are going to get these people killed. You know that, I know that. Let's say you and your men do continue on. Do they survive? Not even a night."

"Not if you lot stay," she countered.

"Even if we stay," I objected. "These attacks are getting worse. The one attacking you when we arrived was the worst we've seen since the big one attacked the city. Maybe the soldiers get them cleaned out soon, but not soon enough to save everyone. We can save this lot by going further inland, and if we return home, I think aid will quickly be on its way. My order would almost certainly want to help if they knew."

We were keeping secret for now that there might be another portal. If it panned out, it would be world-shaking that nobody had disclosed it, and it would probably destroy trust in the kingdom, but it would allow us to help. Of course there was still the option that it didn't exist, and in that case, we'd be giving hope where none existed.

"We'll give them an option—go with you or stay," the Elven woman declared before leaving us. It was easy to tell she wasn't happy about our refusal.

I held Omos back while everyone else went to find a bunk. "You will make sure that someone comes to aid these people, right?" I asked him.

"If Father won't send someone, I'll fight my way to the gate and come back myself." He scratched his head. "Look, I can tell that you are conflicted about this, and if you want to stay, or go with the soldiers, I won't object. I'll admit that what I am doing is a bit self-serving, but getting to that gate could get them both material and physical aid, and I'm not letting anyone else take that mission from me. I can't trust them to."

"I'll come with you, so long as they do," I told him.

Alana

Stupid kids, doing stupid heroic kid things. I'd nearly revealed myself during that battle to pull them out of the fire. This was getting completely out of hand, and these little idiots needed to get out of here.

The moon was bright, and I teleported myself past the wall, quickly popping down the road they were supposed to be headed for. So long as they didn't try to go anywhere else tonight, they'd be fine, but I was going to clear the way ahead as best I could.

The moon was unusually bright as I headed for the highest places I could find, looking outward. I climbed atop hills and into the highest trees and buildings, using my lens trick to look for any lingering monsters. An hour in I found what I was looking for.

A group of those things was swarming a house, and there were nearly as many of them as there had been at the little makeshift fort. Several were chewing on dead bodies while a few others were . . . molting? Oh, hell no! Quickly, I began to spin up a spell, gathering the potential until the air seemed to crackle.

The spears of lightning I sent down arced between each one. While it took me a few moments, when I was done there was little more than smoking shells left behind. These days I seldom found myself in fights, and while I wasn't quite as good as Dras in a fight, I was still one of the strongest mages in our kingdom. Give me another thirty years and I might even start calling myself an archmage.

Unfortunately, the people in the house all appeared to be dead, which saved me from having to try and help them, but it was still depressing.

As soon as my mana had recharged, I leapt up again. I could spend a couple hours out here doing this, and if I could get them all, my kids would be safe from their own good intentions.

CHAPTER 54

CHILDREN CHANGE

Illa

Battle mages," I declared as we looked over the dead crabs. "At least one, probably more than one judging by the destruction."

"But they didn't come to say anything to us?" Omos asked. I could only shrug in response.

"Smells good though," Amara commented. I hated to agree with her, but there was a roasted crab smell that was absolutely lovely.

"I don't know, their diet is throwing me off wanting to try it," Rodrick said as he pointed to another of the beasts; this one had half an elf in its mouth. There were a couple more in the area beginning to decay.

My body instantly rebelled at my brother's words, bile moving up my throat. I'd been thinking of eating one of these things. Even as I tried not to puke, my brain summoned the smell of butter and herbs.

"We should bury them," Lena said.

"That's not how we do things here," one of the refugees said. There were dozens of them following us.

We were quickly shown how elves dealt with their dead. Lena happily gave up some of her seeds, and less happily some of her mana to grow plants on the bodies of the dead. She took care of several of the fallen elves, while my brother helped with the others and the crabs. He'd learned an Elven song as part of our schooling because it was a good way to pick up words quickly. He sang it now, a lover's lament. Maybe not perfect for the occasion, but it worked.

Luckily, we weren't attacked while we worked. It looked like some of the Elven mages had run through last night slaughtering monsters as they went. I briefly wondered where they'd gone, or where they'd come from. Why hadn't they come to see us in that little fortress? Perhaps they'd been swamped, or just missed us. It was impossible to know.

Even if yesterday had been a brutal slog, today was rather uneventful. The whole time I was looking around for more enemies, but it seemed that there were few, if any, in the area. That was fortunate, at least. We even decided to take a slightly longer lunch.

Omos was doing the rounds, checking on people, and eventually made it over to where Lena and I were standing guard.

"How are you doing?" he asked. Everyone had been a bit on edge.

"Conflicted," Lena said, looking at him. I'd known she had feelings about our path, and if it was the right one.

"That's understandable, but we can't change the past. Things have worked out well so far, so let us hope that they continue to do so, and focus on the future." He gave her shoulder a gentle pat before turning and heading off again to check on others.

"He's not a bad guy, is he?" she asked.

"Omos? He's all right; used to be pretty immature, but I think he's trying," I answered. I didn't spend a ton of time with my cousin, but I knew that much. "If you really want to know about him, you should ask my brother, but don't expect any kind of a straight answer from him."

"So . . . what do you do when you're not . . ." she said, waving her hand around and indicating the whole situation.

"Really? That's what you're going with?"

"Got a better conversation topic?" she snapped.

"Don't laugh," I told her, and she nodded. "I'm trying to learn to fly."

She laughed, the traitor. "You know that's nearly impossible, right?"

"I need something," I griped. At those words she raised an eyebrow. "My family is . . . They're all big and important or strangely good at things, but I'm not. My grades are good, sure, and I'm a decent wizard, but I'm not 'Kingkiller Alana;' nor do I have my brother's insane memory. I feel . . . subpar. Like I'm the one left behind. Nobody really cares about me."

"I heard your mom hates that name," she said curiously.

"Oh, violently. If she heard me using it, I doubt I'd sit right for a week," I agreed.

Only a few people had ever called Mother that to her face; fewer still had eardrums left after they did. It still made the rounds though. People saying she killed one, or both, of the kings that night, along with all inheritors of the royal title. People thought I didn't hear about it, but I did—how we'd taken the royal family by force.

"Flight's pretty cool," Lena said after a while. "I mean, nobody our age can do it."

"I know. I can sort of hover, but it takes a lot of mana."

"When we get out of here, will you show me?" she asked. I could tell she was just being nice, but I didn't really care.

"Yeah, of course," I said with a smile.

Our lunch break was over, and we had to move. There was still so much ground to cover, so much left to do, and so many people to get to safety.

Alana

I frowned as I looked down at Illa from the tree I'd perched in. Was that how she really felt? How had I failed to miss it, that she was hurting, feeling left out? I wanted to do something for her, but honestly, I didn't know where to even begin. Mostly I just wanted to hug her, but now wasn't the time. Clearly I'd have to make some time to spend with her, one on one. Maybe we could work on some spells, or I could help her with flight.

As the thought passed through my mind, I froze. Was I doing the same thing my mother had? Had she had those same worries or thoughts about me being left behind? I'd certainly not fit in where she thought I should. This is not a problem I had with Illa, but maybe I was going about this the wrong way.

I needed to spend some time with her; that much was clear, but I should figure out what she wanted to do, not decide myself. I'd been on the receiving end of that before, and I remembered vividly how I'd hated it. Then again, I did still use my sewing spell from time to time, so I couldn't really fault my mother.

Also, did she really think I'd be that upset over her using that stupid name? Sure, I hated it, but I still loved her.

Illa was so different than how I saw her in my mind. She was no longer the small girl who wanted to play with her dolls or her grandfather. That time had passed years ago, years I'd missed while working. Rodrick was the same—so different from when he'd been little, so changed from how I'd seen him. They'd been out of the house and in school for years, and it seemed I needed to see them again, and more often. They'd have to fly on their own one day, but I didn't want to lose them completely.

✦

CHAPTER 55

CITY

Rodrick

I moved to stand next to Veska and reached for her hand, giving it a light squeeze.

"First live one we've seen in days," I said as I looked down at the dead crab. It was true, but the thing was bigger than I'd expected.

"Yeah, the numbers are definitely thinning out the further inland we get," she responded.

"And someone's killing them."

"Good to see some of the elves are carrying their weight," she griped, frustrated that these people who'd acted so superior were not helpful to us at all.

"No, I think it's one person, maybe a team," I answered.

"There's too many though? We've found dozens of them dead."

"All dead in the same couple of ways, all freshly dead, and all on our path." I was giving the whole area a hard look. "I'm betting Lena has realized it too; maybe even some of the others."

"They didn't look that similar to me," she said, then thought about it. "All right, maybe if you squinted, there were some similarities."

"No dead soldiers, no cuts or breaks, and many of them looked to have died while eating. Something is taking them out hard and fast, lots of lightning damage, odd injuries, a few burnings or freezings, and some that just looked to have fallen over dead."

"Maybe one of their bigwigs? But why? Why not just tell us?" she asked, suddenly concerned.

"A hundred possibilities, sweetie, or maybe I'm just being paranoid. It could also be that they've got teams going around hitting these things. You'd think that would make them look different though. Different teams would use at least slightly different styles."

We were at least seeing less of the crabs overall as we worked our way inland. Looked like they did indeed prefer the seaside, and every step took us further from both them and the desolation caused by their mother. Slowly, the signs of damage had dissipated, the spared hills getting lower and lower as we passed them. Now, it looked as if the tidal wave hadn't even hit.

There were almost no new elves on the road. I had to ask myself where they were? Were they all in hiding? Had that many died? No, that didn't make sense. We'd seen enough survivors that we should have met up with more by now. Maybe they were getting to safety faster since there were less monsters and debris in the way.

Regardless, we'd soon be finding out. Because of our route, we'd been on quiet roads since the beginning, but if the locals were to be believed, we'd soon be approaching both a main thoroughfare and a small city. The elves seemed to like cities, but there were very few of the small villages that would have dotted the countryside of human lands in comparison. Perhaps it was due to the higher concentration of magical beasts in these lands.

We found the road first, and while still quite empty, it was far larger than any road we'd seen since beginning our journey. There had to be at least four different lanes for carts to pass by in each direction, complete with inlets and outlets. While as a feat of engineering it was pretty neat, I couldn't imagine that they even had a need for such a large road. I'd seen the Elven populace, and it just made no sense. Unless, of course, they were moving something massive up and down the road, there'd be no purpose for it.

It looked like either the wave hadn't hit this road at all, or someone had already cleared it of carts. There were no abandoned vehicles anywhere. Though, there were signs indicating the distance to the city. Iriatol was, once the distances were translated, only about a three-hour march from where we stood. As a group we decided to skip lunch. While we were all hungry, stopping would keep us from potential safety, and we were all ready to meet up with other people.

As we crested a small rise, the city came into view. It was smaller by an order of magnitude than Atal itself but there were three- and four-level buildings visible. There was also a wall, a massive construction of white stone that had clearly been erected long ago. All along the wall were sentries with pikes, and the surrounding grounds were cleared within bowshot of an unenhanced man.

We spotted them only moments before they spotted us, and soon the elves of Iriatol were moving. The large gate that faced the road rolled upward and a line of carts and cavalry exited, speeding along to meet us. The horsemen made it first, their group consisting of twenty. From here I could see auras—five of them were either casters or physical magic users, though weaker than our group.

"Who's in charge?" the elder man at the front asked.

"I am, and it is quite a relief to see a friendly face," Omos told him, stepping forward with his head raised high. The elf gave him an odd look, since Omos was clearly young, but he nodded.

"The same son, the same. We've not seen any other groups your size, and even the smaller ones are few right now. You have injured?"

"A few, but stable thanks to our healers," Omos told him.

"Plural?" he asked as his eyebrow raised. "You've multiple magic users?"

By way of answering, Omos let his aura loose just a smidge, followed by his sister, me, my sister, and finally Veska and Lena. None of us really tried to impress, but seeing how our casters outnumbered the ones he had with him brought a smile to the leader's face.

"All young. You're from the academy?" he asked as the carts finally began to roll in closer.

"Yes, visiting students from abroad. I regret to inform you that the academy was destroyed. We didn't have time to assess the full damage, but it was significant," Omos said.

"We'll have some questions, but for now let's get you all inside. No need to sit out here and risk any more of those abominations coming."

We were all loaded into the backs of the carts, aided by a few nurses who'd come along to help. The guards didn't lower their attention at the world around us for even a second as we moved, wheels clattering along the pavement.

As we passed through the small gatehouse, I got my first look at the city, and it answered at least one of my questions. I knew exactly where all the elves were—right here in Iriatol. The place was visibly packed to capacity. Small shelters had been set up on the edges of the road where people were trying to rest in what was little better than a tent. Enough space had been left for the carts and soldiers to pass, but no more than that. There were lines outside of what looked to be a tavern that serviced visitors, and judging by what people were carrying, it was now functioning as the public restroom.

Well, at the very least we would have somewhere safe to sleep, and magic users often got preferential treatment.

✦

CHAPTER 56

SUBTLE ADVICE

Alana

I followed the kids inside, but I was more than a little worried. These people's needs weren't the children's. What the children wanted was certainly not what the protectors of this city did. At minimum, I anticipated that they'd try to delay my students so they could extract mana from them to power the city wards. If things went truly wrong, they might try to press them all into the city's protections—in a back-line position, of course, for everyone's benefit.

Should I let them handle it? Should I just go to the leaders of the city and tell them what they needed to do? The answer was unclear at the moment, so for now I would wait and watch. It would be easy to do something if it came down to that, but I'd seen the little birds fly, and stepping in where I wasn't needed would only hurt them.

It was a good sign that they were being checked out by nurses, and if I wasn't mistaken a priest first. None of them were hurt in any meaningful way, so that was quick, but it was there that they were pulled away from the rest of their little group.

The mayor's house wasn't far, but the trip there let me see just how many people they'd packed in here. They were like sardines in a can, and I understood why. Some of the people looked broken or exhausted, but most of them looked to be all right. That was a good sign; the administration wasn't completely broken yet, I'd seen what that looked like, and this wasn't it. There was still hope for the people here.

My childhood had some darker moments, and I was worried that I might see some more of that in the people here. To be fair, some did look terrible, but I'd seen worse. The elves weren't starving, they weren't being beaten down by those in power, they weren't suffering, at least not right now. No, right now they were scared, but still making it.

"Youth, ah, the future of nations, welcome. I'm afraid you're not seeing me at my best right now, but I do hope you'll take a moment so we can speak. I hear you're from abroad," the mayor said. He was on the larger side and looked exhausted, with black bags under his eyes and a strained expression. An aide joined him, standing to his side.

The kids told him about how they'd been separated from their group. How they were trying to make it inland to meet up with a potential way home, along with a few small details about their trip so far. They left out anything about portals, thankfully, as well as the fact that two of them were the heirs to the throne. Progress might be slower than I'd like, but it was happening.

"I see, and I understand your desire to return home, but this isn't exactly a normal situation," the mayor told them.

"Sir, we cannot and will not stay here for an unknown amount of time," Omos said, straightening his back.

"No, no young man, I wouldn't try to make such a thing happen. I will, however, ask for a couple of days though. Let me try to get word to the city of your whereabouts, as I'm sure they're looking, and make sure the worst of these monsters is passed. If it is so, I'll certainly send you on your way, and perhaps even manage a few soldiers to go with you."

"Two days," Amara told him, backing her brother up. "No more."

"Patience, please. For the time being, I'll host you. After all, there are no rooms left in the city and my house is the safest. Now, if you'll follow my aide, he can show you to a room, and where the baths are. I'm sure after such a journey a relaxing soak would be nice, hmm?"

The besieged leader didn't wait for his assistant to come back before he went back to his office. There were a few others present, all chest deep in paperwork. One tried to speak before being quieted with a raised hand. They were waiting for the aide to come back, it seemed.

"How are they settling in?" the mayor asked.

"They don't trust you," he replied.

"Well, I did just lie to their faces. Kids from another country, lost, in the middle of this? No, we're not letting them run off where they please. That's a diplomatic disaster waiting to happen. Even if we have to force the issue, and they hate us, their parents will understand."

I began checking my protections as they continued to speak.

"What about contacting the capital?" the aide inquired.

"Oh, we will. If for no other reason than we need someone to come and take them out of here. I'm not holding my breath though. The fighting's still going on over there and a gaggle of lost children isn't their first priority."

"None of them look weak, sir. Not sure how we'll keep them here if they choose to fight us," the aide told him with a furrowed brow.

"Well," I said, letting my voice be heard as I pushed out and made bubbles fill the room. "You won't."

The mayor tripped back and nearly fell on his face. One of the people doing paperwork also paled and stood, looking all around for me. I gave it a few seconds and then revealed myself, stepping out into their midst.

"W-who are you?" the startled leader asked.

"Well, I'm generally considered the most famous assassin on Hediza," I told him, using their name for the continent, from which I hailed, "but I also happen to be those children's . . . chaperone."

"They didn't say anything . . . No, they don't know you're here, why?" I'll admit I was impressed. I'd just scared them all shitless and he was quickly putting some things together.

"Reasons," I answered shortly. "Those don't matter though. What matters is what you're going to do. What you're going to do is let them rest a couple of days, refresh themselves, and then let them be on their way. Their travel arrangements are already in place, and I can't have you waylaying them. Also, don't mention me. We good?"

"And if I refuse to let them go with some hidden killer to wherever they're going?" he asked, and I smiled. He really did want to protect them, didn't he?

"We'll see, won't we?" I answered with another smile before turning in a quick dance move and rendering myself unseen once more. At the same time, I withdrew my aura, leaving the room much as it was when I first appeared.

The aide who could see auras was the first to speak. "Is she gone?"

"I don't know, but if she is, I suspect she's not far," her boss responded.

"What are we going to do?" she asked.

"Send word to the city. Then . . . take it from there." He was still looking around, for me. This mansion was definitely going to be swept soon, so I left. I suspected he'd do as I asked, and if he didn't? Well, I guessed I would take it from there too.

A Certain Councilor's Office

"Sir, letter for you. Looks like there's word on the missing students," a secretary said as he appeared at my door, paper in hand.

"Wonderful news, let's see it." I took the letter and read it over. We'd not managed to find any of the human students, which was worrisome. On one hand, they might have made it home. On the other, they might all be dead.

It was straightforward enough—a list of a few students who'd appeared at a certain official's city and brief descriptions. It wasn't addressed to me, but a subordinate had thought to bring it to me, and that was the right choice. A quick glance through my memories told me that among them were the ones I would worry for most. Good, good. Oh, and what was this?

"Is this accurate?" I asked the secretary.

"As far as I know, sir," he replied.

Looks like Alana had appeared and briefly threatened him. Normally, I'd take that as a viable threat, but a mother bear was well within her rights to be defensive of her cubs. If she actually did stab the man, though, I might need to do something, but she didn't seem the type.

I took a piece of paper and quickly jotted my response.

"Let them go." Those three words were followed by my signature and seal. Let the mayor make of that what he would.

The fighting here had reached manageable levels, and I wasn't needed at the moment. As a matter of fact, so many of us councilors all working at once had become a tad stifling. Perhaps a quick jaunt would do me well. I'd been prepping for that beforehand anyway, and based on their direction of movement, their destination was clear.

"Return that to the sender. I've a few things to take care of, and then I'll be heading off. Good job bringing that to me," I told the assistant. Positive reinforcement was important, after all.

We were all busy, and the casualty count hurt, but honestly this might be the most interesting month I'd had in the last couple of centuries.

Soon enough, I was flying through the sky once more. The city proper was well enough, but everything around it was still in shambles, or just gone. For a disaster of this magnitude, and an unexpected one at that, we'd done better than predicted. Perhaps with the right leadership, we might have stopped the waves completely. Perhaps I could get that leadership back.

"See you soon, boss," I whispered to the wind. "Maybe this time you'll come home."

CHAPTER 57

SUSPICIONS AND FRUSTRATIONS

Lena

We'd only been settled into our room for a few hours when someone came by. The maid's eyes flicked to the corners of the room, as if she were looking for something. A brief smile flashed across her face when she realized I was watching her. Odd, very odd.

I was grateful for the hot bath, the light meal we'd been provided, and even the change of clothes someone had sent up. None of it was top quality, but none of it was bad either, and after days in the same outfits, all of us needed to do laundry. The stink was palpable after the wash. Perhaps we could even buy a set or two of clothing before we left, assuming leaving was easy.

"Not that I don't appreciate the dress, but isn't this kind of . . ." Illa said looking down at the cloth with a frown.

"Awful?" Veska replied. "Yeah, one of the main exports here is cloth and bulk fiber. Hate to be the bearer of bad news, but the ones available to the elves sort of suck. Or at least most of them do. I heard that some of the really premium ones are nice, but painfully expensive."

"Didn't know that," I said, as I, too, examined the rough textile. The weave looked good from what I could tell, but it was still a little scratchy.

Amara didn't speak, instead pointing to her ear. The meaning was clear—privacy. The two wizards in the group shared a look before Illa took up the mantle, her hand flipping and a light glow surrounding the walls.

"Not sure if it's perfect, but I'm guessing you want to talk about something other than itchy clothes," she said to her cousin.

"They're searching the premises," the princess informed her.

"For what?" asked Veska.

"Or who?" I added. Giant crabs stuck out.

"Don't know," Amara said. "They're being quiet about it, trying to be subtle, and failing. I can hear them, though, going room to room, spending a few seconds in each, then moving on. Something's spooked our hosts."

"Shit, that's not good," I said. "Should we tell the boys? Not sure they'd notice. Need a reason to see them though."

"I got it. Mind dropping the barrier?" Veska asked as she began to gather up our clothes into a nearby basket.

The princess began writing in fluid calligraphy while Illa turned her hand, the glow fading.

"These stink," Veska said. "Think there's a washing room?"

I picked up what she was saying instantly. "Yeah, let's grab the guys' stuff too. Hate for them to stink, and they'll probably try to foist it on one of the staff." That was true too.

With a conspiratorial smile, we headed to their room, where they too were chatting, though, about nothing important.

"What's up?" Omos asked.

"We're going to go do some laundry. You need us to take yours?" Veska smiled while the prince's sister pushed the piece of paper into his hand. He read without speaking and nodded.

"Uh, no, we're good," Rodrick said without thinking. "I have a spell for that."

Every girl in the room turned at the sound of his proclamation, and I could hear the bells already, signaling the impending execution. With a glance, I confirmed that Omos had changed, his other clothes looking fresh and folded neatly.

I didn't much mind washing clothes. Goodness knows that I'd done enough of it throughout my childhood, but I didn't like it. We each had a servant when we were at school, an old tradition that had been carried over from the old kingdom. Those had been left behind in human lands, though, so all of us had to keep our own messes clean for this trip.

"Since when?" Veska asked, eyes locking on his.

"What? Since like, always," Rodrick responded foolishly. "I hate doing laundry."

"Are you telling me," she said, letting the venom creep into her voice, "that I've been walking around in progressively grosser underwear for the better part of the week, and you have a clothes washing spell?" She breathed in. "That throughout this entire trip I've been manually cleaning my clothes when my boyfriend could have sung them sparkling new for me?"

I could see him floundering, looking for the words to get him out of this mess.

"I . . . sort of like the way you smell when you're all sweaty?" he stumbled.

Wrong answer.

The basket of dirty clothes was dropped very close to his foot, and the furious redhead pointed one angry finger at the basket.

"You. Wash. Now!"

I put a hand over my mouth and giggled as his two female relatives descended upon him, eager to express their own displeasure at this secret he'd been hiding. Omos, now left on the sidelines, looked over, seemingly wondering if I would get in on it too. There was no reason for that. It's not like I'd known the guy for very long.

"I . . . didn't know until just a little while ago," the prince said by way of explanation. He looked like he was worried I might take the chance to jump down his throat.

"It's fine. Wanna leave this to them?" Our message had been delivered, and it didn't look like there was an immediate threat, so I didn't really need to be here for Rodrick's punishment.

"Yeah," he said, rubbing the back of his head.

We moved into the hallway, leaving the argument behind, and started walking toward one of the nearby windows. There was a small alcove there, looking out on the city. With nothing else to do, it seemed not the worse place to go.

"I'm not mad. Though if I hadn't had a wash and gotten something fresh to wear, I might be a little irked," I told Omos with a smile, trying to get him to relax.

"That's . . . good, and the dress looks good on you too," he said.

I blinked and tilted my head just slightly as I looked at him. The small smile, the little blush creeping up his cheeks. Was he flirting? I'd seen Omos take command of people, take charge when things were bad, and then decide what to do. I'd seen him face down adults who'd normally try to order us around, but I'd never seen him like this. He looked nervous, a bit lost. Maybe he was afraid I still remembered how he'd peeped on us girls in his younger days. That had been rude, but since he'd apparently stopped, I wouldn't hold it against him.

Honestly I'd not really considered it with all that had been going on, but he wasn't bad on the eyes. We were both separated from our home, alone, stressed, trying our hardest to stay strong. So maybe that wasn't the worst thing, and I could use an outlet for some of that stress. At any rate, how often did someone get a chance to bag a prince? It wasn't like princes were exactly common.

Deciding, I leaned in, pressing my lips to his. Maybe nothing would come of it, maybe it would. If it did . . . well, I had a certain tattoo that would prevent consequences if things went further than I was expecting. At that thought, I pushed some mana into the mark on my lower belly, feeling the slightest jolt as the spell inscribed there pushed out and into me.

For the briefest of moments, I worried that I'd messed up, that I'd gone too far. I could see him pushing me away, angry. Then hands settled on my waist, pulling me closer, against him. As I opened my mouth to breathe, and a tongue that was not my own entered, seeking to taste me more deeply.

Score!

CHAPTER 58

✦

SHARING AND CARING

*O*kay, I thought to myself. *When exactly did this happen? How exactly? Why? What had I missed?*

One hour. They couldn't have had more than one hour out of my sight, and suddenly Omos is hanging over little Lena like he wants to drag her off to the nearest closet for some "alone time," and she's sitting there looking not only like she might be up for it, but like she's the cat who caught the canary. Either I had to reveal myself to them and put this down, or I had to figure out how exactly I was going to explain to John how that had happened.

The answer was obvious, of course. I'd not done all this work to throw it away. Both my children and the royal ones needed this. They needed to have a chance to move on their own and to prove to themselves that they could do it. They could do it. And, letting them know that I'd been quietly helping from the sidelines this whole time would destroy their confidence. The girls, though, might be getting a visit from me soon.

If those two started going at it, did I need to tell my brother who she was? Did I need to tell her who she was? Shit, what if they got married? Could I just keep my mouth shut and let them live their lives unknowing? What if someone else found out and told the parties involved? What then? That asshole bishop already knew for sure, and if it went too far, he really might tell them.

The kids didn't look like they knew. Veska and Rodrick both looked like they would be searching for information as soon as the group split. Illa looked amused, if anything. Amara, I could at least agree with; she looked irritated with the priestess, something I could fully get behind.

They all chatted, hanging out and relaxing for longer than I'd hoped. Perhaps they needed this break. There was even some card playing. The two new lovebirds were huddled up together, leaning on each other.

Eventually, though, everyone needed to rest, so the group split. I followed the girls. There was no doubt Rodrick would get around to pulling the details from his cousin, but how long that would take was anyone's guess. Perhaps they'd dance around it for a while; perhaps it would take days.

"All right, spill!" Veska demanded as soon as the door was shut. I'd barely even snuck into the room in time.

"I, too, want answers," Amara demanded, much more harshly. "You're not the first girl to go after Omos, and if I find out you're playing with him for status, not even your magic will be able to put you back together."

"Seems harsh," Illa said, eyeing her cousin.

"My brother's proclivity for thinking with his dick has gotten him in trouble before, so I don't wanna hear it right now," Amara said.

"That's all men, not just your brother, Amara," the redhead said, waving vigorously at the princess to quiet herself. "Now let her answer." It was a bold decision, but she got away with it.

"Well, you three were going off on Rodrick, and we didn't really want in on that, so . . ." She sighed. "We just sort of went for a walk, and then there was a window, and we talked for a bit, and I don't know. I guess we ended up making out after he flirted with me . . ."

"So, are you going out, or what now?" Veska said excitedly.

"I don't know. We didn't really talk about that."

"And your intent?" Amara inquired, arms crossed over her chest.

"Nothing. I mean, I like him. He's nice, and I like the way he handles things." That statement sent several pairs of eyebrows right up, and she quickly corrected. "Not like that!" she added as red crept into her face. "I mean, he takes the lead, like . . . with getting us here."

"Very well." Amara really wasn't much for talking, and after so much time in her 'serious knight' voice, finally settled. "Remember what I said though."

"Okay, more details. We're not done," Veska said, pulling the priestess off to discuss exactly what had happened.

I didn't need to listen to that. It was enough to know that they were now, something, and that they'd not discussed too much of it yet. If something more came of this, then I'd have to make more decisions, but at least until we got back, it could hold fine. That was assuming that neither of them did something tremendously stupid. Just thinking about it sent shivers up my spine.

Now it was time to wait, hang back, watch, and royally screw over a particular elf if he tried to hold my children against their, and my, will. For the next day and a half, I did exactly that, interspersed with watching the area around the city for any more incursions. They seemed to have the latter part well in hand with only minor incidents. It seemed that for now the monsters had been beaten back.

When the day came to leave, Omos and the others packed their things before heading to see the mayor. They were ready, and it was clear they were not willing to take no for an answer easily. The man didn't seem pleased to see them at all.

"I see you still wish to leave," he commented.

"We do," Omos said, eyes locked on him.

"Well, you should know that I received word from the capital just this morning." That had my attention. If they'd managed to get word there and back so quickly, then maybe things really were settling down. Also, it begged the biggest question of all.

"Oh? And what did they say?" Omos inquired.

"You're free to leave if you so wish. For my part, though, I do hope that you'll consider not doing so. I've received my orders to let you, but if you choose to stay, know that you'll have a place here." His eyes spoke volumes, imploring them to reconsider.

Perhaps I shouldn't have been so hard on him. After all, he had really wanted to protect the kids. Maybe I didn't like his methods, and maybe he was a jerk for lying, but there were worse people in the world.

"We'll continue on. I hope there are no hard feelings," the prince said with a slight relaxing of his shoulders.

"No, none. I can't offer you much, and sadly supplies are scarce, but we do have a small scouting party heading inland soon. If you wish, we can send you the same way. They're not going far, but . . ." That was at least a partial lie. He was sending them some guards for a day or two, and everyone here knew it. Maybe they did need to scout, but that was just too convenient.

"That would be much appreciated. Thank you."

Omos was handed a slip of paper, directing him to one of the gates in just a few hours. After agreeing to one final meal from the kitchen, the children took off. I stayed behind, watching the mayor. Once the children were gone and out of earshot, he spoke again.

"My office is warded. Are you still around? Satisfied?" he asked the air.

I summoned a small illusory voice to whisper in his ear. "Yes." Being mysterious was always good.

"We take care of our children here in Atal. I'd ask you take care of those I cannot."

"I will. Goodbye, Mayor," I had the voice respond before leaving.

"Farewell."

CHAPTER 59

✦

PEEPING

Lena

Days passed as we made our way deeper and deeper into the interior of the Elven lands. For the most part, we were avoiding settlements since our escort had left us. We didn't want to get caught up and held in one again. It was slow going, passing through the deep forests and backroads, but we proceeded well.

The monsters grew fewer by the day as we made it further inland. There were even less signs of them, proving that most had been keeping near the coast. It made the whole operation easier, more relaxing, as we slowly trekked on. There were signs of cultivation here and there, farms that had been taken care of that were now all but abandoned. Some of them looked recent, and others could have been ancient orchards that had been left fallow for a long time.

It was in one of these overgrown copse of fruit trees we stopped for the day. The gnarled and twisted forms of the branches above created a thick canopy. Nearby, a brook gurgled softly, forming a series of pools.

"Don't see any fruits here," Omos said, looking at the trees.

"Wrong season there, cousin. Lena, would you be willing?" Rodrick asked.

Certainly I could make some of these trees bear fruit for us, delivering a bounty for our little group, and it wouldn't even be too harmful for them. On the other hand, it would still hurt them, and it had been drilled into me that allowing these little harms brought on much bigger ones. If we needed food, that would be one thing, but wants and needs weren't the same.

"We have enough supplies that it would be a waste," I told him with a shrug.

"Aww, but fresh fruit," Veska pouted.

"She's right though. We do still have a good amount of dried food," Omos responded without looking. It was nice to have him stick up for me like that.

The other girls had gone to gather some wood while we set up camp. With magic, it wasn't much of a chore. A few walls of dirt and foliage, a quick roof, and we were done. There wasn't even much need for a fire, as it never got that cold, but the smoke was a wonder for dealing with bugs, and the light was pleasant.

"All right, girls, I don't know about you, but I stink," Rodrick declared once everything was done. "Think I'll go for a wash."

"Right now?" his girlfriend inquired.

"Why not? Do you have plans? Thinking of joining me, perhaps?" He inquired, raising his eyebrows suggestively.

Veska responded by helping him, in the form of throwing a sizable ball of water his way.

"Oh look, you're already half done," I snarked to the now soaking Rodrick.

"So I am," he said shaking his head like a dog and sending a spray of water over all of us. "And you too!" This didn't actually win him any points with anyone, but in retrospect, it was kind of funny.

"Come on, you idiot. Now that I'm soaked, I need one too. We shouldn't go alone anyway," Omos said as he grabbed his cousin and began to march toward the stream.

"But I don't wanna see you naked," the other boy objected as he faked resisting.

"Idiots," I said after they'd left, earning me a laugh. "Well, I'm going to see about shoring up the roof a little, maybe go relax in the sun."

For a while I did just that, using some of the native vines to decorate and improve the strength of our dwelling. We'd leave here soon, but this place could stay, letting the plants live longer and in a better place than they had. Perhaps it was whimsical, but I liked it.

As the minutes wore on, I looked to the path. I knew where the boys had gone, where they'd retreated to bathe. There were really only so many pools in a couple minutes' walk, and one of them was perfect. The crystal-clear water poured over the rocks just right, and the small clams that lived in the river were pushed out of the way.

Checking to see that Veska was still inside, and the others hadn't returned yet, I went to go find some mischief. I slinked along at an angle to the path, carefully picking my way along through the brush and staying as low as I could. Soon I heard the water, splashing, and the sound of voices.

Getting as low as I could, I crept forward until I came to a small break in the leaves. There, I peeked out. Omos had spied on us, and well, maybe turnabout was fair play; it wasn't like I was planning to stay long.

The two boys had put their clothes on a rock to dry and were scrubbing, waist deep in the cool stream. I couldn't make out all the words, but it seemed they were chatting about what they were going to do when they got home. As I looked on, Omos started to move to the nearby waterfall . . .

"Hey, what we looking at?" A voice whispered in my ear.

I jumped and almost screamed, only to find a hand over my mouth and Veska's grinning mug inches away from mine. I wasn't sure how she'd snuck up on me, but she had. Before I even had the chance to form thoughts, she slipped up to the hole my face had been in, looking. As she did, I felt the heat creep up my face, threatening to make my cheeks as red as her hair.

"My, my, what a view!" she continued low. "And you coming out here to spy."

"Veska!" I hissed, trying not to get attention.

"Lena!" she returned in the same small voice sounding scandalized. "Oh my, did you decide to join them? HEY OMOS!!!!"

I nearly jumped up and ran, only to be pulled back down by the wizard. "What are you—"

"Don't worry," Veska laughed. "I put up a sound barrier before I said anything. Didn't want you to spook them."

"Well . . . thanks," I said, trying to figure out how to get out of this.

"Of course, peeping is a longstanding tradition, isn't it?"

"Not really?" I said. "But I mean, Omos spied on us."

"Oh, fair is fair, isn't it?" she said with an evil grin.

Soon we were cheek to cheek, peeking out. We didn't get to see much though. With Veska's running commentary, you'd think something truly dirty was going on. As both of the boys turned to the rock upon which their clothes lay, a single bubble floated down into our view, settling before popping.

Instantly I pulled back, turning, looking for wherever it had come from, and Veska wasn't far behind. Every hair on my neck stood straight up, like someone was breathing right behind me. But, there was no one there.

Another quick peek and my partner in crime tsked. "Missed it, we need to head back before they do, unless you want to be discovered." There was a hint of invitation in her voice, a maniacal laugh hidden below the surface.

"Let's go," I whispered, still afraid of being found.

We got back to camp just in time, our companions arriving soon after. Illa and Amara strolled into camp seconds before the boys did, looking at us strangely as they deposited the firewood. The boys looked at us askance upon their return.

"What, did you two roll around in the dirt while we were gone?" Rodrick asked.

It was then that I realized lying on the ground had gotten my clothes covered in dust.

"Um . . . I fell, and grabbed Veska on my way down. It was sort of a mess," I answered, trying and failing to keep the heat from my face as I lied.

"Yeah, let's go wash," the redhead answered, and our other female companions readily agreed, joining us immediately.

Alana

I watched as the little perverts wandered off, not sure if I should laugh, punish them, or just not care. Certainly they were out of line, but of course that line of thought pulled forth images of some of the parties I'd attended in my youth. So, I wasn't sure I could judge them too harshly.

This particular section of river was also really, really familiar. I couldn't quite place it, but I was sure I'd seen those rocks somewhere. Maybe we'd camped here on our way inland all those years ago? No, that would just be too much.

"So, Omos, want to . . ." Rodrick said, tilting his head toward the same path Lena and Veska had taken.

"Rodrick, our sisters are there," the other boy answered, killing the suggestion instantly.

"Fair point."

I rolled my eyes. These kids were all way too horny.

CHAPTER 60

✦

RETURN TO ERATOL

I was all smiles as I watched the kids approach the little village of Eratol. The folks I knew there were good. As long the kids met up with at least one of them, there shouldn't be any problems. It was now time for me to get to some important work, preparing the way home.

The forest reminded me of the time I'd passed through here, huddled against my friends as we hunted down a shadowy beast. It wasn't fun but, in retrospect, those were some of my most important memories. It was where I'd met Ulanion, where we'd found the first portal and learned how to create more. It was also where we'd lost people, where they'd fallen against the beasts we sought to kill.

It took a while, with several missteps while deciding which path I needed to take, but soon enough I found Justin's facility. I made my way down to the very center of the crater, where it lay hidden beneath the dirt and stone.

This time I had the ability to appreciate the place. Before I'd been harried or just too tired, but with some breathing room, I had no problem taking some time to see what had been built here. The outside was dirty, but inside was in perfect shape because of the magic being used, albeit, covered in leaves and debris. There were even a few sections where dirt had built up over the years.

After a short jaunt through the courtyard, I returned to the atrium where Olnir had died. The arched door leading in, the high stone columns and balconies looking down from above. There was no evidence of our battle, not a speck of dust or crack to indicate what had happened all those years ago. As a point of fact, it looked even more pristine than it had back then—the lights on and the floor shining. I wondered if I could one day get the enchantment used for keeping things immaculate; it would be a terrible waste of magic, but a self-cleaning and repairing building was just fancy.

I'd barely made it up to the long reception desk, which was completely clean now, before I heard a noise. It was the clicking of metal on the white stone, echoing through the empty room. It wasn't rushed, or slow; it wasn't even loud, just a faint sound, almost like claws scratching the rock.

"Greetings, your Highness," the wolf golem said as it appeared. "The administrator would like to see you."

"Good, I'd like to see him too," I answered. I didn't like the form of address though, something my husband still used when he wanted to tease me.

The machine wasn't talkative. As it led me through the building, I regretted not having someone to speak to for so long. I wondered how Justin did it, alone in his cave. Maybe it was an elf thing, or maybe he was just weird. I never had found out.

We did not go down into the bowels through stairs and elevators this time, but rather to a relatively nearby room, where a portal sprang into existence across the wall. There wasn't really any clearer invitation than that, so I strolled through.

I recognized Justin's lab, the one that held the portal back to my place. I was pretty sure, though not completely, that this was a little far from the room with the eggs. He'd never gone into detail about how things were laid out, and I'd never needed to go wandering far from wherever he brought me.

The man himself sat in a plain robe at a nearby desk, sipping some tea. "Of all the people to stroll up to my front door, I didn't expect you," he said.

"Really?"

"We do have a portal we normally use? I'm guessing you've got some problem that needs resolving, which somehow brought you here?"

"That predictable?" I asked.

"Do you ever come to see me for anything else?" There was somewhat of a chiding tone in his voice.

"Er, sorry about that. You don't really seem the type to entertain visitors, and you won't come over to my place. You're welcome to, as far as I'm concerned though."

"Fair, I suppose. So, what brings you here?"

I told him about the trip to Atal, about the kids' field trip, and the general plan. He smiled as I explained what we'd done so far and how the trip was supposed to go. When I got to the part about the attack on the city, he seemed concerned. Long ago he'd abandoned his post, but I got the feeling he still cared about his people.

"The city?" he asked.

"Seemed intact, though there was fighting going on. The wards held the creature back while some of the heavy hitters dropped it," I reassured him. "Will you go help?"

"There are some things I can and will do without revealing my presence, depending on how bad it is."

With a small smile I continued. I got a laugh out of him when I recounted threatening the mayor, and I gave him a brief rundown of the kids' actions. I left out how they seemed to be intent on spying on one another; no reason to give him a bad impression.

As I began to wrap up, there was a long, loud tone, followed by a calm feminine voice. "Incoming mana signature. Identification Councilor Chien."

"Um?" I said, confused.

"I updated the wards and cleaned up after you lot left. Didn't want anything else nasty moving into my attic," Justin said, frowning at what looked to be a monitoring panel. "Hate to be a poor host, but I must deal with this. There are cups and tea in the cabinet there. Please wait for me to return."

"Should I come with?"

"No, our history is . . . complicated, and if he came to fight, you'll only get yourself killed." There was no room for argument in his tone, and I'd seen him fight before, so with a frown I nodded.

I made it through a full cup and was considering another when the tone sounded once more. "Incoming mana signatures. Identification unknown humanoid, six."

I barely had time to register the message before it sounded off again. "Incoming mana signature. Identification unknown monstrous."

Illa

The villagers were surprised when we appeared, all blinking at us as we poured into their front gates. Before we could even begin to ask questions, an old elf moved to the front of the group, his eyes lined with wrinkles and hair white. He regarded us for nearly a full minute, the others silencing as he did so.

"Ah, forgive an old man his quirks," he finally said. "It's just that you reminded me of a group that passed by some years ago. Particularly the girl there, looks just like that bard . . ." he said, pointing to me. "I'm Indriel, the village elder."

I blushed. It was true that I did indeed look similar to my mom. Though, her hair was a shade lighter, and I'd not quite inherited her figure, but in the face and eyes, we looked alike. My brother, who was chuckling, took more after my father. Amara even looked more like me than he did.

"Don't suppose her name was Alana?" I asked.

That question caused the man to go into uproarious laughter. "My, my, it was! And I suppose you're looking for some old ruin in the woods?"

"Hmm," I mumbled.

"Well, come in, girl. I feel you've a story for me. And, luckily this time around, we're monster free."

With his apparent approval, our group was led forward, with he and a few others just spinning up the first of the questions for us.

✦

CHAPTER 61

LAST HURDLE

Illa

This little village, Eratol, was really quite pleasant. It wasn't a bustling city or an ancient monument by any standards, but it was quaint, homey. I'd never lived in any of the villages back home, but I'd passed through from time to time, and it rather reminded me of them, mixed with a fair bit of a nature style magic. Perhaps one day I'd retire in a place like this, when I was old and gray.

The village elder was so pleased to meet us too. All smiles as he led us to his house.

"Well, since you've come all this way, perhaps you'd like to hear the story of how I met your parents and how they saved our village?" he asked, smiling at me and my brother.

"I would, but unfortunately, not at this moment. We're in a bit of a hurry, you see, and lives could well be on the line." Was that true? Maybe, but we'd taken a lot of time to get here, and I really wanted to have a route home before reminiscing with this man.

"Something's happened?" he asked.

"Yes," Rodrick answered. "We were staying at the capital, and there was a sizable monster attack. It's only a theory, but we've come to believe there may be something in the ruins that could lead to establishing a connection with our home and bringing back help. A way to provide aid should it be needed."

"Monsters? What kind?" he inquired.

"Enormous crabs," my brother told him. "Have you seen any?"

"We found a large shell, but we haven't seen any living specimens. I'd call it odd, but now and again we get magical beasts of some form or another. That's just part of living this far from the cities," he explained with a shrug.

"Our thinking was that they probably couldn't survive so far from the water anyway," Lena told him.

"Mayhaps so, mayhaps not. We do have a few species like that—little animals that live in the lakes and rivers. They're not like the ones in the coastal cities, but they do exist," the man replied.

"Regardless," Omos interrupted, "could we get a guide to those ruins?"

"None of the guides are available right now, but it's not far if you're in that much of a hurry. You could walk the path yourselves in a couple hours," the elderly elf offered.

"That would be much appreciated," I said, hoping we could meet again so I could hear his story.

We didn't stay in the village long. Gathering a few supplies and getting directions was fast work; we were eager to be on with it. The elves seemed a smidge put off that we wouldn't at least stay the night, but our group really, really wanted to be home.

In under an hour we were back on the road, marching off into the woods.

"The first thing I'm doing when I get back is taking a bath," Amara declared with conviction as we sped along the path.

"Stellar idea," I replied. "I may go for food first, then a bath."

Each of us told our own plan, be it food, or washing, or sleeping, many nods went around the group about having proper beds once again. At the idea of a proper soft bed, my back began to ache.

"Not that I haven't enjoyed it. Perhaps I'll even go and explore again one day. See the world." Amara was a weird one, but she seemed honest enough, and I wished her the best.

Omos, on the other hand, had a different opinion. "Not me. I think I need to take a long look at how our kingdom would deal with a monster like that. If it were to land on our coast, I pale to think of the casualties."

"Luckily, we don't get the same kinds of beasts they do," I pointed out to him.

"Maybe not, but it would still pay to be prepared."

The path followed along the banks of a creek, which seemed to be as old and meandering as time itself, weaving in and out of the trees. Small animals and bugs buzzed by on occasion. We were close, so close. It was just as the path turned from the creek that I noticed something amiss. I couldn't quite put my finger on it, but something felt wrong.

"Why did the birds go quiet?" Veska asked, nailing it.

There was a shuffling of the trees and branches, and then across the bank from us a leg appeared, then another, the beast pulling its way into the opening in the canopy created by the passing water. It was one of our old friends, but this time on another scale. It was easily three or four times the size of the others we'd met, the shell darker and splotched.

As one, we launched into our favorite spells, and together we slammed into the carapace of the beast. Bolts of death and ice-cold mist rained down upon it but had little in the way of effect, and as we broke to check on our progress and let Amara move forward, we saw that we'd done very little damage.

With what could only be described as a look of simple confusion, the crab stumbled before lifting itself once more. There was a clicking of claws, and the stream around it began to move. It reminded me of the thing's progenitor, a massive abomination that moved the sea. This smaller version didn't have that much power, but the creek began to rise into the air, water flowing around it and around its claws, one of which pointed at me.

"Oh shit," I managed before it loosed a crushing geyser of liquid in my direction.

But, I wasn't alone. Before the blow struck, many things happened. Shields snapped into place before me, trying to slow the cannon, and a dark-haired blur reached me, scooping me off my feet and out of the line of fire.

"To the ruin! We need to get it away from the water!" Omos yelled.

Alana

"Shit, shit, shit, golem, how do I get to the meeting room Justin went to?" I yelled at the automaton.

"The path to that location has been locked, your Highness," it replied.

"Then alert him to a monster on the premises! He said that he'd upgraded the wards to do so."

"Affirmative, your Highness."

Behind me there was a sound not unlike that of a cell phone ringing, a persistent attention-getting one. It emanated from a point on what looked to be one of the workspaces. Sensing my eye beginning to twitch, I walked over and pressed the big friendly answer button on a small blackish square.

"Unknown monster on premises," a slightly feminine voice echoed out.

"What is the point of this if he doesn't carry it with him!?" I roared. "Screw it, which door leads to the surface?" I asked the golem. It didn't verbally confirm, but did move to stand before one of them.

Of the magical items I'd brought with me, only one had a chance of opening the door. I raised my hand, the bracelet glowing bright red before sending a maximum power attack at the portal. It failed, bouncing and not even leaving a scratch. When Justin got back, I was going to give him an earful about emergency exits, and heaven help him should anything happen to those children.

CHAPTER 62

◆

ATRIUM BATTLE

Omos

Our trek to the ruin was blessedly short, shields and trees covering our escape from the monster we'd clearly underestimated. Even so, as I ran beside my friends, I could hear it smashing into the trees behind us and the crash as it sent jets of water slamming into them.

"We need a plan," I shouted, trying to keep my voice steady.

"Carapace is too hard, can't cut it," Amara said from ahead of me, still carrying Illa.

"Normal spells aren't working," Veska confirmed.

"We need to hit the world around it, not the creature itself!" Illa shouted as she was bounced around.

Seconds later we hit the clearing where the ruin stood. If this were any other time, I'd have taken a moment to appreciate the beauty of the place—the open courtyards before the perfectly maintained arches that led inside—but I didn't have the time. We ran for the archways, our enemy close behind us.

The atrium had multiple levels, something we could use to our advantage. This wasn't something I needed to tell Amara either. She grabbed Veska and jumped for the higher areas. From there, those two could rain down damage, while the rest of us would take on the beast from below. With enough angles of attack, we might manage to take this thing down.

"Rodrick!" I tried to tell him what to do, but the creature smashed in the front of the building, claw ripping the door clean off. "Screw it! Darkness around the eyes; can you?"

"Got it!" he replied and began to sing.

Our crustaceous enemy scuttled into the room, huge legs struggling to fit as it slid inside, but we didn't let up our assault. My spells were kinetic, grabbing any of the rubble it created and hurling it at the thing's joints as fast as I could.

I didn't know what Lena should be doing, but she seemed to have a plan of her own. She was beside me, and sweat began to pour down her brow. I wondered what she was casting, but then I saw her hand flash forward, little green lights shining, and the vines sprung from the floor. Crawling plants worked surprisingly well, seeming to dig into the joints they found and wrap tightly, sucking out nutrients and water from this creature, which we were all having trouble even damaging. Had the room been a little bigger, the thing might have struggled and pulled away, but it couldn't with two of its legs disabled by the grasping green.

Rodrick's cloud of darkness was not blinding our foe completely, but it was helping. The monster bucked and turned, trying to escape the blinding effect. The crab eventually stopped, claw opening and a slight aura seeping from it. I wondered what it was doing until I saw the flow coming in through the door. It wasn't as much water as before, but even a little at speed could be deadly.

"Freeze it!" I shouted to the other two wizards, who did exactly that, bolts of blue impacting the fluid before the creature could form its spell properly.

The whole time, Amara was a blur, ducking and weaving as she used her sword against any point she could reach. It didn't look terribly effective, but she was distracting the creature by hitting its legs, causing tiny cuts.

"I need to get under it," she said as she landed beside me.

"I can get you an opening, but only one," I answered, grabbing the biggest of the boulders the monster had left when it tore the door open.

"On your mark then, brother." She crouched, tensing her legs.

With a heave, I tossed the projectile at our enemy, and two of its legs rose to meet it. The claws were too far away to reach just yet, but this would be enough. My sister ducked, seeming to slide into the gap.

Amara's sword shone blue as she stabbed upward. It had some form of enchantment on it. Though I didn't know the exact details, I knew that she seldom used it, since it apparently took some time to recharge. The blade slid between two of the sections of the creature's body like a hot knife in butter, hilt deep into the crab's body.

The monster did not take kindly to that, rearing up and turning hard and fast. There was a flash of movement, and Amara was sent flying, a leg having smacked her in the gut. Time seemed to slow as she arced through the air.

I sent out a cushion of air where she would land, but even as it began to form, I knew it wouldn't be enough. It helped, slowing her body's momentum, but she still slammed hard into the stone, enough to crack it. The world dropped out from under me as my sister, who'd always been made of steel, slouched, coughing and sending a spurt of red from her mouth and down her front.

In the moments that I had been distracted, the battle had changed. The beast pulled forward, one claw latching onto the ramparts as it tried to pull itself upward toward the two girls up top, ignoring the rest of us. The creature seemed to have decided that they were the issue. It pulled back one of its massive claws for a sweep.

Veska and Illa were nowhere near fast enough to make it to safety, even as they tried to flee. However, while rising like it did, the monster had shown me its belly. For a second, I didn't recognize what I was seeing, still shocked by Amara's injury. I saw a glint of something—the hilt, still buried in the monster's body.

When I was younger, I'd asked my aunt about one of her favorite spells, one she was well known for, lightning. It was a powerful weapon, one I longed to wield. She'd told me at the time to wait, that it was too dangerous for someone my age to play with, but that she'd teach me once I moved to her new school. That, however, had not stopped me from searching for everything I could in the library, learning as much as possible.

Lightning wasn't my strongest spell, or even in my top five, but if it could be applied to a body, it was potent. Normally I wouldn't bother, but with that shard of steel . . . It took only an instant to form the concepts in my mind, imagining the hilt as the highest point in a city, reaching skyward, and then directing the bolt.

With a scream of effort I poured myself into the spell. The result wasn't the thunderous boom made by a true expert, but a wave of crackling arcs, each smacking into the little metal protrusion. The crab seized as the first wave hit, claw unable to keep swinging at the girls.

Moment by moment, I poured magic into the metal. First, it glowed orange, then, red, then yellow, gradually brightening as more and more energy was poured into the steel, smoking and burning the creature from within as it grew. The monster screamed and its legs twitched. It was shaking but unable to go anywhere. The claw it had used to pull itself upward locked in place and was unable to release its hold.

Now that the girls above were freed from the threat of imminent death, they took up some of the new rubble, and my old position. A grim smile crossed my face as one of the rocks landed true, crushing a pair of eye-stalks.

Eventually, I ran out of power, the mana refusing to come from my now tired body. I slumped, but so did the crab, the beast no longer able to move. It fell, charred and smoking, onto the ground, the last of its twitching fading quickly.

It was then that I looked to Amara. During my final attack my cousin had made it to her side, singing a healing spell for herself. Lena made it to her first, raising her hands and letting a yellow light flow over the injured knight. Amara was moving, and that meant she was alive. A small miracle.

I tried to make my way to Amara's side, struggling as the exhaustion from spending all of my energy washed over me. To my surprise, Illa grabbed Veska, and the two shakily floated down. That wasn't easy magic at all. They took my arms and helped me make my way to my sister's side.

"Will she be okay?" I asked, looking at Lena.

"She's hurt bad, but she'll live." Lena didn't even look at me, instead concentrating on her magic.

With that assurance, I slumped against a pillar, exhausted.

CHAPTER 63

✦

HOMEWARD

I cannot believe you left me here with no way to contact you and no way to get out!" I yelled at Justin as soon as he reappeared.

"I was gone for five minutes. Why are all these alarms going off?" he replied with equal frustration.

"The kids arrived, followed closely by *something*. Your system didn't tell me what, and then everything started ringing and turning red." I gave him a second to process that. "Now I need to get up there and see that everything's all right, and quickly, please! My children are up there."

That seemed to strike a chord. Justin nodded and reached out, wrapping me in whatever spell he used to teleport and moved us both up into the building proper. I recognized the entry I'd been in not so long ago, and the enormous monster taking up nearly half of it. I had us hidden seconds before we found the kids, lying down and looking broken.

"They look well at least. Is that all of them?" Justin asked from within our hidden bubble.

I wanted to object and punch him for saying they looked fine. Amara was currently being treated by both Rodrick and the priest girl, and the rest looked ready to pass out. Amara was still coughing blood.

"It is, but Amara—"

"I've seen worse injuries treated by healers who were nowhere near as competent as those two appear to be. I'm sure she'll be fine, and if her situation begins to degrade, there are things we can do." I turned to glare at him, but he was looking at me with a tolerant smile. "Look at her, she's a warrior. This is the path she has chosen, and she will be hurt on her journey. If she cannot take the pain, then she'll need to know early and find a new path. Perhaps I seem cruel, but it's best if she goes through this and survives now."

I sighed. He wasn't completely wrong, and while I didn't like it, I knew this old man had perspective I might never get. "All right, maybe you're right, but could we please set up the gate so we can get them home? I don't even know how you want to play this one."

"Will you trust me to handle it?" he asked, and at my apologetic nod continued. "Good, please stay here with them while I take care of things, Alana."

I did as he asked and got closer to the children. If it looked like they couldn't handle Amara's injuries, I could step in. While I'd never been the best healer in the world, I was still trained in the basics, and I had plenty of mana to throw at the problem. As I calmed and took time to examine her, I realized that wouldn't be necessary. She was injured, but not too badly.

Illa

Around the time that my cousin started to look well again, there was a sound. Soft shoes on stone was something I was well enough acquainted with, but this time it was joined by a tapping of metal. I stood, as did several of the others, to face whoever was coming.

An Elven man entered through a side hall, followed by a golem of unusual make. It looked almost like a dog or wolf, but it moved so well, so naturally. Golems, even simple ones, were notoriously difficult to create, but this model was sleek and quick.

"Goodness, what a mess," the pale-haired elf said, looking around. "Is there a reason you six are here? Or did you just seek shelter from this thing?"

Rodrick was busy, so I decided to take the lead. "My mother came through here some years back and supposedly found a way home for us. You see, sir, we're kind of stuck here. Our way home was destroyed in a disaster at the capital."

"I was recently informed of the tragedy, yes. Your mother, you say? Blonde hair, pointed ears. I heard Alana had ended up with that boy, but it's a shame she never introduced us. I'm a research colleague of sorts, you may call me J."

"Um . . . Dad's kind of old," I informed him.

"Not to me. Now, you said you were stuck?" The way he said that told me to drop it, that I didn't get to know too much. As long as he could get us home, I didn't really need his secrets.

"Yes, sir," I said as politely as I could.

"Good, if you don't mind getting your friends together and following me," he said.

As we began to move through the facility, he told us that while he didn't begrudge us our trespass, he also didn't particularly like visitors, so we were to keep our mouths shut about him being here. That was the condition for his aid, one all of us readily agreed to.

"Ah, we were hoping to send some aid when we get back," Omos told him.

"It won't be needed, though the thought is appreciated." This, too, was said with finality. "In fact, once you're through, I will be closing this gate for a while, to prevent you from being tempted."

While I would have loved to tell people that we surged through the ruins, overcoming traps and dangers to finally reach the gate, I'd had more than enough excitement to last me several years. Now I just wanted to go home, to see my parents and my friends, and to rest.

"Your golem is magnificent," I said to him as we turned down one of the halls. "However did you get it to move so smoothly?"

That got me a smile. "Golems are tricky things, and to make one work properly, even more tricky. In my youth I had a phase where I was quite into them, and I made a number of them. Is it an interest of yours?"

"Well, it's not really something I can study, as there are no working ones anywhere. They are neat though— magical automatons, capable of action without supervision."

"I don't recommend no supervision. Golems are unbelievably difficult to get right, and when they go wrong, they can go very wrong. You always need safeguards upon safeguards for them, my dear, just in case," he said, speaking lightly of something few could really lecture on.

"Mother has one, and she said that it came with a big red button to turn it off, with signs and stuff." Now he actually laughed.

"Yes, the big friendly red button is a good extra, just in case. There are other methods as well." We turned into what looked like a pristine work-room, and there it was, a portal. With a wave of his hand, the mage turned it on, probably some unseen switch somewhere, and he was just showing off.

"This is it then?" Omos asked.

"Yes," the elf told him. "The other side is in Alana's workshop. Off you go."

"Wait," Rodrick uttered. "We get to see mom's lab!" That said, he ran forward and through the glowing opening like an idiot. Seconds later, he reappeared on our side once again, looking at our stunned faces. "Just kidding. Needed to make sure it was safe; it is, by the way." Then he leapt through once more.

When the others recovered, they followed him in. At least he'd saved us the drawn-out questioning of how to make sure this was what the unknown man said it was. I took one last look at the dog before heading that way myself.

"If you want to learn about golems I can send you some notes," the elf offered.

"Actually I'm more interested in flight. Any suggestions?"

"Yes, a lot of people try to push themselves up, but that's a slow way to go about it. You'll find it much easier if you can instead consider negating the force pulling you down, then build from there."

I stopped, looking at him. The pull of gravity was everywhere, and I'd never really put too much thought into it. Things fell. That was just what they did, but what if I could make it so I didn't fall? The implications. I might need to rethink my whole methodology, start over again.

"That's . . . a thought."

J chuckled. "Now, off you go, lass, and good luck. Remember that most shouldn't fly. There'd be all kinds of trouble, but letting a few who are responsible is okay."

With one final thanks, I stepped through after my friends.

CHAPTER 64

◆

UNTIL NEXT TIME

After giving my host a quick goodbye, I followed the kids through the portal. I was going to have to do something to repay Justin, but I was unsure as to what. Right now, I needed to get things back together as they should be, though I supposed that was mostly done.

My lab was, to my relief, still sealed from when I'd left. While the young ones were quickly getting their bearings, and Rodrick was examining every surface like an excited gremlin, I waited. Eventually, one of them tried the door, and in that moment, I managed to slip out. We were back in our own country now, and there was nowhere near enough time for the ruse I needed to set up to keep all the work I'd done in place.

I flitted through the halls like a speedy ghost, heading straight for my room. It was late in the day, and if Ulanion was keeping to his normal schedule, my husband would be there right now. Luckily for me, I knew this place better than almost anyone else, and being able to bend space meant that I could be there quick as lightning.

As I threw open the doors, I saw Ulanion blur and then stand, barely taking the time to register me, and then he blurred again, his arms appearing around me and lips on mine. After a rushed kiss, I pulled away, looking up at him.

"We should continue this later. The kids are at my lab. Can you go quickly and get them back to the palace? Don't tell them I was with them," I said as fast as I could.

"I have questions," he said, not quite letting me go, but not trying to stop me from ducking under his arms and slipping into our rooms.

"Later!" I answered with a yell. "Need to change, be right behind you."

I heard a sigh and Ulanion leaving to go do as I'd requested. Soon, I'd be done with this mess, and we could spend as much quality time as he wanted talking about everything. He knew what living with me was like, and being gone for a few weeks had been expected. So there was no real issue, right?

With a fresh dress, and a hesitant use of magic to clean myself, I hurried back to the lab where the kids were being corralled by various staff. They'd found someone on their own, and there was no small amount of confusion that followed. Once Ulanion arrived, there were a few tearful greetings followed by the kids being quickly herded into a portal leading back to the capital.

There were no portals in the palace proper. This was inconvenient but a simple security feature. Well, actually there might be a portal there made by Dras, but if there was, I didn't know of it, and I hoped to all things good and decent in the world that they'd kept it sealed. This meant that the collective of our group had to take a carriage to the palace, and we were beaten there by messengers.

Unlike the previous king and queen, my brother and his wife cared little for formality when it didn't suit them. Therefore, as soon as the kids made it into the palace with guards in tow, they appeared. Etia scooped her two up into a hug as soon as she saw them.

"I was so worried. Where were you? How did you get stuck over there? Are you hurt? Amara, IS THAT BLOOD!?" she asked as she finally looked at her daughter's clothes, the stains from her injuries in the battle standing out brightly on her chest. Unlike me, she'd not cleaned up at all.

Veska and Lena stood back, trying not to catch the attention of the royal couple while my own two looked quite relieved. They had a pretty good relationship with their aunt and uncle, after all. Our family might have changed, but we still cared for each other, and the infighting that occurred between former royals hadn't struck us, at least not yet.

"Where is Alana?" John asked Rodrick, who clearly didn't have an answer.

"Here I am," I said appearing out of the air. Unveiling yourself from invisibility was a party trick that never got old.

"Did you just walk through most of our security and wards?" he asked, seemingly surprised.

"Brother of mine, I designed most of those wards," I replied. Getting past them had been a breeze, and not because I hadn't tried to fix the holes. Just that there were some holes that really couldn't be fully patched. "And I knew the moment this lot made it into my workshop."

"That is . . . fair." I could see the flash of understanding in his eye. I hadn't mentioned that I'd been with them the whole time, and he wouldn't either.

"Mom! Where did you come from?" Rodrick asked as I approached him and his sister. They both needed a hug, and I'd been holding off on that for too long.

"Your mother is everywhere," I replied mysteriously.

"But—"

"Everywhere . . ." I made it sound like my voice was coming from every direction.

Illa held me tight, speaking softly. "Missed you," she said.

"You, too, sweetie. We should talk later, maybe do something fun." I wasn't sure what she'd want to do, but I'd promised that I'd spend more time with her, and I planned to keep that promise.

"Okay," she agreed.

Etia was still fussing over the prince and princess while John turned, looking at the two oddballs in the group.

"And I don't believe I know either of you? You traveled with my children, though, and I am glad you all made it back together," he said, rather more politely than a king would be expected to.

"I believe the redhead is dating my Rodrick," I informed him, causing the girl's head to snap in my direction and her eyes to go wide. They'd been keeping that from me, of course. I just looked at her and mouthed "everywhere" once more.

"Oh, and this is Lena, Father," Omos said, pulling away from his mother briefly. "We've been . . . seeing each other recently as well."

"Is that so?" John said, looking down at the girl in a way that made her freeze up. "I'll have to meet her then, won't I?"

"Oh, me too," his wife agreed, giving little Lena an even more harshly appraising look. It seemed the royal couple didn't plan to let their son be led astray if they could help it.

Eventually, the greetings came to an end, and the story of how the kids had survived was told, at which point they were ushered off to go clean up. All of them were exhausted and dirty, and I think everyone wanted a good, warm meal. Since they'd be nicely distracted, I pulled my brother and his wife aside.

"They don't know I was with them," I told the royal couple, "and I think we should keep it that way."

"Is this another of your 'being mysterious' things, sister?" John asked tiredly.

"No, they gained a lot of confidence in their abilities, achieved things by their own merit, and succeeded. Letting them know that I was watching over their shoulders for it and making sure they didn't bite off more than they could chew would destroy that confidence, something they'll all need."

"You did keep them safe though?" Etia asked.

"Of course. I even cleaned up a lot of the messes ahead of them. They still had their struggles, though, and those will build them up." I left out how I'd been pulled away a few times during the crisis. "If I'd thought they couldn't deal with something, I would have stepped in to aid more obviously, but they handled themselves marvelously."

"Fine, what about the girl?" John asked, seeking my opinion of her.

"He seems to really like her, and while I'm a tad nervous about it, she seems genuine. I'd appreciate it if you kept an eye out, but let them be." That was the best I could do for Lena, a girl whose parents I'd killed. She seemed a good apple to me, and I hoped that I wasn't wrong.

"She's a priestess though; won't that cause problems?" Etia asked.

"I've got connections in the orders, and if you think it's going to work out between them, I'll call those in." Those might be some powerful casters, dangerous even to me, but I could go to Linden and visit their head. He at least seemed reasonable and I didn't think he'd try to split them up.

"Settled, what next?" John asked.

"What next? Next, I'm going to spend time with my children and husband, John. We've only so much time, and how many lives do we get? I'll be around if you need me."

"Until next time then, Alana?" he asked with a smile.

"Until next time," I replied.

EPILOGUE

♦

Ten years later

I stood back, watching, waiting for all of our people to come into position. It was strange, no longer running most of the activities. At times, I needed to step back and let others take up the work and prove themselves. This joint operation was going to be something.

"We don't have time to stop. If the king's men or the Worldsingers find us . . ." one of the men before me said, his voice enhanced by my magic.

"Shut up, you idiot. I know, I know, but the horses have to rest or they'll die, and we're not getting anywhere without them." The one who issued the reply went to turn, but there was a change in the air and he faltered, falling to his knees where he barely caught himself.

A dozen men let out curses and tried to rise, only to fall. The first speaker was on his knees, heaving, trying to get up, and failing as the plan fell into action.

"Hate to be the bearer of bad news, boys," Rodrick said as he stepped out from a patch of darkness, fading into sight as his illusions fell, "but you're already way too late."

One of the men managed to raise his hand and point at my son, letting loose a blast of flame and surprising the now adult Rodrick. Of course I was here, and so with a note sung loudly, I quashed his spell like brushing aside a gnat.

"Secure your prisoners first, son, then gloat," one of my illusions said as it appeared beside him. It remained best to keep out of sight in any operation, something we'd be talking about later.

The offender was now unable to move, gasping for air as the pressure pushed harder and harder upon him, unable to do much more than sputter and wheeze. He couldn't even raise his eyes to see Illa floating down from above, glowing like an angel as she descended, dress and hair floating and fluttering.

"The next one to attack gets crushed into paste," she declared with finality, her shields pulsing with power.

While they were talking, over a dozen men and women—some mine, some my nephew's—poured in from the woods around us. Spells were taking shape, and one by one the thieves were being bound, magical restraints affixed before they were pulled from Illa's high gravity spell. Once all were in custody I joined the rest.

"Good work," I said, finally stepping out into view. "Though not great. There was no need for either of you to reveal yourselves," I chided my kids.

"It sends a message," Rodrick objected.

"Yes, it does. It says 'Look, kill me!' in bright letters. If you want to be seen, use an illusion." They both frowned. I was well enough known, and my penchant for remaining unseen was pretty much my calling card. "But, you did well tracking them, son. And Illa, that use of gravity was exceptional."

The three of us, along with some of the other officers here, moved to one of the carts. There was a woosh as the cover was pulled away, revealing a gate buried under the many boxes.

"I can't believe they actually managed to steal one. Just getting past the wards was impressive," Illa said.

"I can't believe they did it during Omos's coronation," her brother replied. "You should have seen him; hate to be those poor bastards."

"We'll get our answers as to how and why soon," I told them. "Yes, I imagine they'll regret their decision. Though they may not regret it for terribly long."

My kids moved off to their own jobs, now that we had the gate back, and I couldn't have been prouder of them.

Illa had grown so much and was now the premiere expert on gravity magic in the kingdom. Originally, she'd mastered it to learn to fly, but she'd taken it so much further. I suspected that if she really applied herself, she might even be able to bend space to speed herself up like I could, but so far as I knew she hadn't yet. We were supposed to have tea tomorrow. Perhaps I could ask her then. Those weekly meetings were always a joy.

Her brother was working with me. Rodrick would never be in any administrative role if he could help it. As a field agent he was magnificent. His memory meant that he could gather mountains of information and process it with ease, connecting dots so few even saw. Though it pained me that he'd failed miserably when it came to trying to learn to make gates properly.

I'd have to deal with whatever we learned from the criminals. Even if Omos wouldn't directly order me on most things, we agreed on this one. I suspected it was an attempt by one of the surrounding kingdoms to secure portal technology, one that would fail, but we still needed to know who was trying.

His father was also being a pain. John had followed our father's lead and stepped down as soon as it was clear his son could rule, joining Dad in semi-retirement. This was something I couldn't approve of enough, as it really did make for a more reliable transfer of power, a more stable base. Perhaps one day there'd be a succession issue, but so long as one or two old kings were there to pull everyone back together, there shouldn't be a civil war.

Thirty-six years later

My black dress fluttered in the icy wind. I couldn't bring myself to cry again. I'd done so too many times in the last couple of days. As the tomb was closed, I just couldn't. It was too much.

Ulanion had fallen, and not to some enemy or monster, but to the one thing that wouldn't be denied to those with human blood. Age. He'd outlived so many that I almost couldn't believe it. He'd seemed immortal, but he wasn't.

Before I could fall too deeply into thought once again, a hand touched my shoulder. With a small, sad smile, Rodrick helped me, his sister joining him in leading me back to the school, the fortress, my home.

Even looking at my own children brought up dark thoughts. Would I bury them too? My attempts to wage war on my aging had been more successful year by year. Time was still coming for me, but at a snail's pace. These days my little Illa looked like my mother, not the other way around. Her hair was graying, as was her brother's.

It seemed that all of the people I knew were dying, each year causing me to lose more and more of my friends. I even found it harder to make new ones as I aged, the pain of loss hardening me.

There were a few ceremonies over the course of the day, a few moments where people wanted to talk, or see how I was, or something else that I had a hard time caring about. Most of them were dissuaded when it became clear that I wanted them gone. When the last of them had left, I almost went to bed, but that seemed hollow.

So instead I went to my lab. Here, I could visit the one man I doubted I would outlive. Over the years, I'd tried to visit him more, even if he was as prickly as I felt now.

Justin joined me soon after I stepped through the gateway, gave me one look, and sighed.

"I'll get something stronger than tea then," he said as we went to his sitting room.

"How'd you know?" I asked.

"Other than the solid black dress? You look horrible, Alana." The ancient king handed me a glass of some liquor, the amber fluid giving off a powerful, smokey aroma.

"How do you . . . How do you deal with it?" I inquired, begging him for an answer.

"Alana, I live alone in the middle of nowhere, barely talking to anyone else. If there's anyone less qualified to tell you how to handle grief, I'd like to meet him." There was another sigh, and in his eyes I could see it, the pain of millennia. "I think it's worse for us, though, and maybe better too. My memories don't fade. I see lost loved ones in my mind as clearly as if I were looking at them now. I remember every conversation like I'm watching a movie—every good word, every angry one, every fight and hug and tear."

"I want to just lay down and die," I admitted. "Let it all go."

"I've been there, too, you know, but I don't think they'd want us to."

"They're gone, so we can't well ask."

"Not here, but gone? Come on, you and I both know that dying doesn't have to be the end. I don't believe in suicide; I think it's wrong, but it's hard to fear death when you've already been through it. Perhaps we'll meet them again on the other side; perhaps not, but I don't think those I've lost would want me to die, and I don't think those you have would want you to either." He was right, and I sort of hated that.

"So what do I do?"

"Start with finishing your drink. Then, why don't you tell me about those you've lost." That seemed as good a suggestion as any.

Sixty-four years later

So many years had passed since I'd come to this world. I even had a few gray hairs. These days, I mostly kept to myself at the school, only coming out to advise the king and attend to things, like I was today. I passed through the halls of the royal palace like a shadow, heading to the wing where the former kings and queens had resided. There was something I needed to do before it was too late, a secret held too long.

When I knocked, I was pleased to find that the owner of the room was awake and not alone. There were servants, of course. There were always servants here, but one of the princesses was here, too, speaking to her great-grandmother at her bedside, the older woman smiling as she looked at the young girl. It was heartwarming to see that the kids were so loving.

"Hello, Lena," I said with a sad smile. She looked horrible, but she was smiling. Priestess or not, her body was failing. The healers said she'd likely not survive the week.

"Oh, if it isn't my old teacher. Serena dear, have you two met?" she said, introducing us.

"Ma'am," the young girl said, making to rise. "You're one of my father's advisors, right?" Being that she was maybe eight or nine, that was all she needed to know.

"Something like that, dear. I hate to ask, but do you think we could have a moment alone? There's something I need to speak with your great-grandmother about privately."

Serena looked over, asking, "Granny?"

"It's fine dear," Lena said, patting her hand gently. "Why don't you wait just outside? This shouldn't take too long."

After she was gone, I put up a privacy barrier. I really didn't know how Lena would react, but I couldn't hide it from her any longer, and there was no point.

"I am sorry for disturbing you, but there is something I need to tell you, before it's too late," I said, struggling to get the words out.

"About my parents?" she said with a smirk. My face must have shown some amount of shock because she continued. "You're not the only one with connections in the orders. You know that, right?"

"When did they tell you?" I asked.

"That I was the true heir? Just before I married Omos. The same time they told me how you fought to let that happen. Thank you for that, by the way. He was a wonderful husband."

"You never brought it up," I said softly, saddened that she'd kept my secret for so long.

"You seemed content to let it be." She didn't even seem angry.

"You're not mad that I killed your parents?" I asked, still stunned.

"Not as much as I could be. You forget that I learned of their crimes long, long before I learned who they were. It was painful to learn that I'd hated them so. Yet, I was also told that you saved me, tried your best to give me a peaceful life."

I sat down beside her. "You shouldn't have hated them. Your father was my enemy, and he caused a lot of pain, but I've met worse men. I think he really did want to do right, but went about it in the wrong ways. As for your mother . . . Her death is one of the things I've regretted more than you can imagine. As far as I know, she was just another victim, and she just wanted to protect you."

"And you killed her?" Lena looked taken aback.

"I wanted surrender, not violence with her. She attacked me, and things went badly. War is like that sometimes. Had we had just a little more time, perhaps it would have turned out differently. I'm sorry." It wasn't much, but it was the best I had.

"I forgive you," she said, and I felt the worry fall off of me. "You forget that I've known you most of my life, that I've seen you at work for that time. I've watched you advise and tell Omos that he needn't fight some of those fools, even if he wanted to, because you'd tell him how much pain it could cause. At any rate, it seems pointless to hold a grudge now."

"Thank you." It was all I could manage to say to this woman, who had every right to hate me.

"Will you do me a favor though?" she asked.

"Of course," I replied. If I could, I would. I owed her that much.

"Look after them, the kids, as long as you can." Her eyes began to cloud.

"I will," I promised, leaning up to kiss her on the forehead.

"Good, now send Serena back in. She's a lot more fun to talk to than you."

I did just that, promising myself that I'd be here for as long as I could and keep an eye on all of them.

Over two hundred years later

I stumbled through the portal into Justin's domain once more, leaning heavily on my staff as my muscles rebelled. I had to hurry, but everything hurt so badly. As usual, the man took his time to join me, but as soon as he saw me, he rushed over to help. I felt frail, so frail.

Magic or not, hundreds of years had taken their toll. My bones were no longer strong, my skin was loose and wrinkled over muscles atrophied from age. And, I was in pain, so much pain. I gritted my teeth as I walked beside him, happy for someone to lean on this time.

"Alana, what are you doing? What's wrong? You look like you're dying," the ancient king said as he tried to pull me toward a chair, but I resisted. I couldn't sit down.

"Not dying; dead. Body just hasn't caught up with it yet. Heart gave out two hours ago, my boy," I laughed. "Only reason I can still move is that I'm keeping it all together with magic, and that won't last."

"Why are you here!? You need a priest, you daft woman!" he roared, far too loud for my taste.

"Can't help. Even you know there's a point at which it all falls apart. Maybe they could keep me alive a bit longer, but it's all coming undone, and I'd rather go out standing up than as a vegetable lying in a bed. Now listen, because I don't have time." I affixed him with the harshest glare I could manage, and he stilled.

"What do you need?" he asked, eyes in pain. We'd known each other for so long, and I knew he'd already lost so many. It hurt to do this to him, but my time was over.

"The pool. I want you to take me to it. I'm going to drink, see what happens, see if I end up going back. Bet none of us have before, so let's do it. We'll use the walk to talk, because I need to tell you about some things too," I said, struggling, leaning on him even more.

I felt magic wrap around me, and I was somewhere else. It was clear now how he was doing this, the method of teleportation, but it didn't matter, not today.

"This is as close as we should teleport. Let's hurry, if things are that bad." I was glad that he wasn't going to argue.

The giant cave was much as I remembered it. Perhaps just a bit brighter, the plants just a little fuller. The magic was thick, almost visible in the air; you could very nearly taste it. It was a shame, a true shame that I'd only been here a few times.

"There's another like us, at least one other. Met him a while ago in a city called Exion. Another point for your data there," I said.

"I see," he said as he helped me hurry forward.

"I also want you to know that whatever happens, it's not your fault." He looked at me with furrowed brows. "Oh, don't give me that. I know you were a naughty boy when you were younger, and you went and hid here to pay for it, but you need to let it go. Forgive yourself; nearly everyone else has. If those priests had half a brain, they would too. That's not what I'm talking about though. This, whatever happens here is on me. I'm the one drinking that water to try and find out what happens."

As I spoke, I felt the spell I'd woven around my heart lurch. At this late phase, even my magic was starting to fail, as if it knew my time was up. I'd already put too much into making that spell in the first place, and my mana was running on fumes. I pushed more mana into it, trying to stabilize it, but there wasn't enough left to make it fully functional.

"Alana?" Justin's voice reached me.

"Can't . . ." I'd fallen almost to my knees, and try as I might, I couldn't push myself back up. My staff clattered to the floor.

"I've got you," he said, and I felt a mix of magic and muscle wrap me up, scooping me off my feet and carrying me toward the glowing pool.

"Of all the money I ever had, I spent it in good company," I sang, trying to get just a tad more mileage out of the magic to keep me alive.

"And of all the harm I've ever done, alas it was to none but me," Justin joined me, and I felt the gestalt hit like a freight train, bolstering and shoring up my weaknesses.

"And all I've done for want of wit, to memory now I can't recall," I saw him smile at that, for we both knew his memory.

"So fill to me the parting glass, good night and joy be with you all."

I could feel him rushing, hear him singing, but the edges of my sight began to dim. The only things I could really see as we moved forward were the light from the pool and the tears streaking down my friend's face. The song was working, though, and as we moved, I could feel my heart thump to the beat, the beat of that old farewell song.

"Of all the comrades that 'ere had, they're sorry for my going away
And all the sweethearts that 'ere I had, they'd wish me one more day
But since it falls unto my lot, that I should rise and you should not
I'll gently rise and softly call, good night and joy be with you all."

As we neared the end, I was placed gently down on the vines, Justin rushing forward and producing a small glass, which he filled with the water. He had to help me raise it to my lips so I could drink. The water was cool, not the burning pain I expected, but refreshing, welcome. Had it been like that the last time I drank it?

"So fill to me the parting glass, and drink good health whatever befalls."

Then the fire hit me. Strangely, it didn't hurt that badly. One by one, the bubbles of my aura burst, releasing small explosions of fiery magic. I rose, strength pulsing, but I could see it wouldn't last. My aura was burning, and when it was gone, I knew in my bones that it would be the end.

"And gently rise and softly call."

So I rushed forward, my companion saying something behind me that I couldn't make out as I dove into the pool, like I had all those years ago, still singing, still wishing him goodbye. Even as I floated toward the center, though, I could feel the effects. My body was coming apart, flaking away like dust.

Once more I could see clearly though. I could see the pool, the elf weeping beside it on his knees. I could see others too, all those I'd lost over the years. My husband was here, the children I'd buried so long ago, and their children. Off to one side were my closest teachers, looking on with smiles, Mystien and his friend Lucien both shaking their heads. To my right, just out of reach was my family—my parents and . . . both of my brothers.

It was Rod, the first of all to fall, who stepped forward.

"Hey there, little sister. You ready to go?" he asked, offering me his hand.

I reached my own hand up, which was odd, since it had fully turned to ash, but the idea was still there, a spectral hand. I knew in my heart that I wasn't going back to Earth, but instead to wherever it was we went upon death.

As the song came to a close, I touched my brother's hand. The moment it met mine, my body sped up its destruction, the slow burn speeding to consume me, but I had just enough time to finish my song.

"Good night and joy be with you all."

ABOUT THE AUTHOR

Wandering Agent is the North Carolina–based author of the Melody of Mana and Elevation of Mana series as well as other fantasy and isekai stories.

Podium

DISCOVER MORE

STORIES
UNBOUND

PodiumEntertainment.com